Regina of Warsaw

Love, Loss and Liberation

Books by Geri Spieler

Regina of Warsaw Series

BOOK ONE
Regina of Warsaw
Love, Loss and Liberation

Coming Soon!

BOOK TWO
Revenge of the Sisters
A Tale of Retribution

BOOK THREE
The Family
Love and Death in WWII Poland

For more information
visit: www.SpeakingVolumes.us

Regina of Warsaw

Love, Loss and Liberation

Geri Spieler

Inspired By Real Events

SPEAKING VOLUMES, LLC
NAPLES, FLORIDA
2024

Regina of Warsaw

ISBN 979-8-89022-149-0

To Rick Kaplowitz,
my ever supportive and loving husband.
You make my writing possible.

Acknowledgments

Thank you to my mother and extended family who helped me pull together the history of my maternal grandmother, Regina Anuszewicz. I am grateful to them for enlightening me about events and documents and generously leading me to new relatives around the world.

A special thank you to two sets of cousins I didn't know existed until circumstances brought them into my life.

Aleksandra (Ola) and Jarek Minor live in Warsaw, Poland. I had the good fortune to visit them there and also meet Januz and Joseph Anusevwicz, my grandmother's surviving nephews.

Another set of cousins I met in Paris are Josette and Alain Chabay. Alain's genealogy research connected many pieces of the puzzle regarding what may have happened to my grandmother's siblings. Josette, Alain, and I shared happy tears at our good fortune in finding each other.

My biggest sense of gratitude goes to my loving and patient husband, Rick Kaplowitz, who has been stalwart by my side. I'm so fortunate to have such a wonderful and supportive partner.

While this book is fiction, the excellent advice and information I received about this historic period helped me frame many of Regina's life events.

Beyond extended family, I had the good fortune to connect with Professor Robert Blobaum, Eberly Family Emeritus Professor of History at West Virginia University and president of the Polish Institute of Arts and Sciences of America. Professor Blobaum was patient and generous with his scholarly and friendly advice.

Craig Horning, Vista Del Mar Archivist, allowed me to "see" what the orphanage looked like and how it ran when my mother and her sisters lived there in the 1930s. Sherly Postnikov, the Hebrew Immigrant Aid Society (HIAS) Archives Manager, found my grandmother's immigration papers when she came to the United States. Thanks to both of you.

Writers and friends Joan Gelfand and Nanci Lee Woody provided warm and generous support and were so important and necessary for me to keep my eye on the meaning of this book.

I must also include my many colleagues at the San Francisco Peninsula branch of the California Writers Club.

Finally, I want to thank my fabulous literary agent, Nancy Rosenfeld, and AAA Books Unlimited. You believed in me and found a fabulous publisher, Speaking Volumes. Thank you, Kurt, and Erica Mueller, and thank you, Nancy. You are more than an agent.

And a hearty thank you to my editor, David Tabatsky, for his wonderful and detailed work in making this manuscript as clean and clear as possible.

A Note from the Author

The idea of writing a book about my family only began to take shape when I told my son about my mother and her sisters, who lived in a Jewish orphanage in Los Angeles for most of their school years. It took me a while to realize that their experience was not normal, even though it seemed that way to them at the time.

As I grew up and learned more about what my maternal grandmother, Regina Anuszewicz, survived, I realized I had never given her the respect or credit she deserved. I also knew that I didn't have the whole story. By the time I recognized the amazing and courageous life she led, and that without her guile and guts I wouldn't be here, she was gone. So, through her bravery and determination, I'm here to tell her story.

Regina, who grew up in Warsaw, Poland, was a very private person when I knew her. After she died, when I was pregnant with Josh, we learned she had been corresponding with two of her nephews, Joseph and Januz Anuszewicz, the sons of one of her brothers, Zelman. She never told anyone, not even the family. I only learned about it when I visited Warsaw twenty years after her death. I had an address my mother gave me that she found in Regina's effects. I learned her story from those nephews, my mother, my aunts, and my uncle, the baby she brought with her when she left Warsaw.

The events that inspired this book are real. They happened once upon a time, but we should all be aware that history can repeat itself, and often does. So, while Regina's story is meant to inform and entertain, I know she would also want you to see it as a cautionary tale.

Regina's Glossary

These words and phrases are a mix of Yiddish and Hebrew.

Bar Mitzvah
Religious initiation ceremony of a Jewish boy at the age of 13.

Borscht
A sour soup made with beets.

Bund
A secular Jewish socialist party initially formed in the Russian Empire.

Challah
A loaf of bread, typically braided, served on the Sabbath and holidays.

Cheder
A private Jewish elementary school.

Cholent
Sabbath dish of meat and vegetables prepared on Fridays to cook overnight.

Chutzpah
Supreme self-confidence; audacity or nerve.

Dayenu
Enough!

Gett
Jewish divorce document.

Golabki
A popular dish in Central European cuisine, made from boiled cabbage leaves wrapped around a filling of minced beef, chopped onions, and rice.

Holishkez
Traditional dish, cabbage stuffed with meatballs, with tomato gravy.

Kalduny
Stuffed dumplings made of unleavened dough.

Ketubah
Jewish marriage contract.

Kiddushin
Engagement.

Kippah
Small, round head covering for observant Jews.

Kissel
Dessert of fruit puree, boiled with sugar, thickened with potato/cornstarch.

Kosher
Jewish dietary laws.

Kugel
A baked casserole with starch, usually noodles or potatoes, eggs, and fat.

Le Marais
Jewish district in Paris, France.

Matzo ball
Typically made of matzo meal, fat, and eggs, and usually put in soup.

Mazel Tov
Congratulations!

Minyan
A quorum of ten men needed for a traditional Jewish service.

Mitzvah
A good deed.

Oneg
A small celebration.

Pale of Settlement
Western region of the Russian Empire from 1791 to 1917, where Jews were allowed permanent residency only inside specific borders.

Pierogi
Dumpling stuffed with potatoes or cheese, served with onions or sour cream.

Pletzl
A "little place," i.e. the Jewish quarter in the 4th arrondissement of Paris.

Pogrom
A violent riot that aims to murder or expel an ethnic or religious group.

Rebbetzin
A rabbi's wife.

Resztki
Leftovers, scraps or remains.

Schatzeleh
A term of endearment, like Sweetheart.

Shabbos
Jewish day of rest, 24 hours, beginning Friday before sundown

Shadkin / Shadchanit.
Matchmaker /Marriage Broker.

Shanda
Indicates something scandalously shameful.

Shiddach
A Jewish arranged marriage.

Shiva
A period of mourning following a death.

Shomer
To guard, watch, or preserve.

Shtetl
Small town or village.

Shul
A synagogue or temple, a place of worship.

Tante
Aunt.

Tenaim
Formal prenuptial agreement.

Toda Raba
Thank you.

Yiddish
The language of Ashkenazi Jews from Central and Eastern Europe, written in Hebrew script.

Bialystok, Poland
1906

1

Pierogis and Pogroms

Regina Anuszewicz squeezed her eyes shut as she hid inside the closet of her sister's room. Her breath tightened as she heard Russian soldiers stomping their feet downstairs. As she heard them shout, she tried to make herself as small as she could, blending her body in with the clothes, scarves, and shoes.

I wish I could just disappear.

She tried to slow down her breathing as she felt the pounding of her heart in her head.

A loud bang and a thud sounded like the front door had been kicked down. Heavy footsteps continued from room to room, and shouts in Russian came closer and closer to the closet.

Regina, 16, had come to Bialystok to visit her older sister, Chaja Fajga, who worked as a spinner at the Lewandowski textile mill, situated along the Bialy River. They had plans to meet when Chaja Fajga finished her shift and enjoy a picnic with the special pierogi their mother had made for them.

When Regina arrived for a lovely June weekend, she dropped her bundle at her sister's boarding house and stepped outside to walk several blocks to the mill. She stopped suddenly when she heard loud voices and saw soldiers running down the street, some on horseback, some on foot, wielding their swords at anyone who did not run away fast enough. Blood dripped from their blades, and the wounded lay screaming on the ground.

As Regina scurried back inside the building, locked the door and ran up the stairs to the bedroom, she heard gunfire coming closer. She had read about pogroms after a wave of anti-Jewish riots swept through Ukraine and Poland. They had begun in Russia and devastated several Jewish communities. Soldiers were known to rape women and often killed them. When some women realized that soldiers were coming for them, they killed themselves rather than suffer such horrific abuse.

Gunfire echoed throughout the streets, and the pitiful screams of people begging for their lives was mixed with the soldier's jeering and laughter. Regina couldn't bear to imagine what was taking place outside the boarding house. She knew the soldiers would behead their victims, even gutting babies and children in front of their parents.

The footsteps inside the boarding house came closer. She squeezed her eyes tight, hoping the soldiers wouldn't open the closet. After the noise finally stopped, she didn't trust the silence right away. She remained frozen, afraid to come out, until she heard a woman's voice.

"No, please don't!"

Then she heard laughter and loud voices in Russian.

Regina could barely breathe.

Is that Chaja Fajga or some other unfortunate woman? How can I tell?

She knew it was probably her sister because who else would be there at that time? The other girls were working at the mill.

What should I do? Should I run downstairs?

Regina didn't know if she could save anyone from what she imagined was happening.

"Please. Don't. Stop!"

More laughter, grunting, and silence.

"My turn! Let me at her!"

More grunting.

"Ah, that was just what I needed."

Regina felt sweat dripping down her forehead. She didn't move.

Will they rape me and kill me next?

She didn't know how she could stay safe while her sister was being horribly abused. She wondered if they were beating her while she was raped.

She heard a deep Russian voice.

"Leave her. Maybe she will have your baby!"

More laughter. More stomping.

Are they coming upstairs?

4

Regina's head was spinning with the worst thoughts possible.

What if my sister is not dead but is being beaten and raped while I stay here in safety and do nothing? How can I be such a coward? Surely, Chaja Fajga would come to my rescue.

Regina rationalized that she could not stop the Russian soldiers and would become a victim, too. That is what she decided to tell herself, that it made no sense to lose two daughters to the pogrom instead of one.

Am I being callous? If Chaja Fajga is alive and knows I am hiding while she is being beaten and raped, how will she feel?

Inside the closet, Regina couldn't move, even when she no longer heard any soldiers. She wondered if the girl screaming was her sister, and if she was, she didn't understand why she didn't hear her.

Is she dead? Is it even Chaja Fajga? Is she still alive?

She heard more crying and then someone gasping for air. Finally, a voice. "Regina? Are you here? It's Chaja. Are you here? Please, say something." More sobs.

Regina held her breath and squeezed her eyes tight as her body continued to shake. She didn't trust her ears. She wanted to hear her sister's voice but couldn't be sure the Russians wouldn't use her as bait to get Regina to respond. She wanted to run and hide.

Chaja Fajga can't find out I've been hiding the entire time she was being raped and did nothing. Could I have saved her from the soldiers?

She did nothing. She saved herself and let the soldiers do whatever they wanted to the girl downstairs, and she felt sure it must be her sister.

Regina hadn't moved for what felt like hours and her legs were cramping. She was still not sure that the voice was her sister's. She stayed quiet, afraid she was imagining something that was not real.

She knew that Chaja Fajga would blame herself for allowing her sister to get caught in a pogrom. She also knew that the Russians could still be hiding, waiting for her to come out and look for her sister, only to be caught. That's what the Russian soldiers often did, using one family member as bait to catch another. But those pogroms had seemed so far away. Regina never expected to be caught in one so close to Warsaw, where she and her sister were born.

Regina heard Chaja Fajga call her again, but she was still afraid and too ashamed to respond. Finally, when the pain in her arms and legs became too much, she decided to risk answering her sister.

She cracked open the closet door.

"I'm here Chaja Fajga. I'm safe."

Regina pushed the door open so she could see. Her sister had come upstairs alone. Regina carefully unfolded herself, one stiff limb at a time, and took Chaja Fajga in her arms, holding her close as she cried. Her dress was torn, the bodice ripped to her waist, exposing her breasts. Her face was red from being slapped and punched into submission.

Regina was stunned to see how her sister had been so abused, especially while she stayed safe. She cried, ashamed of her behavior, and slumped on the sofa as exhaustion overcame her. She nearly choked as she tried to explain how she had panicked and frozen when she heard the soldiers.

Chaja Fajga said nothing. Neither spoke for several minutes until Regina managed a whisper.

"Did they slap you?"

She didn't know what to say or ask, but it was obvious that her question was stupid.

Of course, they slapped her.

"I was luckier than most other women, Regina. It was quick. I guess I should be grateful because at least they let me live."

Chaja Fajga said nothing about Regina hiding in the closet until she realized what had happened.

"I'm glad you were small enough to fit inside."

Chaja Fajga was taller than most women in her community, with soft, light brown hair worn in a braid at the nape of her neck. She was fair and lean, unlike Regina's dark solid frame. They shared their father's deep blue eyes.

Regina wasn't sure if it was a criticism or a sincere comment.

"I'm so sorry, Chaja Fajga. I'm so sorry. I didn't know what to do."

"They would have done the same thing to you, Regina. Then, we both would have been raped and maybe killed."

6

Chaja Fajga fell onto the couch, hands over her face, her chest heaving in great sobs.

"I'm ruined for life. I'll never marry and have children if I'm not pregnant already. I've shamed our family."

As Regina embraced her sister, she still felt ashamed that she had done nothing to stop the abuse.

Chaja Fajga rocked back and forth.

"I wanted to come here sooner from the mill and take you back with me, but they locked the doors before I could get out. I thought it was safe, that the soldiers had left."

"Chaja Fajga, you can't live here anymore. We must return to Mokótow, even though the soldiers may come there, too. We must leave now."

Regina hung on to her sister as they sobbed.

"Chaja Fajga, come home with me right now. Tonight. You can't stay here another day. Come back with me."

"Why should I go home? What will they do with me? I'll bring shame to our family once they know I've been raped."

The sisters sat quietly for a few minutes before Regina spoke.

"What if they don't know? Only you and I know what happened here. There are no witnesses except the Russian soldiers."

"What if I get pregnant?"

"Let's just wait and see what happens. When is your monthly due?"

"Soon, I think."

"Let's hope you get it. And if you miss it, we'll think of something. We can explain your bruise by saying you fell while running up the stairs at the mill, and you hit your face on a sharp corner. No one needs to know, my dear sister. It's our secret,"

Regina held Chaja Fajga by the shoulders.

"It's our secret."

She took a deep breath and smiled.

At least I can help my sister look forward to a life free of shame and sorrow over nothing she could control.

Geri Spieler

Regina knew that Chaja Fajga was right. If their parents knew the truth, it would shame the family. She hoped it was behind them, but there was still one thing that could cause a problem. All they could do was wait. Regina would do what she could to help her sister.

It's the least I can do.

They peeked outside to see if any soldiers were still around and then they piled furniture against the door, hoping it would help keep any more bad men from getting in the building. By the following day, they no longer heard screaming but they did hear crying, so they decided to wait longer. Finally, when the streets were quiet, they decided it was safe to leave. They gathered up whatever items they could carry and looked outside.

Regina imagined family members bent over their dead relatives, powerless to do anything to stop the slaughter. She fought back the vision and tried to continue.

"Do you have another dress here you can wear? There must be something here in a women's boarding house."

They found a dress that fit Chaja Fajga. As they stepped outside into the sunlight, they were shocked to see dead bodies with pools of blood around them and limbs scattered along the ground. Dead mothers held dead children to their breasts. Frozen eyes stared at Regina, reminding her of the guilt she felt for remaining safe while so many suffered and died.

She bent over and vomited.

They walked toward the train, stepping around the carnage, not sure if the train was even running.

"I've read about what is happening in Russia, that the soldiers are marching on any town they think they can overrun with their pogroms. They have started to move to Poland now, as we can see. Chaja Fajga, you will be safer with the family."

The General Jewish Labor Bund had offices in Lithuania, Poland, and Russia. Usually called the "Bund," it was a secular Jewish socialist party initially formed in the Russian Empire.

There was speculation as to why and how the Bialystok pogrom took place. It was just a mill town, and there were just as many Christians there as

Jews. Usually, pogroms took place in strictly Jewish communities. News traveled quickly through the region with reports of armed soldiers and police shooting in the streets and brutally raping Jewish women and girls, with bandits breaking into Jewish houses and robbing Jewish stores.

Regina read descriptions of soldiers gouging people's eyes out with their nails, cutting their abdomens open, and stuffing them with feathers. They removed the heads and organs of small children. Several Jewish leaders risked their lives by appealing to the authorities, pleading with them to stop the killing and looting, to no avail. One leader managed to get out of Bialystok, and from a neighboring town he sent a telegram to the Duma of Russia, reporting on the horrors he had witnessed.

As the girls made their way home, they ate their pierogis. Regina worried about their parents and if they would believe that Chaja Fajga fell on the stairs and got injured.

I can only hope our plan will work.

She and her sister would find out soon enough.

A Secret Bond

Regina knew that her parents and siblings would wonder about the bruises on Chaja Fajga's face. She hoped they wouldn't jump to conclusions, thinking she had been attacked. They would share the story they came up with and pray that their secret would not be revealed by too many questions.

No one else needs to know.

Regina knocked on the front door the family normally kept locked.

"Mama! Papa! It's Regina and Chaja. We are home."

Yosef opened the door and stared at his girls.

"My daughters, you are safe. I was so worried."

He looked closely to see if they appeared normal.

"Chaja Fajga, what happened? Are you okay? Did someone hurt you?"

Regina spoke first.

"She's fine, Papa. She fell at the mill, trying to get out to come to me as soon as possible. She tripped and hit her head on the stairs."

Their mother, Lena, slim, with curly brown hair and bits of gray pulled back into a bun, looked at her daughters.

"Chaja Fajga, is that what happened? Are you okay?"

"Yes, Mother, just what Regina said. I was trying to get out when the mill unlocked our doors. I was in a hurry."

Chaja Fajga and Regina locked eyes.

This is our secret to keep.

The family gathered to discuss the events in Bialystok. Regina's younger brothers, Zelman and Aleksander, and her younger sisters, Dina and Kejla, gathered around the large wooden table, which was covered with a crochet tablecloth made by their grandmother years earlier before she died. It had become the official cover for all their family dinners, and that night was no exception. Everyone had to be present to discuss the pogrom in Bialystok, and the fact that Regina and Chaja Fajga could have died.

Lena sat at one end of the table, and Yosef, tall and broad with dark blonde hair and blue eyes, sat at the other end. As the matriarch and patriarch, they held family court at these dinners, when vital matters were discussed, and no one could be excused from participating. When parental decisions were made, they were final.

That evening meal consisted of traditional stuffed cabbage and holishkez, which were stuffed with meatballs and served with sweet and sour tomato gravy. Dina and Kejla placed the cabbage heads and bowls for the borsht at each setting. Other platters held golabki and a rare serving of beef. No one had to get up during the meal to get more helpings.

Regina eagerly ate the borscht, one of her favorite dishes, and added potatoes to give the soup more flavor.

As the family ate in silence, Regina locked eyes with Chaja Fajga. Suddenly, Lena declared that Chaja Fajga would not return to Bialystok and continue her job at the mill.

Regina stared at her plate. She didn't know what to say about the pogrom. It was too awful to talk about what they had experienced. Everyone kept eating and passing dishes around the table, filling their plates with food, and savoring all the rich flavors.

If only we could just eat and enjoy our food.

Lena sipped the last of the borscht, put her spoon down, wiped her hands, and looked at the family. Regina knew this was a sign that the family meeting would now begin. She recognized her father's serious face.

"Children, we are living in dangerous times. We must be careful where we go, and we must not be out past early evening."

Yosef said that if anything happened in their neighborhood of Mokotów, the family would gather in the barn behind the house.

As she listened to her father and remembered what she had just seen during the pogrom, Regina thought about taking a more active role in fighting antisemitism. Working for the Jewish Labor Bund had provided Regina with first-hand news of antisemitic activity around Poland as well as in Russia, Lithuania, and Belarus. She could tell her parents what was happening, and they could act if necessary. But that was not the direct subject of the discussion during that evening's meal.

What to do about Chaja Fajga?

Where she lived and worked was no longer her decision. It was customary for the family to oversee all its young women until they were married. Young men, however, had more authority over their work and where they lived.

On their ride home, Chaja Fajga had confided in Regina that she didn't know what she would do now that she had been raped. Sitting at dinner with the rest of their family, Regina didn't know what to say, so like her siblings, she stared at her plate and remained quiet, waiting for her parents to continue.

"Chaja Fajga," said her mother, "what about Regina? Look what you did to your sister. She could have lost her life because she wanted to see you. Don't you feel bad about that?"

Regina stood up.

"It's not her fault, Mama. It's not fair to blame Chaja Fajga. How could she have known?"

If they knew what really happened, they would never ask such a question.

When Regina stopped shouting, the room fell silent. No one said a word, and everyone except Lena looked down and fiddled with their food. It was not a good idea to go against her like Regina has just done. Even Yosef knew well enough to keep his own counsel.

Please, God, let Chaja Fajga get her monthly. Soon.

Friends and Enemies

The next day, Zelman, and Aleksander, both solidly built with bulging muscles, accompanied Chaja Fajga on the train back to Bialystok to help her pack what was left of her belongings.

Regina stayed home from her job at the Bund, where she translated documents. She feigned being ill but in fact she was still shaken from the effects of the pogrom in Bialystok. Chaja Fajga hadn't gotten her monthly yet. She didn't want to nag her about it, but she was worried.

What if she's pregnant? What will we do?

She knew of a midwife who could help with unwanted pregnancies, but would it be possible to keep Chaja Fajga's secret so the family wouldn't find out? There was a rumor that the midwife gave girls and women medicine to help with their monthly but was really being used to stop having a baby.

While Regina's mother busied herself in the kitchen, Regina replayed the events of the pogrom over and over in her head, second-guessing that she could have done at the boarding house to interrupt the attack and maybe hit the soldiers with a lamp or some other heavy object. She knew that she really couldn't have stopped the attack and most likely would have become a victim herself, but she still felt cowardly hiding upstairs while she knew what was happening to her sister.

Why wasn't Chaja Fajga upset with me for not coming to her aid?

Her sister didn't blame her so Regina guessed that she didn't know she could hear the attack. She never said anything about that. She was too paralyzed with fear in that moment.

Her thoughts moved to the politics of the situation. It was not just Poland fearing Russian men rampaging through their country. People in Lithuania and Belarus were growing increasingly troubled by the news. Russian soldiers were rampaging through Jewish villages, killing, burning down stores and homes, and raping women of all ages. At the Bund, the reports were becoming too prevalent, and Regina was relieved to have a day off from hearing more.

She listened as her parents talked about the future of their children. She knew they wanted more for them than what they had, but Regina felt they lived well compared to her friends at school and work. Her father was a respected leather worker who worked long hours to provide for his family. Some of her friends lived with more than one family in their house. Owning a home was only possible if you built it yourself.

Education in Poland had a history of being tied to the Catholic church especially for those who eventually entered the clergy. For others, higher education meant a more advanced status for those who continued school past the tenth grade. Regina didn't have the same educational opportunities as more wealthy and elite children. For some wealthy Jews, separate educational opportunities were offered through the synagogue and available for those who passed a test and demonstrated special abilities. Boys could spend time studying the Torah and hone skills that would support a family. Girls had to forge a more creative path if they wanted to pursue a dream outside the family.

The house was quiet after the children went to school and Regina's father headed out to the leather shop.

"I'll be home before nightfall, of course," Yosef said, with a tinge of sadness in his voice, as if he wanted to stay home and make sure his wife and daughter were safe.

Education for Jews was becoming more limited, so much of their education occurred at home, reading from the classics and the Torah, while Yosef taught them mathematics.

Regina sat quietly for a few moments, holding her head in her hands, trying to collect her thoughts before she began the daily tasks of cooking, mending, and cleaning to help their mother.

The past two days had changed everything the family used to take for granted. Everything they used to know and trusted had been stripped away.

If our secret gets out, it will blow up our world. It can't!

Regina knew that their story had to remain secret for Chaja Fajga and her future. Her chest tightened as she considered what could happen if Chaja Fajga was pregnant, especially from being raped by Russian soldiers. Her life would be restricted to living at home and raising a child, and the family would have to live with the shameful consequences.

Even though it was not her fault, the circumstances would essentially remove the family from the society they had always known. Who would come to their defense? Would their friends defend them from the people who would say they should no longer be included in the Jewish community?

Our life in Warsaw will not remain peaceful if that happens.

Regina's heart fluttered at she thought about the possibility that she could have lost her sister as well as become a victim herself. Sweat broke out on her forehead. She wheezed, stood up, and grabbed the back of a chair.

My family is in danger anywhere outside of Warsaw. What can I do to keep them close? Can we feel safe anymore living under one roof?

She had first-hand knowledge of the region's politics through her job at the Bund. She decided she must be responsible for the safety of her family.

This must be my new responsibility.

By taking on a new role as someone well-informed about the current situation, Regina thought her family might take her announcements more seriously when she told them about the notices that came in at the Bund and that she was not being paranoid for no reason.

Mokotów, a residential section of Warsaw just south of the city center, was a quiet community. People knew the Anuszewicz family. Their friends included Christian and Polish Lipkas, who were Tatars that had settled in Lithuania, where they tried to preserve their shamanistic religion and sought asylum among non-Christian Lithuanians. Their friends, the Ratkewitch family, had emigrated from what was then Polish Lithuania, which had become an integrated part of Poland. Regina's family had many Muslim friends who lived in the same neighborhood.

When Lena did her usual shopping at the market square, she bought meat from Bashar's meat grocery, where each month the Muslim owner invited the Jewish shochet to examine the shop's hygiene and make sure the kosher rules were observed, while the Islamic Imam examined for cleanliness and to ensure that the similar rules of Halal were also being followed.

Local residents with different religious affiliations observed each other's holidays and celebrations, such as weddings, Christenings, Bar Mitzvahs, anniversaries, graduations, and birthdays. They ate at each other's homes. Jews were an integrated part of Polish culture. Regina knew they all had to stay as close together as possible to ensure their mutual safety, which she hoped would continue, but since the pogrom, she was not so sure that Warsaw was a safe place to be.

Regina normally accompanied her mother to the greengrocer for fresh vegetables and potatoes. After they shopped, she would carry home whatever they bought.

On that day, as Lena pulled a shawl over her shoulders and put on her boots to walk several kilometers along the dirt streets, she stopped and looked at Regina. It had been an exhausting two days and Regina noticed how tired her mother looked. She slumped and put her head in her hands.

"Mother? Are you alright?"

"I'm just so tired. What if we don't shop today? What if we just have some of the resztki from yesterday? Surely, we have some extra vegetables we could put together for tonight."

Regina stood over her mother, not sure how to help her. She had never seen her look so defeated and it frightened her. Her parents were always in control, yet at this moment, she felt her mother could not deal with even the smallest decision.

"I can go for you. Just tell me what you want me to buy."

"I'm too tired to even do that, Regina. Just stay home with me. That is all I need."

Lena sighed, removed her shawl, and put down her bundle. As she and Regina sat together, holding each other, they heard a knock on the door, and then a voice.

"Lena? Are you there It's Sonya. Lena?"

The sound of her mother's friend was welcome. Regina was glad to know that Lena had friends who looked after her to see if she needed anything. She found it warm and comforting.

"Yes, Sonya, I'm here."

Sonya was a diminutive, birdlike woman with large brown eyes and straight brown hair, pulled back in a bun. While her physical stature was not imposing, she created a large presence in the warm she cared for her friends and family.

Regina went to the door and invited Sonya inside.

"I just heard about the pogrom in Bialystok and thought of Chaja Fajga! Is she all right? Is she here?"

"Yes, yes. Chaja Fajga is safe. She went back to Bialystok with her two brothers to fetch her things. She will be home later. She won't be going back there to work, though."

"Yes, that is best," Sonya said. "Did you hear about Jakub Geremek? He was clubbed by Russian soldiers as he left the mine. Now, he can't see anymore. Heathens. Monsters. Jakub must live at home where he can be cared for, but he was the one making money for his family. Now, what will happen to them? We all must cook for them and give them food."

More terror from the Russians.

Regina sat down with a heavy heart for the Geremeks, a nice family that lived close by. Sonya sat next to Lena and took her hand in hers.

"Lena, you are so lucky that Chaja Fajga and Regina are safe. Be grateful and thank God you were spared. They must not go back to that terrible place. We are safe here."

Just then, another knock on the door startled all three of them.

Who else is coming to our home at such a time?

Lena looked at Regina and shrugged as she walked toward the door. "Who is there, please?"

"Lena, it's Chayana Achmatowicz, your neighbor across the square. I heard about the pogrom in Bialystok, and I'm worried for Chaja Fajga. Please open the door. I have some food for you."

17

Chayana was a Lipka Tatar, portly and square with a mass of black hair and piercing brown eyes. She offered Lena a dish of kalduny, stuffed dumplings made of unleavened dough.

"I heard about the pogrom in Bialystok and was so worried about Chaja Fajga. I also heard Regina went to see her. I know they are home now, and praise to Allah they are safe. You must have been frantic!"

Years ago, Chayana and her husband, Azgar, were the first family to welcome Lena and Yosef to their Mokotów neighborhood. Although the Anuszewiczs were Jewish, they still welcomed them with a gift of potato pancakes, which were like the latkes Lena made for Hanukah.

Chayana approached Lena with open arms, ready to give her friend a loving hug.

"I hope I'm not bothering you. I didn't know you had company."

Chayana and Sonya looked at each other. Finally, Lena invited them to sit with her on the couch on one side of the room while Lena sat in the chair usually reserved for Yosef.

"It's fine, Chayana. You are always welcome in my home. Now, you and Sonya can get to know each other."

Sonya said nothing as she looked at Lena.

"This is so nice of you to let us in at the same time," said Chayana. "I'm sorry, Sonya, that I didn't bring more kalduny to share with you, too."

Sonya stood up straight and offered her own apology.

"Oh, no, it is me who should have brought food for us all."

As she observed the interaction, Regina felt the tension and wished that both women would leave.

Mama is so tired.

Since she was only a daughter, Regina couldn't dismiss these two nice women who came to her home to offer support and food for her family.

"You are both so nice and caring," she said. "It was not necessary or expected, so please don't feel you have failed us in any way. On the contrary, my mother has always said you are both wonderful, and we so appreciate what you have come to check on our family. But I'm sure you can see that my mother is quite tired."

Chayana and Sonya looked at each other.

"I'm so sorry. I don't mean to intrude," said Sonya.

As tears streamed down Lena's face, Sonya crossed her arms.

"We are neighbors," she said, "and we both care about your family."

Chayana and Sonya moved to hug Lena.

"I'm too tired to cry anymore," Lena said.

She looks to be beyond exhausted.

Sonya spoke up.

"It's a sign that we need to stay in Warsaw and not to go too close to Russia. We are not welcome there. It's no better for us, either. The Russians are persecuting Muslims, too, especially Lipka Tatars. We are all in the same place with those heathens."

Sonya looked at Chayana.

"It's time for you and me to be friends now. We share more than we differ. Please come and feel welcome in my home, Chayana."

Regina was surprised but impressed by Sonya's candor. She observed the interactions between the three women and felt especially touched by the way Sonya and Chayana cared for her mother.

"You are both brave and caring friends to my mother and I'm so touched by your invitation. We will happily accept and share it with my father, telling him how loving you are with our good friend here, and that we must extend our family to you both. Thank you."

With that, both women stood, gathered their wraps, and left together, leaving Regina and Lena to sit in silence.

Finding a Mate

Regina had overheard her parents talking about finding a mate for Chaja Fajga and knew it wouldn't be long before they discussed finding a husband for her, too.

What if she's pregnant? When will Chaja Fajga have her monthly?

Her parents had met for the first time at their ceremony, a traditional fate Regina wanted to avoid. Arranged marriages were how women and men were joined. Her parents' marriage was set up by Lena's parents when they learned about a respectable man, her father, who was eligible for marriage and looking for a suitable wife.

Her grandparents, Schlomo and Audria, had been eager to get their eldest daughter out of the house so they could make room for her younger sister to begin the process of finding a mate for her.

Regina had heard family stories about Yosef being considered a prized catch, a skilled leather worker known for superior products that brought top prices in the village where he worked. Her father could cut, sew, and prepare leather trim and benches, do repairs, and create gun slings, straps, and similar articles. He also did his own clothing designs, which was considered quite desirable among the high society of Christians who frequented the shop where he worked.

Regina was proud that her father could cut and sew so fast without sacrificing the quality of his work.

When the matchmaking was finalized, Schlomo and Audria put together a nice dowery to sweeten the pot, as Yosef used to say. He also came to the wedding with a horse and bundles of wheat for Lena's family.

It was customary for the local rabbi to create a ketubah, the Jewish marriage contract, for a newly wedded couple. Lena explained to her daughters that it was an integral part of a traditional marriage, as the ketubah outlines the rights and responsibilities of the groom in relation to his bride.

I'm glad I'm still on the young side to become a bride, even though Mama married at 17, when she was just a year over the legal age.

Regina couldn't imagine that her parents didn't meet until the day of their wedding. She felt sure that if she was in that situation, her nerves would be on high alert about meeting the man she would be spending the rest of her life with as his bride. While looks were not primary, she wondered about the person's character.

When it becomes my turn, which I hope is years away, my partner should have a more righteous upbringing than an attractive face.

Regina had heard stories about her father's reaction to seeing her mother's face for the first time. The family had enjoyed many laughs about Yosef's pleasant surprise when he lifted Lena's veil and saw her natural beauty, with her hazel eyes and full lips. Apparently, her brothers and sisters snickered.

That's why Mama became pregnant so fast!

It was also why there was a constant flow of children, one after the other every year and a half, keeping Regina's mother continually pregnant and the midwife in their small town very busy.

Having several children meant that Yosef needed to find more work than he could find in Mokotów, which is why he went into Warsaw to find a job that would pay him enough money to support his growing family. The small leather workshop in his village did not allow him to earn enough money to purchase even the lowest cuts of meat more than once every two weeks. To keep his family in good health, it was considered acceptable to provide meat at least once a week.

The family also enjoyed Yosef's talent at home. He set up a small studio next to their house where he turned the skins he bought into stools, table tops and even clothing, such as vests and pants for Regina's brothers. Everyone in Mokotów recognized the quality of his work and Regina enjoyed knowing that her father had a reputation for being extremely talented.

21

However, Yosef had to be careful not to sell his private work to friends and neighbors because that would have been seen as stealing customers from the place he worked, so he limited his personal creations to his own family.

I wonder if Papa will have to make maternity clothes for Chaja Fajga.

Since Regina worked outside the house, she had opportunities to do some stealth investigating about resolving Chaja Fajga's potential pregnancy. She did some research about the different herbs women could use for their monthly or to stop a pregnancy. Regina read that various concoctions were made from tansy oil, pennyroyal, rue, ergo, and perhaps opium, but they could have dangerous side effects, such as damaging internal organs, triggering seizures, or even death. When used in correct doses, however, they could be effective in causing a miscarriage.

If the midwife is not eager to do this without our parent's knowledge, could I be comfortable trying to do this on my own?

Regina felt desperate, as though she were possibly pregnant herself. She also felt guilty about staying safe in the closet, even though Chaja Fajga never said a word about it.

I can't bring it up.

It was time to act. Everyone knew where the midwife lived, and Regina was determined to talk to her.

She didn't go directly to the Bund office. Instead, she took a detour to see the midwife. Regina knew this was a difficult errand, and she wondered if other women who suspected they might be pregnant also wanted to do something to stop it.

How many other women do this in secret?

She walked slowly up the flowered walkway and rapped on the door. She realized the midwife did not have regular hours, as babies can come at any time of the day or night. After several minutes, the door opened, and a plump, sleepy woman showed her face. She had long, gray hair twisted in a loose braid over her shoulder.

"Can I help you? Oh, it's Regina Anusevicz, is it?"

"Um, hi Miss, uh, Mrs., uh . . ."

Regina wasn't sure of her name. She only knew her as the "midwife."

"Never mind that. Is something wrong at your home?"

"Yes, sort of. Can I come in to talk about it?"

"Yes, yes. Sorry, I was up very late last night with a difficult delivery." She moved back so Regina could enter.

How do I ask what I need from her?

"Thank you. Um, you know my sister, Chaja Fajga, was in Bialystok during the pogrom."

"Yes, everyone knows she was there and that she was able to escape the violence from those heathens."

"Well, that is why I'm here. She didn't escape the violence, but no one knows what really happened. Not even our parents."

Regina looked down, afraid to continue. The midwife touched her arm and nodded, urging her to continue.

"Okay, I'll just say it."

Tell her, Regina.

"She was raped, but not killed. Obviously."

The midwife looked confused and took a deep breath.

"Oh my, how?"

"We told our parents that Chaja Fajga fell on the stairs at the mill and banged her head, and that she changed into another dress. No one questioned her explanation."

"I think I know why you are here."

"She hasn't gotten her monthly yet, and we are very concerned. We have heard there are medicines you can take."

The midwife sat down and put her hands to her face.

"Yes, that's true, but they can be dangerous if they are not taken properly. I think you are asking me for them so you can give them to your sister yourself without anyone knowing. Is that right?"

"Yes. I'll be with her."

"That will not do. Without the right guidance, Chaya Fajga could hemorrhage and die. Regina, I can't let you give these medicines to your sister without my guidance. I'm sorry."

Regina sat still. She had hoped their conversation wouldn't end like that.

"What are we going to do? She hasn't gotten her monthly, and she could be pregnant. Our parents will be horrified, and Chaja Fajga's life will be ruined either way. Our father will make her a spinster."

Regina let out a cry as the midwife watched her pace back and forth, explaining how she felt for keeping the rape a secret and making up a lie to protect her sister.

"I feel guilty for not trying to rescue Chaya Fajga. Maybe I could have hit the soldiers on the head with a heavy object. It doesn't matter now, does it?"

"Regina, it would not be right for me not to be with your sister when she takes the medication. How do you think your mother would react?"

"I don't know. I'm scared it would go badly. It didn't occur to us to only tell our mother and not our father."

Regina sat back down.

Would our mother keep it a secret from our father?

"Couldn't we just do this, the three of us? You could be there."

"I can't disrespect Lena that way. You must not try to do this without help. I won't sell you the herbs. You could kill your sister."

Regina thanked the midwife and left, not at all sure what to do about her sister and the possibility of her being pregnant.

I need to take responsibility for the situation.

Another week went by, and still nothing. Regina was distracted at work and at home. Chaja Fajga told Regina she was close to telling their parents what really happened and was ready to face the consequences. Staying silent was becoming impossible because Lena kept asking Chaja Fajga is something was wrong.

"It must be a remnant of the pogrom," Chaja Fajga said, "and Mother must be afraid that I was traumatized."

Regina suggested to her sister that the midwife would tell only their mother and see how she felt about keeping the secret from their father. They couldn't imagine Lena would go along with it, but they had to do something or face the consequences of having a baby from such an awful act.

Chaja Fajga stared at the patterns she used to make clothes. She sighed, and when Regina asked her what she was sewing, Chaja Fajga had no answer.

"I don't know yet."

In that moment, Regina realized that her sister was no longer capable of rational thought.

It's up to me now.

She decided to stay home from work so she could talk to her mother without the rest of the family around. She insisted that Chaja Fajga be part of the conversation, even though Regina would be the one suggesting such a difficult act.

The next day, she put her plan into action.

"Mama, I'm staying home from work today. I'm a bit tired."

"I'm sorry, Schatzeleh. Do you need to lie down, my sweetheart?"

"Maybe."

Chaja Fajga watched from a corner of the room. Regina caught her eye and made a small motion with her hand to come to her. They had the house to themselves until their siblings came home from school.

Finally, Regina knew it was time to tell their mother the truth. She inhaled deeply, as she dreaded what was to come when their world would change and not for the good.

"Mama? Can we talk to you for a minute?"

Lena looked at her daughters with a puzzled look on her face.

"Of course, my darlings. What is it?"

Tears streamed down Chaja Fajga's cheeks, and she lifted her hands to cover her face. She hurled herself onto her bed, leaving Regina standing alone next to their mother.

Lena shrieked.

"What is going on? Why is Chaja Fajga acting like this?"

Regina froze. The answer was all up to her. She couldn't move, as her eyes darted back and forth from her mother to her sister.

"Someone tell me what is going on!"

"Mama," said Regina. "Oh, Mama."

"What is it?"

Just say it.

"Mama, Chaja Fajga was raped in Bialystok."

Lena looked at Regina and shrieked.

"What are you talking about? She fell on the stairs at the mill. What do you mean she was raped?"

"I lied. She never fell on the stairs. She was raped by two Russian soldiers, and we are not sure she is pregnant, so we went to see the midwife to get some help making her monthly start."

Lena didn't move. She looked at Regina and then at Chaja Fajga, still lying on her bed with her hands covering her face.

"So, it was a lie. Why didn't you tell us when you came home? Why was this a secret?"

Regina waited for her sister to say something.

"Chaja Fajga, aren't you going to tell Mama what we decided to do? Are you leaving it all to me?"

"I can't. I can't."

"Okay, here is what happened. After I got to Chaja's boarding house, I started to walk to her mill to meet her for our picnic. I had your pierogis with me, too. Then, I saw Russian soldiers running down the street and realized there was violence coming fast. I ran back upstairs and hid inside one of the wardrobes. I heard voices and a woman screaming. I didn't know who it was, and I hoped it wasn't Chaja. I stayed in the closet until much later when I heard Chaja calling me. I wasn't sure if it was a trick, so I stayed quiet. Finally, I came out and saw what had happened."

Regina sat down next to Chaja Fajga.

"We are hoping for her monthly to come but it hasn't yet, and we don't want to wait too long. The midwife won't give us medicine because she said she needs to administer it herself, and she won't do it without you there."

Chaja Fajga sat up in bed.

"Mama, I'm so sorry. We hoped that we wouldn't have to tell you what happened. I'm ruined. I know that. Father will be furious with me. I'll never marry. I'll be a burden to you forever. Our family will be shunned."

No one spoke for a few minutes.

Finally, Lena addressed her daughters.

"Listen to me. We need to reach the midwife as soon as possible and take the medication she uses for such circumstances. This will be just between the three of us. It will be our secret. Chaja, if you get sick, we will say you have an illness and that you need time in bed. No one can ever know about this. Do you understand me? Regina, go and arrange with the midwife to come here when everyone else is at work or in school."

Thank God.

Regina nodded as Chaja Fajga wiped her eyes. They both felt a sense of relief even though they were still frightened about what was coming.

5

Lonely Protest

Regina sat on a chair in the main room, reading Bolesław Prus's *The Doll*. She put down her book and sat back in the chair, reflecting on the day the midwife came to their house to administer the medications to Chaja Fajga.

It was not a good day. Regina sat on the edge of her bed with her sister after she took the medicine. The midwife stayed for a couple hours, waiting, and watching Chaja Fajga. It didn't take long before she felt cramping and doubled over in pain, holding her stomach.

"Oooooh. My stomach, it is cramping so. What is happening?"

Lena sat next to her daughter with her arm around her shoulder.

"Be strong, my love. It won't be long."

The midwife explained that it might take a couple hours before any discharge would begin. She didn't know if it was just her monthly or something more. She said to stay home for a couple of days to be sure it was over and that she would check in again the next day.

I hope Chaja Fajga finds an excuse to avoid being at the dinner table.

Regina was concerned about what might happen if their secret was revealed in front of everyone. She and her sister were barely two years apart. They had much more in common with each other than with their siblings. If there was any friction in the family, it was mostly between Zelman and Aleksander. The two older girls were responsible for managing their younger brothers and sisters. The eldest brother, Zelman, had black hair and their father's blue eyes. He was tall, with a mild manner, the one who always smoothed out tension or arguments at school and at home. Chaja Fajga usually decided who would do what chore, such as going to the grocer or butcher. She also chose which sister would help Lena after school.

To Regina, it seemed like her younger sisters, Dina and Kejla, giggled all day, braided each other's hair, and talked nonstop about boys, especially when they were not washing clothes, sweeping floors, or peeling potatoes.

When it came to assigning chores, Regina and Chaja Fajga were careful not to show favoritism as their mother had instructed.

Regina loved languages. She used those skills to work her way into local politics by offering to translate documents from Polish to Yiddish or Russian. Working at a textile mill was not something she wanted to do until she got married. However, it was not uncommon for Lena to grow exasperated with Regina's alarmist lectures about why they should consider living someplace else to avoid what she believed was antisemitism marching its way through Poland from Russia.

Her brother's route out of day labor was a bit simpler, although there were still several limitations for Jews. Many of their friends had businesses, such as a bakery or greengrocer, a butcher shop or selling textiles.

Regina saw how hard her father worked just to keep food on the table and have textiles for Mama to make the family clothes. She loved her siblings, but she wanted more in her life than just the day-to-day tasks of caring for them. She didn't tell anyone, but she was not eager to get married. She was still only 16, but it wouldn't be long if Chaja Fajga were married off before her, making her the next in line.

None of that was on her mind when the family gathered around the dinner table to talk about Chaja Fajga's plans to stay in Warsaw after the awful experience she had in Bialystok. Was there a nearby Jewish-owned mill where she could work?

Chaja Fajga is so good at sewing. Maybe she could make clothes to sell from the house. Everyone knows she is very talented.

On more than one occasion, some of their Christian neighbors asked Chaja Fajga to pick out fabric from the mill. They gave her money to buy it for them; then they took the bolt to a seamstress in town to sew a special dress. These women had money because their husbands worked in the government, and they always needed fine clothes.

29

Regina figured that if Chaja Fajga offered to sew their clothes, they would hire her. However, there was a question about how she would buy a bolt of fabric if she didn't work at the mill.

Nothing was decided that night because the family had to absorb what almost happened in Bialystok. The only thing they knew for sure was that Chaja Fajga would not be returning there, which meant they now had other options to consider.

We must make sure that Chaya Fajga is not pregnant while we keep the rape a secret.

Regina said nothing about keeping the information from her father. It just was not discussed. The only thing anyone in the family knew was that Chaja Fajga was not feeling well from all the events of the past several days.

The major topic at the Bund was how the Jewish community in Warsaw was growing more and more on edge, even though the pogrom took place in Bialystok. Regina did not tell any of the other workers that her sister had been raped. They knew she had been there, but that's all they needed to know.

Regina didn't remember hearing about antisemitic attacks as she grew up.

Maybe because our parents never talked about it.

But now she had access to news from all over Eastern Europe. The repeated alerts from Poland, Lithuania and Belarus continued to come in and it was Regina's job to send the information out to the public. This was why the Mokotów office was so glad they had Regina to translate notices to other languages, increasing the opportunity for more people to read the alerts. Regina's career was launched much earlier than most. In fact, having a job translating was unusual. She wondered if she wanted to do it for the rest of her life.

Will I finally get tired of constantly being on edge and sounding the alarm of danger at our door?

After the midwife administered the herbs to Chaja Fajga, it took three days for her to finally finish bleeding. It wasn't clear if she was pregnant or not, or if it was just her monthly, but because of the amount of blood and clots, it could have been the beginning of a pregnancy.

"It's over now," said the midwife. "At this point, it doesn't matter. You can relax and get your strength back. Call me again if anything changes."

After the midwife left, Chaja Fajga spoke to Lena and Regina.

"Do you think anyone suspected anything?"

"If they did, they didn't say anything to me," said Regina.

"I agree," said Lena. "Now, we can focus on the future, and you can be thankful that you still have your reputation. This was our secret and it's over. Let's forget about it and move on."

Regina thought about her mother keeping the secret from her husband. It had to be difficult to refrain from sharing something so awful about her daughter and keeping the story private. She understood about the need to protect Chaja Fajga from a stained life as a spinster. Regina was in awe of the strength this took for her mother.

Now, it was time for her two younger brothers, Zelman, and Aleksander, to begin thinking about a profession, or at least find work that would enable them to earn a decent living and eventually support a family.

Except for a small minority of well-off Jewish merchants, bankers, and factory owners, the options were to become a trader in fur, own a small shop, or as her father had done, to become a skilled craftsman. The textile industry was always looking for new skilled workers, even Jews.

Regina reflected on her father's family. She wondered how he would feel about his daughter being raped by Russians. She realized that by not telling him and keeping it to herself, her mother did the right thing to spare her husband's anger and helplessness that he couldn't protect her. It would have changed everything in the family.

Regina knew that work for Jews was becoming limited and education was the key out if they could get it. For years, the only opportunities for Jewish children were the cheder, a private Jewish elementary school where the kids studied Hebrew, the Bible, and the fundamentals of Judaism.

That is not going to get them a job.

Yosef told his children that he wanted the boys to learn a craft and for the girls to learn sewing and dressmaking or how to run a bakery.

Regina knew that newly married men needed to create a home quickly because their women traditionally got pregnant right away and it would take too long to build a dwelling. They needed to have a place for their wives and new infants. Once the family started, between working as many hours as required, there was no time to build a new home or add on to one they had.

Regina had read that during the last 20 years of the 19th century, Jewish merchants and factory owners developed markets in other countries. They did not feel comfortable with their "small town" status. Never again would the modest wooden dwellings they lived in be adequate. At the first opportunity, and sometimes even without the necessary funds, people built multiple story houses with every modern innovation known at the time. New apartment houses sprang up out of nowhere.

Although she had suffered horribly in Bialystok, Chaja Fajga told Regina that she missed her young friends there and wondered if their families were also demanding that they stay home and not return to Bialystok.

"I know what happened, but before that, I enjoyed the friends I made, and I miss them. I hope they are doing well."

She giggled.

"One of my friends was crazy silly over one of the boys at the mill. She talked about him constantly. I think he knew it because he gave her the eye when he was on our floor. It was so much fun."

Regina knew that for Zelman, life was about to get complicated. As the oldest male child, he would bear a lot of responsibility if their father died, including providing for the family once he completed his studies. With so many siblings, Zelman confessed he was confused about his future. Was he supposed to become a leather worker like his father? He had told Regina about his vision of owning a farm outside of town, with his own cows, horses, and sheep, where he could grow delicious fruits and vegetables to sell to wealthy families. His products would be prized by the best society.

Where would he get the money to buy the land and the animals? Who would buy from him? He would have to build a reputation, which takes time.

Zelman told Regina that if he brought his best to the market and the women saw how much better his carrots and beets looked compared to the others, his reputation would build quickly.

Her younger sisters, Dina and Kejla, were still too young to think about their future. Their life was attending school and helping at home.

When Regina went into the Bund office on Monday, she found several notices from the Warsaw office. Under the election campaigns for all Dumas, the most recent election aggravated relations between Poles and Jews, culminated in an anti-Jewish boycott by local Christians.

Regina was keenly aware that the crushing events in Russia had now seeped into Poland. She read that the intensity of the Russian revolution, beginning in 1905, had led to a major setback in the growth of the Polish community that supported political liberation.

How am I going to keep my family safe when they don't want to hear what is coming?

6

Leopold and Aron

It had been three weeks since the pogrom in Bialystok, but to Regina and Chaja Fajga, it seemed like ages since they had returned from the scene of the rape. Chaja Fajga seemed fully recovered, and except for the terrible memories, life appeared to be back to normal and relatively good. They could go on with their lives without the threat of pregnancy hanging over them.

It's history now. I hope my sister can put all of this out of her mind, but I'm not sure if she can.

It didn't take long for Chaja Fajga to find new work. Friends who knew she was looking for help with her dressmaking business introduced her to Kasia Kowalski, a well-to-do Christian woman who was highly regarded for her skills making dresses for women and pants and dress coats for men.

Kasia's husband worked for the Jewish Poliakov family, headed by the brothers, Samuel, Yakov, and Lazar. They had invested in a company that built and operated railroads connecting central Russia's main cities. They were considered well off compared to Regina's family.

She was excited for Chaja Fajga to take the job because it allowed her to stay in Warsaw. Her sister was less than inspired, however, and she told Regina she felt isolated, as the only person to interact with was Kasia. Her clients would never know that Chaja Fajga was doing most the sewing, even though Kasia told some of them she had help.

"Mrs. Kowalski is careful not to give out my name because she doesn't want to lose any of her clients. Mama thinks this is a good job for me. I don't want to make her feel bad because she was the one who reached out to Kasia on my behalf but working there feels so isolating compared to what my life was like at the mill with my friends."

Regina's life at the Bund became a bit more exciting when a young man, from Warsaw, named Leopold Frenk, showed up. He was 22, tall and fit with deep brown eyes and wavy brown hair. He had been working in the Jewish Labor Bund office in Moscow for two years after he finished school. Leopold was now back on a three-month assignment to help organize and strengthen the growing Bund office in Mokotów.

Regina was deeply committed to translating the news that came through each day. She still shared it with the family, even though they were less than thrilled to hear about antisemitic attacks in Russia and Poland. They preferred to focus on finding a husband for Chaja Fajga, as she was getting a bit older than some other eligible, young Jewish women.

Early Thursday morning, as Regina was getting ready to leave the house, she heard a light knock on the door.

"Lena, are you home? It's Doria."

Regina knew Doria as a lovely and somewhat outspoken woman. She had four children, three boys and a young girl, who was a bit slow-witted.

As Lena greeted her friend, Regina watched, pretending to put her bundle together to leave for work.

"Doria, what a pleasant surprise. Come, we will have tea and the apple cake I just made for the kids. There should be plenty for us."

She gestured for Doria to sit at the family table.

"Thank you, Lena, you are always so welcoming. I enjoy visiting with you for any reason, but I have a special one today. But first, let's enjoy your apple cake."

Regina was curious about the surprise visit. She knew Doria had a son who was studying to become a rabbi and wondered if that had anything to do with why she showed up.

Lena poured tea and cut pieces of apple cake that were still warm from the oven.

"I'm glad you stopped by. I can use some pleasant company these days."

"Oh, yes, I heard about Chaja Fajga and you, too, Regina, and all terrible events in Bialystok. Lena, you must have been so horrified until you knew the girls were safe."

"We are not allowing Chaja Fajga to go back to work in the mill, even though they said all the women were safe from the soldiers. I don't care what they say now. They can't prevent the Russians from returning and breaking down the doors as they did before. She must stay here. We found her a good job with Mrs. Kowalski, the dressmaker. Chaja Fajga will sew many of her clothes and make good money while she improves her skills. Mrs. Kowalski is an expert and sews for the wealthy society set."

Lena looked closely at Doria.

"This is just between you and me, of course."

Doria nodded.

"It is fortunate that she found new work here," said Doria. "It is not easy for women to find non-factory work outside of the home before they marry and have children."

"Well," Lena said, "hopefully, she will be married soon, although nothing yet has developed. We are not wealthy, and our dowery is not as much as some other families."

Regina was anxious to hear why Doria was visiting and was not surprised at what she overheard. She wondered if it had anything to do with Doria's son, Aron, the future rabbi, and if he was interested in marrying Chaja Fajga.

Doria could not help but smile.

"Chaja Fajga's work situation could change. You remember our son, Aron, who studied to be a rabbi? He has completed his studies and is ready to settle down and make a home. Aba and I were talking about the eligible young women in Mokotów, and even in other parts of Warsaw, but Aron remembers Chaja Fajga from when they were in school together. He asked us if she was already married, and of course we said no. Aron has had his eye on her since they studied at the state school."

Doria was flushed and couldn't get the words out fast enough.

"Oh, I'm so sorry. I didn't even ask you if Chaja Fajga is already promised to someone."

Lena took a breath.

"Oh, my goodness, Doria. This is such good news. Of course, I remember your Aron, such a studious young man. But won't he want a wife who wants to be a rabbi's wife?"

"All I know is that he asked about Chaja Fajga and wondered if she had already been promised or married," said Doria.

"This is something Yosef and I will have to discuss. I can't promise Chaja Fajga without talking to him first."

"Of course. I know my coming to you directly is highly unusual and I'm sure the shadkehn (marriage broker) would not be amused. However, I'm making her job easier, right?"

"That is true, so if we allow her to broker the process and she gets her fee, she will be just fine."

With that good news, Doria said goodbye.

Regina kissed her mother on the cheek.

"Marrying Aron would make Chaja Fajga a rebbetzin, right?"

Lena turned to Regina and pointed a finger at her.

"A rabbi's wife, yes! Regina, please don't share this with your siblings, not just yet. Your father and I must talk privately first with Chaja Fajga."

Regina tried to imagine being a rebbetzin.

Is it something my sister would want to be?

She felt happy and distressed by the news. On the one hand, she was happy about her sister getting married if she was ready. But she was also concerned about Chaja Fajga marrying a rabbi. Being a rebbetzin was not an easy life. All day and night, everyone in the synagogue wants something from them. A rebbetzin also needs to take care of household responsibilities, tend to the children, and support the rabbi with his teaching and studying.

And what about being a rabbi now in Poland? It's becoming increasingly antisemitic, which means rabbis and their families will be vulnerable.

Regina wondered if her mother would insist on Chaja Fajga accepting this marriage agreement. She hoped her parents would allow *her* to make such an important decision.

All I know is, I would never want to be a rebbetzin.

7

Can't Escape the News

Regina walked every morning to the Bund office at Rakowiecka and Kazimierzowska Streets, about 15 minutes from her home. On this day, she smiled to herself as she approached. She had worked hard to learn Russian at school and Yiddish from her grandmother. She wanted to know what people were saying, and learning those two languages gave her great satisfaction.

It had never occurred to her, though, that she could parlay those skills to get a job translating. In fact, her friends and family were surprised, too. She was also lucky to be around smart people who were interested in what was going on in the world around them, even though Regina wished they would stop grunting and groaning about the notices that came from Russia.

Most of it was not good, but at least they were all aware of what was happening. She was frustrated with her parents and siblings because she felt that they didn't pay enough attention to the political and societal happenings, even in Warsaw, and how it could eventually affect all of them.

A notice came in that a young boy had been hassled by some kids who called him a "Jew" and that he should leave Poland because he wasn't welcome here.

There are too many of these notices coming in.

Regina knew that while Mokotów was considered a genteel neighborhood of Warsaw, and that life was peaceful and people got along, she also knew that violence would not remain restricted to one place.

Her family finally said that they no longer wanted to hear her "news" at the dinner table.

"It's just not appropriate during our meal," Lena said.

It wasn't always bad news, though. Regina saw more women appear in larger public forums. She read the poetry of Maria Konopnicka, as well as the novels of Orzeszkowa, Gabriela Zapolska and Zofia Nafkowska.

She heard that Konopnicka and Orzeszkowa were becoming respected as national treasures, now comparable to their male contemporaries, Boleslaw Prus and Zelman Sienkiewicz. Women were playing an important role in the emergence of Poland's modern political movements and had a strong voice in elaborating their ideologies. Ester Golde, Rosa Luxemburg, Cecylia Sniegocka, Iza Moszczeiiska and Helena Radlinska, though of different ideological persuasions, were all connected to an unprecedented creativity that marked the era's social-political thought.

Polish science would eventually lay claim to the achievements of Maria Sklodowska, who later became known as Madame Curie.

Regina researched countless other women and she came to believe that. her skills could be valued, too, even though she was a woman.

What will the boys feel about my accomplishments?

While these women were successful, Regina didn't know anyone among her family or friends who could compare to these women.

Who will want me?

Documents that passed through Regina's hands at the Bund included developments in Jewish communities outside of Poland. She wanted to warn her family, but her mother and father made it clear it could not be discussed while they were eating their meal. It would have to wait until later.

But later never comes!

Soon after, some good news arrived for a change. Highly talented Jews were making a name in the arts, sciences, and humanities. Regina read about a Czech writer, named Franz Kafka, and she heard about Jews writing music in Vienna. Berlin had become a center of Jewish writers and journalists as well as actors and theatre directors. Berlin was also hosting a strong scientific community, including Albert Einstein.

Despite sharing good news about the growing role of women in literature and their scientific breakthroughs, Regina's feisty personality was met with a stern rebuke from Yosef.

"You are spending too much time outside your role as a dutiful daughter, and all this talk could be seen as setting yourself above other women in the Jewish community. This could cause problems for you, Regina, and for our family, too, because all your talk could be met with disapproval from the Christian community, too."

Regina stopped talking about her work and what she was learning. Instead of participating in the usual dinner banter, she stayed silent. She did, however, keep her ears open when visiting friends, a group that included a couple of Christians who had access to news from outside Warsaw. Much of that news was not good.

Regina had enjoyed the circle of friends that Yosef and Lena had acquired within the Jewish, middle-class community of Mokotów. It consisted of leather workers, builders, professionals in the healing arts and even some educators. While Lena and Yosef were not professionals, they were respected for their intellect, even though they avoided talking about problems in Poland.

Regina liked to be around for their visits and discussions, but when she shared what she had learned, she encountered mixed reactions. More often than she liked, her parents' friends quickly changed the topic.

"Regina, why do you listen to such negative opinions about Poland, and especially Warsaw? Look how many Jews here are professionals and community leaders."

Even so, the events in Russia fed her fears, such as the establishment of the Pale of Settlement, which were boundaries set up by Russia that included Belarus and parts of Poland, Lithuania, and Ukraine—basically the Russian Empire, where Jews had to live.

One night, Helen, a friend of her parents, quickly dismissed the news.

"That is no concern of ours, Regina. It's too far away."

"Maybe, but remember we had a pogrom here in Poland just a few months ago. Our government said nothing to repudiate the event. Polish citizens who were hurt were not compensated, and they still haven't received an apology from the Russian government."

Maybe it's just me.

Regina reflected on the physical terror she had felt inside the closet in Bialystok, when she heard the soldiers' boots approaching, and later, when her sister cried out to stop the Russian soldiers from raping her. She knew she was more highly sensitized to the risks and impacts that a pogrom could have on the community.

I cannot get those images and sounds out of my head, but I still can't tell anyone what really happened that day.

Her nightmares continued, which kept her wondering what could have happened if she had come downstairs and tried to save her sister.

Why didn't I beat them to death with a chair or at least frighten them away?

She had tried to talk to Chaja Fajga about the aftermath of the pogrom to see how she was doing, but her sister dismissed any discussion and said it was all in the past, that there was no need to bring it up again.

Regina was also puzzled by Chaja Fajga's indifference to the antisemitic attacks in Poland, especially after what she went through.

"Regina, it's all behind me now. Life is as it was before the pogrom, except I live at home now. Just put it behind you like I have."

Regina stared at her sister, but she found forgetting impossible.

And I'm not the one who was raped!

Despite her sister's request, Regina continued to live with a knot in her stomach that only became more pronounced every time she read of another incident. No matter what her local friends or parents said, she would close her eyes for a minute, take a deep breath and exhale, never convinced that "everything will be okay for the Jews of Poland."

Even her friend Ada, a Bund office colleague, told Regina to keep her worries to herself.

"Regina, stop being so negative."

"I'm not! I'm just sharing what I see. I don't know why you and the others don't see it, too. You hear the same news as me when it comes into the office. Times are troubled, and we all know it."

Ada groaned and threw her hands up in the air.

"Times are not troubled. You keep going back to Bialystok, and that was a freak event. It doesn't mean the pogroms will happen here. Józef Piłsudski, the chief of state and a very important person in government, would never let anything happen to us."

"You are being naïve, Ada. Those citizens' rights are more for Christians than Muslims or Jews."

Enough is enough!

Regina wasn't up to defending her position yet again. Lately, it seemed that every conversation devolved into an argument about the situation for Jews in Poland. She decided that she'd rather read a book than get into another heated discussion with her friends, so Regina made an excuse that she was not feeling well and left for home.

She was angry and exhausted to be left alone to deal with this threat.

Will I have to leave Poland to be safe? But where? I can't go to Russia, Lithuania, or Belarus. What about France or England?

She took a deep breath and held her head in her hands. Since she stopped bringing up her fears with her sister and the rest of her family, Regina was feeling more and more isolated.

One day, Yosef took her aside.

"My dear daughter, I know you are trying to help us understand what is going on in the country. We are not unaware, but your constant lecturing only makes us feel defensive. Where would we go? Where will things be different? How could we speak a new language? So far, nothing bad has happened to us or our friends. Please, stop."

He hugged Regina.

"You know we love you."

8

She Must Decide

Regina watched her mother as she rubbed her neck. She sensed that her anxiety was about a possible marriage between Chaja Fajga and Aron. She was more sensitive to what Lena was going through because the rest of the family didn't know what had transpired between Lena and Doria.

Her mother had told Yosef that she was concerned because they did not have a dowery, like upper-class Jews. They also did not have domestic help, an assortment of fine clothes, or a house with two floors. Finding a good husband who could provide well for her daughter and their future children would be challenging. A rabbi would always have work, a community around them, and she would be living with a learned person, which was a good thing.

But the wife of a rabbi is automatically considered to be his adjunct, even though he is the only one who signed the contract. Who she is and how she interacts with people could affect his work positively or negatively, and this would impact her husband's reputation within the community.

Regina expected Lena would want to talk with Yosef about such an important decision. She wondered if they would proceed with the kiddushin (engagement) of Chaja Fajga to Aron.

He will be a wonderful husband and he deserves a wife who will happily fulfill her wifely duties as the wife of a rabbi.

Throughout dinner, Regina looked at Chaja Fajga differently. She tried to imagine her as Aron's wife, visiting a family with a new baby, bringing sweets, and making affectionate comments about the newborn. Then, she would visit a mother who was ill and bring something to help her feel better, along with food for the family.

After dinner, Kejla and Dina removed the dishes and soaked them in a large pot before moving them to a rinsing pot. It was a process the children knew well and each of them took a turn after every evening meal. For the more extensive Shabbos meal, one more child participated.

Regina felt her mother's nervousness all through dinner. She wondered when her parents would finally talk to Chaja Fajga about the potential shidduch with Aron. She hoped her own anxiety didn't show, but she was sure everyone could see that something wasn't right with their mother.

Is it just my imagination?

She went in the living room and forced herself to work on her latest knitting project to try to stay calm. She watched Kejla and Dina kiss Yosef and say good night. The same ritual was repeated with Lena. Then, it was time for Lena and Yosef to retire to their room. They asked Chaja Fajga to join them. This was unusual, so all the children knew something was up.

After several minutes, Regina heard Chaja Fajga.

"Aron wants to marry me, and he is becoming a rabbi?"

"We are going to let you make this decision because becoming a rebbetzin is a big commitment."

"I didn't think he had eyes for me," said Chaja Fajga. "I always thought he was very nice and a good son. This is a surprise."

"You don't have to decide tonight," said Yosef. "It's a very big decision, a commitment beyond just being married."

"Now I would like to go to bed," Lena said. "I'm exhausted."

Regina sighed. She was glad they were letting Chaja Fajga make the decision. Everyone knew being a rebbetzin meant much more than just being married. It was a full-time job. She knew her sister could do it well, but she didn't know if she would want to.

Aron is a good catch, but is that enough?

9

Family Expectations

After attending Shabbos services and relaxing at home, Zelman asked Regina if she would like to take a walk to look at some new flowers that were just blooming. Regina raised her eyebrows. This was an unusual request, but she would not say no.

What could this be about?

She was happy but concerned. Nevertheless, she jumped up from the chair where she had been reading.

"How nice of you to ask!"

She knew that Zelman's was not interested in flowers, but she wanted to accept his invitation because she knew there was something he wanted to share with his big sister.

As soon as they walked away from the house, Zelman stopped and looked at Regina.

"I need to ask you something. I don't know how to tell Mama and Papa that I want to become a farmer and that I don't want to work at a leather shop or in a factory."

Regina took a moment to consider her brother's situation.

"What type of farmer would you like to be, Zelman? There are different kinds. Do you want to raise cows and sell the milk to stores or plant vegetables and fruit?"

"I knew you would ask that. I want to make fancy cheeses and grow some vegetables, the best in all of Poland. People will want to buy my cheeses, milk, and vegetables. But I have a big problem because I don't have money to buy land or a farm that might be for sale. I don't know how to get started and I'm afraid our parents would think I'm silly."

Zelman raised his hands in despair.

"I need to get an apprenticeship. I've done some research."

"I have to say I'm surprised. I never thought that anyone in our family would want to farm."

Her brother's passion and preparation took Regina by surprise.

I've been so involved in my own world that I don't know this young man at all. He's growing up and has dreams of his own.

Regina gave Zelman a hug.

"Dairy farmers with prized cheeses are sought out by the wealthiest families in Warsaw," said Zelman. "I've learned that just like a successful businessman, specialized farmers can be invited to fancy parties in the city. Farmers are not just considered to be laborers because the elite society respects the science that goes into making cheese."

"I'm really pleased you've shared this with me, Zelman. I appreciate your passion and I'll support you when you decide to tell Mama and Papa about your dream. Maybe they can find a way to help you start a small farm."

She hugged her brother tight. Now, they had a special bond.

I need to spend more time with my siblings. I've been living in my own world for too long.

Regina's brothers were approaching 17 in a couple years, which meant it would soon be time for Zelman to begin a career. It was already her turn to look for a husband, and she hoped her fierce attitude wouldn't repel the parents of prospective mates. Regina also had Chaja Fajga's potential marriage on her mind.

After the "talk" with Chaja Fajga, Lena had sent a message to Gita, the shadchanit, about arranging the marriage with Aron. Now, she might end up with multiple matchmaking opportunities.

Zelman had one more year to finish his studies. Regina was proud he had passed his lower school final exams and had been permitted to do three more years of education. The government encouraged Jewish students to take the exams, and if they did well, they could do secondary studies that would prepare them for viable careers that would help Poland become appreciated throughout Europe for its contributions to science and medicine.

Back in the house, as Regina resumed her reading, she watched her wiry younger brother, Alex. He was still young enough to not have a care in the world, but that would change quickly enough. Regina had never had a serious conversation with him. He was the quiet one in the family, always first to grab a book and find a corner to read. His intellect was obvious to Regina and from what she heard, to his teachers, too.

The family kept an eye on him as he moved up the ladder at school, on track to pass the tests that would allow him to attend university and become a professional.

Could that happen? It would be a first in our family.

Regina had seen the government become more inclusive as the education department reduced some of the barriers that traditionally barred Jews. She liked to tell people that, her parents taught all their children to read Polish and Yiddish before they even attended school. They would sit with her and each of her siblings and spend time reading with them, and then have each child read word by word until they could pick up any book and read it without help.

This exercise made Regina interested in languages and she eventually learned Russian as well. She wanted to know what people were saying around her and there were a lot of people speaking Russian in Poland.

Regina watched Lena with her two youngest daughters, pointing out words in a book.

"Do you know the word for flower, and can you find it on this page?"

She suddenly noticed Kejla and Dina in a new way. With Chaja Fajga's potential wedding in the air, she realized she had been ignoring her little sisters, assuming they were fine and didn't need her attention unless there was a problem.

With so much happening with her and Chaja Fajga, Regina knew it was easy to let the girls attend school and read at night without ever engaging them in a conversation about their young lives.

Just because they don't actively seek comfort doesn't mean everything is okay. Would I even know if they have a problem? Do I have to wait until I see them crying?

Regina decided it might be her job to check in with Kejla and Dina.

47

After all, they are not dolls. They are people! What if there is a problem in school? What if other students tease them or make fun of them? Should Chaja Fajga and I ask them if they need help with anything?

Despite her desire to be a better big sister, Regina couldn't stop wondering about Chaja Fajga's decision. She knew her parents were allowing her to decide instead of telling her what was best, as they had the right to do.

After Chaja Fajga returned from Kasia's home to collect the patterns and bolts of cloth she needed to sew two dresses, she walked into the kitchen for some apple cake before she started to work.

"How is it going with Mrs. Kowalski?" said Lena. "Is she nice to you? You are doing some very good work for her, you know. She should feel lucky you have taken on some jobs that help her grow her business."

"She's fine, Mama. She is polite and seems to respect my work. She has been able to take on more projects and get them back more quickly, which helps her earn more money. She pays me well, but she is the one getting the clients, not me."

Regina was careful not to bring up any negative news and kept to herself. She wondered what would happen with Chaja Fajga and Aron. It seemed forever before Yosef and the rest of the family came home and dinner was on the table. Lena had made a special stuffed cabbage with more meat than usual since she thought it would be a significant evening for Chaja Fajga, no matter what she had decided.

"Wow, stuffed cabbage, and it isn't even Shabbos!" said Zelman. "Are we celebrating something?"

Nothing happened during dinner. Dina and Kejla cleared the table, Chaja Fajga returned to her sewing, and Zelman and Aleksander curled into their corners with books. The girls gathered their books as well.

Chaja Fajga could do worse, but becoming a rabbi's wife?

A new rabbi could be assigned anywhere, and it probably wouldn't be a plum assignment, as new rabbis were always placed way out of town. They were supposed to work their way up to better assignments.

The bigger question was if Chaja Fajga understood the role of a rebbetzin and would even want to take it on. Regina was beside herself, waiting to hear what Chaja Fajga would decide.

10

No One Is Listening

Regina couldn't sleep. Fragments of the day's conversations with other members of the Student Bund kept running through her head. Some of her friends seemed primarily involved with issues of Polish identity under continuing Russian rule, especially considering the 1905 workers' strikes against the Czar.

She wondered if the possibility of Polish independence from Russia was embedded in the government's actions. Even if it wasn't, she questioned the Polish movement toward assuring at least seven years of free education for all children, boys, and girls, alike, and if providing that education in the Polish language was possible. She worried about the long-term consequences of the Polish boycotts of Russian schools in Poland.

How will these political actions impact our Jewish community?

Ever since she returned from Bialystok, Regina had been frantic to understand how antisemitic violence could have happened in Poland.

Will there be pogroms in Warsaw?

She hoped she could make her parents aware that they were victims like all the Jews in the Pale of Settlement.

Her chest felt tight whenever she thought about violence in her hometown. She was sure it was only a matter of time before she would see blood on the ground in her town. She made plans to bring it up at the next Bund meeting, even though she knew there would be negative reactions and plenty of eye rolling and yawns.

She was pleased, though, that the Bund had at least won some converts to its socialist viewpoints among Jewish artisans and workers, and among the growing Jewish intelligentsia. During the Russian Revolution of 1905, the

Bund headed the revolutionary movement in Jewish towns, particularly in Belarus and Ukraine, and they reconstituted themselves as a separate Polish political party.

Regina was active in the Bund campaign against antisemitism, as well as defending Jewish civil and cultural rights and rejecting assimilation. It led a trade union movement of its own and joined with Zionists and others to form self-defense organizations to protect Jewish communities against pogroms and government troops.

Fighting antisemitism had become Regina's preoccupation, especially after what she experienced in Bialystok. She wondered why Chaja Fajga wasn't more outspoken about it. It was as though she had buried the rape. She did confide that it was too painful to think about what happened and what she had to endure, so she had to put it behind her.

Eventually, the Bund strongly opposed Zionism, arguing that emigration to Palestine was a form of escapism. The Bund did not advocate separatism. Instead, it focused on culture, rather than a state or a place, as the glue of Jewish "nationalism." This approach was mainly influenced by the Austro-Marxist school, further alienating the Bolsheviks and Lenin. It was a tight line to walk for everyone involved.

I must take a more active role in the local Bund.

Even though she was privy to important news about the Jews' situation throughout the region, she knew it was still difficult for her family to take her seriously, and this was due to her being a girl, which she resented.

Regina debated about telling her family what she learned each day. She knew that if she didn't share, it would make her life easier at home. However, her news was about staying safe and being aware of the potential dangers they could face.

How can I make my family take me more seriously?

She thought back to a recent conversation with her mother.

"Regina, my sweet daughter, don't you think what you are doing is dangerous?" Lena said. "Don't you think those Russian antisemites know who you are?"

Regina grunted and let out a sigh.

"Mama, we can't just hide and pretend everything is going to be okay. Our Bund party is the only way we can stop the Russians from creating pogroms in Warsaw. Don't you see that?"

"What I see is a young woman upset and angry all the time. That certainly can't help your cause."

"My cause? This isn't about me! It's about all Jews, in Poland and elsewhere. Don't you see that?"

Regina threw her arms in the air and walked away. Then she stopped and turned around to face Lena.

"Look what happened in Bialystok. They are working to come into our community, but only if we let them. We must stop them, and that means we must work with the Bund."

Regina took a step back and abruptly stopped talking. She sat in silence. She felt tired and folded her arms across her chest as Lena faced her.

"I think you should quit your job at the Bund. It's turning you into someone I don't know. You are alienating everyone. And I'm afraid you will never find a man who will want to marry you."

Lena sobbed. Regina looked at her parents and Chaja Fajga.

My family is not on my side, and they don't care about the news.

They didn't seem to believe the reports she was bringing home, even when she showed them official notices of antisemitic activity so close to where they lived.

How could this be? How could they not believe their own child?

"So, Regina, our political activist," Chaja Fajga said, "all you are doing is putting your family in danger with all your activity with the Bund."

Regina stared at her sister.

Of all the people who should know how dangerous antisemitism can be, how could she say such a thing? What happened to the woman who was raped by Russian soldiers?

For a moment, Regina thought about how to answer such a ridiculous question, as if they had not heard what she had been saying for almost a year. Then, she decided to do her best to be reasonable.

"Chaja Fajga, if they want to come after anyone, they will come after me. But we are not trying to overthrow the government. The Polish party leaders have been very supportive of the Bund."

Chaja Fajga threw her hands in the air.

"You have an answer for everything, don't you? It would be good if you stepped back and saw what you are doing. It isn't just about you, you know."

She put her head down and went back to her sewing. Regina looked down and didn't move. There was nothing more to say. The Bund was her refuge, the only place where she felt she belonged.

Tears ran down her cheeks.

Am I still part of this family?

11

Yosef Tells a Story

Regina was always proud of Lena and her homemaking skills. She felt fortunate to have a mother who took such good care of her family, even though there were clear differences in how they saw themselves as Jews in an increasingly divided country.

Under Lena's watchful eye and loving guidance, her children had learned the skills they needed to be helpful at home, and Regina and Chaja Fajga were now making their way in the world as responsible young women.

Regina knew that some members of the Jewish community thought the Bund was the answer to keeping them safe from antisemites and Russian pogroms. Others thought the Bund was creating too much visibility, making them all targets, even for those Poles who would see their activism as making trouble for the Polish government.

No one else in my family seems particularly conscious of this.

Everyone in the Anuszewicz family besides Regina avoided discussing antisemitism and what was happening in Poland. She kept the news to herself to keep her sanity and avoid more stress.

She knew that when her father grew up, he was busy taking care of his family after his mother died while giving birth to his fifth brother. It was up to Yosef to raise his younger siblings because his father was always working to support the family. He shared with his current family how much he appreciated his neighbors bringing food and offering to do errands. The entire village had pitched in to ease the load on Yosef and his father.

He never had time to just be a young man and spend time with his friends, talking about girls, sharing their hopes about what their wives would be like, and trying to guess who their parents were considering for a shidduch.

Regina's father never had time for such activities, but at least he was pleased with his arranged bride, especially when her initial shyness evolved into caring for her husband and making a family.

Now, it was Yosef's turn to guarantee that his family would have a roof over their heads and food on the table. He often told them how fortunate they were to never have to deal with the sadness he suffered as a youth.

"Our problems today are ordinary day-to-day problems any family can have. It was a tragedy, though, when your mother and I lost our firstborn, but thank God, Mama survived."

Regina asked her father to explain what had happened. He hesitated, but then realized that his children were old enough to hear the story.

"I heard Lena crying and the midwife sent me to fetch the rabbi. It was her first pregnancy, only nine months from our wedding day. She was just seventeen, and her mother was not able to help because she had her own health issues. Our neighbor ran to the synagogue and brought the rabbi to our home. It was late in the afternoon, and he was preparing for evening prayers, but our emergency took priority. When I was finally allowed to see my beautiful, sad wife, we held each other and rocked back and forth, but that's all I could do. Rabbi Simcha was such a comfort. He held his hands over Lena because you know, according to Jewish law he is not allowed to touch a woman who is not his wife. He asked about our child. Doria was there. She was so wonderful. Thank God she was there to help. She took the stillborn baby away from Lena, but the rabbi needed to say prayers over it. He had to gather ten men, a minyan, to say the prayers. It was after sundown, so it was too late to go to the cemetery, but Rabbi Simcha recited the prayers right away to protect our child's Jewish soul, even though it would not be buried until the first light."

Yosef took a breath and swiped away a tear on his cheek.

"The rabbi said, 'God, we are weary and grieved. We were anticipating the birth of a child, but the promise of life was ended too soon. Our arms yearn to cradle new life, our mouths to sing soft lullabies. Our hearts ache from the emptiness and the silence. We are saddened and we are angry. We weep and we mourn. Weep with us, God, Creator of Life, for the life that could not be.'"

Yosef stopped, took a breath, and closed his eyes.

"I was at a loss with my inability to make things right for Lena. This was to be our first child together and it was stolen from us."

Regina considered her father's story. Life was different now. She could spend her time and energy in politics, which would have been unheard of when her father was her age. Being the head of the household back then was not the issue for her.

Political activities seemed so far away back then and had nothing to do with Papa and his family.

Regina's heightened awareness and anxiety after experiencing the terror of the pogrom terror was obvious. But Chaja Fajga had a different way of dealing with it.

She was raped and needs to forget. What else can explain her indifference to the threats we're now facing?

When managers at the mill in Bialystock saw the Russians coming, they rushed everyone to the third floor and locked the mill before Chaja Fajga could leave. By the time she left, the streets weren't safe, and if she had stayed longer at the mill, she might have escaped the attack.

Regina wondered if her family should learn more about the Bund party and their work to protect Polish Jews in Warsaw.

Would that make a difference? Should I invite them to the office to meet my co-workers and see what I do there?

She had heard about Bialystok's Chief of Police Derkacz, a man well known for his liberal sympathies and opposition to antisemitism. He was respected by the Jewish Bund and the Polish Socialist Party. When Russian soldiers attacked Jews in the marketplace, Derkacz had sent police to put down the violence and declared that a pogrom against the Jews would occur "only over my dead body."

His murder on June 11, 1906, foretold the violence to come. Russian soldiers began preparing for the Bialystok pogrom, which took place three days later. His death steeled Regina's resolve to fight against the violence that she feared was growing inside her country.

One Saturday evening, Yitzhak and Agata, long-time friends of Yosef and Lena, came by for a visit. Regina overheard her name during their discussion and wondered if they thought she couldn't hear them.

"Yosef and Lena, remember Regina was recently a student and we all know that young people are very political, and they get excited about anything that has to do with the government."

Yitzhak and Agata had moved to Mokotów to escape the noise and intensity of Warsaw's center city. The neighborhood seemed like a nice place to raise children, free of politics and demonstrations in the streets.

"It may be time to have a serious conversation with Regina," said Agata, "because as you have said yourself, she is changing. She is not the same girl since she came home from Bialystok."

12

My Sister, the Rebbetzin?

At her desk in the Bund office, Regina shuddered as she finished translating a short letter bringing news of another pogrom in Ukraine.

Am I overreacting?

She knew that her parents and friends thought the Polish government had nothing to do with what was going on in Ukraine and Belorussia, which were miles and miles away.

She handed her translation to the office manager and to Leopold.

"Are these pogroms really a threat to us here?"

"Are you serious, Regina?" said Leopold. "Remember how this has been building up in Russia? In the Kishinev pogrom of 1903, forty-nine Jews were killed, hundreds were wounded, seven hundred homes were destroyed, and six hundred businesses were pillaged. Then, we saw more pogroms in Gomel in Belarus, and in Smela, Feodosiya and Melitopol in Ukraine."

Regina nodded.

"What about Kiev in October?" said Leopold. "A hundred Jews were murdered by these savages. They mutilated people. And don't forget about the pogrom in Zhitomir. They are happening in Belorussia, and there have been so many in Ukraine, I can't even count them all. The Russians are in control, and they are sending their soldiers to attack their own citizens."

"You're right," said Regina.

"Yes, I know, and what is going on in Ukraine and Belorussia does have something to do with what's going on in Poland. How could it not? Violence doesn't know borders. Just look at Bialystok."

Regina was concerned about telling her family what she learned from Leopold. She already knew they thought she was exaggerating, that the unrest had nothing to do with their family in Warsaw, that the pogrom in Bialystok was more about Russia than Poland, and that any violence was still far away from where they lived.

Hearing these reminders provided ammunition for her next conversation with her parents and siblings, but she didn't have the energy to get into a debate that night and describe the latest events that should alarm her family. They were focused right now on whether Aron and Chaja Fajga would marry.

Every day, Regina read a new notice of antisemitic events throughout Eastern Europe, with some very close to the Polish border. There were also isolated acts, such as beatings and shouts of "dirty Jew" within Poland, so these threatening activities were getting closer to home every day.

Regina couldn't ignore what she was reading and hearing about each day, and the violence and savagery waged on innocent men, women, and children never left her mind. She knew that her family could be the next ones to suffer from the knives, clubs, and humiliation at the hands of the Russian soldiers.

There is only one way to stay safe and that is to leave Poland and live somewhere where the violence and pogroms couldn't find us.

Regina decided that she would talk about the family leaving Poland at the evening meal.

It's for the family's own good.

Aside from her political passion, Regina recognized her strong attraction to Leopold. He was passionate and knowledgeable about everything, and she was excited to hear him talk. He was pleasant looking, but it was his intensity that made her want to be around him and to follow him anywhere.

I trust him. He seems like a real mensch.

As she headed home, Regina wondered how Chaja Fajga could consider marrying a rabbi.

Ugh, I would never do that!

She was not at all drawn to the numerous tasks of being a rebbetzin. That was Chaja Fajga's concern. Regina wondered what she would think if she fell in love with someone who wanted to be a rabbi. She knew it would be tough. Fortunately, it was not her direct concern. But Regina knew she was getting closer to the age when her family would look to arrange a marriage. She had no interest in maintaining a home for at least several years. For now, all she wanted to do was work with the Bund to protect her community.

As she walked in the door of her home, Chaja Fajga and her mother were deep in conversation. Chaja Fajga was in tears.

"This is so unexpected. I don't know what to do. I've always liked Aron, but I didn't think he ever thought of me as more than a friend. I had no idea he would consider me for his wife."

Lena held her daughter and they rocked back and forth.

"I understand, my sweet daughter. I know this is a big decision, way beyond just marrying someone and being a wife. This is more than that. So, your father and I are letting you decide."

Chaja Fajga let out a small wail.

"I don't know what to do!"

Regina stood still in the center of the room and watched how her sister was suffering. She walked over to her and put her arms around her.

"I'm so sorry you are having to make this difficult decision. I wish I could offer some wisdom, but obviously I can't. I want you to know I love you, and I believe you will do what is right for you either way."

Chaja Fajga hugged Regina tight and smiled.

"Thank you for your love."

Regina felt exhausted, first from the Jewish Bund meeting and now with her sister's situation. She excused herself and moved as fast as she could to her bed, where she flopped down and tried to sleep, vowing to share the important news she had learned with her family.

As she tossed and turned, she put herself in the role of a rabbi's wife.

I would need to know more about Judaism. I would need to be ready to leave home any time of the day or night to tend to new babies and sick grandparents. I would have no time for myself, which is something I crave. I like to read and contemplate the daily news. Would I even have time for my own family? No, being a rabbi's wife would never work for me.

The next morning, after a long sleep, Regina heard laughter as she entered the kitchen for breakfast, a stark change from the previous night.

A decision had been made!

"I know what I want," said Chaja Fajga, "and that is to marry Aron. He's a good man; he was a friend at school, and he is a good son."

The heavy air that had hung over the home for days had now lifted. Lena moved around like her old self, humming, as she tended to her chores. The whole family seemed to be celebrating the news. This was a joyous event for all of them.

"It will be great to have a rebbetzin in the family," Kejla said.

Hearing that, the entire family began to dance a Yiddish tango, clapping and hugging. Regina grabbed her sister.

"I'm so happy for you, Chaja Fajga. I know you will have a fulfilling life with Aron. I'm so glad he didn't forget you and that he wants to choose you for his wife."

Chaja Fajga laughed and hugged her little sister, and then teasingly whispering in her ear.

"You are next in line, you know."

Regina stiffened. She knew Chaja Fajga was right, but she didn't want to deal with such an event for herself. She pulled back just enough to look at Chaja Fajga laughing face.

"Oh, I just finished school. I have plenty of time."

I hope I'm right. Everyone should be busy making plans for Aron and Chaja Fajga so no one will be thinking of me for a while.

Regina was tasked with going to Doria and Ada Neumann's home to invite them to come over for dinner the following evening. She was not supposed to mention Chaja Fajga's decision. That was up to Lena and Yosef.

When she arrived, Doria greeted her. Regina tried to remain low-key and not give away the news, but Doria sensed from her wider-than-usual smile that the news was positive. She kept a straight face as she responded.

"Regina, please tell your family we are looking forward to seeing them at dinner tomorrow evening."

As she prepared a celebratory meal for the Neumann family, Lena put her four youngest children to work. She and Chaja Fajga laid out the items they would need for a small betrothal celebration. The two families would want to draft and read out loud a tenaim, a document stating the conditions of the wedding, including the date. They also selected a piece of crockery to be shattered as a symbolic ritual to announce the engagement.

As she set the table, Regina was glad that all the attention was on Chaja Fajga, and that no one would be paying any attention to her.

It's not my time!

She also knew that the timing was bad to discuss politics.

13

Leopold Comes for Dinner

Two weeks later, Regina joined other members of the Bund group as they waited for Leopold to join them. The conversation centered around the news of yet another incident in Krakow.

Could this be happening so close to home?

Regina watched Leopold enter the office. His face showed that what the others had been saying was true. It was not a full-blown pogrom or riot, but a group of worshipers had been beaten leaving services at the Alta Shul, an Orthodox Jewish synagogue in the Kazimierz district of Kraków. They were clobbered with clubs and smacked across their faces, called filthy Jews, and told to leave Poland because Jews kill babies for their blood to make matzoh.

Regina froze at the news.

It feels like every day brings more bad reports.

She stayed silent, not knowing what she could add to the conversation about the attack. She listened to the others suggest a counterattack, but Leopold thought that would be a futile attempt because the attackers were well-armed and more numerous than our little collective.

Regina crossed her arms over her chest and let out a sigh. She felt helpless and frustrated.

"What can we do? It seems like the antisemitic comments and attacks are growing while we sit here helpless."

The members stared at Regina.

"What do you suggest we do, Regina?" Chaim said. "We are unarmed and a small group of Jews, and mostly a youth group. How can we go up against a group of armed antisemites?"

Regina knew he was right, but she still felt angry and frustrated.

"Of course, I know who we are, but it just feels so hopeless. Do we wait until they storm Warsaw?"

Leopold stepped in to thwart what was becoming an argument with no satisfying answer or solution.

"Listen, what we can do is make everyone we know aware of what is happening and that it's getting closer to home," he said. "The more people know about these smaller attacks, the better prepared they will be if they come closer to us."

Regina wasn't satisfied.

"I can't help it. I want to *do* something instead of just talking."

She felt Leopold's eyes on her as he got up from his chair.

"I admire your gumption, Regina, and I wish I could offer you a way to go up against these monsters. I know if you could, you would, but obviously it's not an option for us, at least not yet."

"You know, I agree with Regina," said Amos.

He was a tall, lanky 23-year-old, one of the older members of the group.

"What if we could get some weapons and stood outside the synagogues to keep those barbarians away? We are not just helpless, are we? We can't just sit here and wait for them to show up at our synagogues, right? I hate feeling helpless like this."

Leopold raised his arms to get everyone's attention.

"I understand everyone's frustration. And I know you want to do more than just hear about it, but we need to be smart and recognize where our power is. It won't make sense for us to try and fight a group of goons with knives and guns. Plus, there are a lot more of them, which means we need to gather more involvement from the community."

There was grumbling among the group, and plenty of angry retorts.

"We should show them what Jews can do when they're angry."

"Yeah. Give them a taste of their own medicine."

Finally, Regina realized that her quick tongue about wanting to fight back wasn't helping at all.

"Of course, you are right, Leopold. I'm sorry for creating a problem here. I know we all appreciate everything you do for our group. But I'm sure you understand our frustration at feeling so helpless."

Regina felt Leopold staring at her again. She blushed and stepped back to sit in a chair.

"I've never seen you this passionate about any of the issues that come through here," he said. "Why is this different?"

"It feels like there is more antisemitic activity in Poland now. This attack was not in Russia, Belarus, or Lithuania. It was within our borders, and I think we need to take more action than just sending out notices to other Bunds."

"I appreciate that, Regina. I'm sympathetic to everyone's frustration. We need to get the Jewish Bund and the Polish Socialist Party to finally take some action against these goons."

Everyone was quiet. Regina suddenly felt tired , as if she would fall asleep on the couch from the sheer exhaustion she felt after getting the news of the attack in Krakow.

I don't know if I can manage my frustration any longer.

There was nothing more to say, and the members began to go their own way. As Regina gathered her belongings, Leopold asked her to stay a moment. Her face reddened and her hands began to sweat.

"Okay, sure, Leopold."

"Regina, I'm impressed with your commitment to translation work and your principles as a member. I don't believe I've ever heard you so intense."

Regina's throat felt dry, and her heart started beating double-time. She swallowed hard and wanted to impress Leopold, but she was not sure what her answer should be.

"Well, Leopold, I'm passionate about our mission. I don't know if I told you, but I was in Bialystok two months ago during that pogrom."

"What? You were there? What happened?"

I'm not telling him about the rape.

"I'm fine, but I was lucky. I was in the boarding house where my sister lived. She was working at the Lewandowski textile mill, and I was visiting. We were going to take a stroll along the Bialy River and have a picnic."

"And?"

"I heard loud noises and heavy footsteps. I peeked out the window and saw Russian troops. No one else was home, so I ran upstairs and hid inside her closet. I heard them push down the door. They were so loud. It sounded like they were standing in front of me, but I don't think they were all in the room, but it sounded like it."

Regina was out of breath just reliving the moment.

"What about your sister? What happened at the mill?"

"Nothing. The mill was locked down, and they couldn't penetrate such a large facility."

I hope he doesn't know I'm lying.

"So, what happened? I hate to ask, but did they find you?"

Regina relaxed. She was flattered that Leopold took such an interest in her welfare.

"No, as far as I could tell they marched around the parlor area and then left. I was terrified. I was sure they could hear me breathing. I could also hear screams and gunshots outside. It was terrible."

"That had to be horrible for you."

"I don't know why I was so lucky, but I couldn't move for hours. I was sure they were waiting downstairs for me. I couldn't trust what they were doing. I also was horrified to think they had found my sister. We were supposed to meet outside the mill. What if she was there when the soldiers came? That would have been awful. Fortunately, she was still inside, and the mill supervisors locked everything down."

Regina stared at the floor, unable to look directly at Leopold. At that moment, she hoped Leopold saw her as more than just a young Bund activist. She felt important and more of a colleague than just one member of the group.

"So, how did you finally get out?"

"My sister, Chaja Fajga, came back to her boarding house after they left. Of course, she was looking for me. She didn't know if I escaped. I heard her in the house calling for me, but I didn't trust if it was a trap. Maybe the soldiers were making her ask for me. It was awful for both of us."

"You finally came out and it was okay, though, right?"

"Yes. I don't remember how long I stayed in the closet, but obviously, everything worked out."

Regina felt bad about lying, but she could never tell anyone the truth about what really happened that day. Now, with so much attention from Leopold, she felt special.

I hope he isn't looking at me like I'm a child.

At that moment, Regina wondered if she could ever be more to Leopold than just another member of the Jewish Bund party. She tried to think of something clever to say or ask, but her mind felt like it was stuck in mud.

"Thank you for asking, Leopold. I'm sure you can understand why I'm so passionate about stopping the Russians and the pogroms, and why I see this recent attack on Jews attending synagogue as part of the larger picture. There must be something we can do beyond just telling people about these events. It doesn't seem like we are making a difference."

Leopold sighed.

"I wish I had an answer for you, Regina. I'm as frustrated as you but I don't want everyone to know how helpless I feel. I know this is not something I should share with anyone else, but I think you understand better."

Leopold shook his head as Regina rubbed her hands together and wiped them on her skirt.

"I can't believe you kept the pogrom in Bialystok to yourself and didn't tell the rest of us."

"I didn't want everyone to see me differently, but I think the experience contributes to my passion for stopping the attacks."

"It's beginning to get dark. Can I walk you home?"

Regina heard thumping in her ears as her heartbeat increased.

Did he just ask to walk me home?

"Oh, I'm okay, but if you would like to, that would be nice."

"It's no bother. I'd feel better if you don't mind. It's getting dusk and it will be dark soon, so I would like to be sure you get home safely after I've kept you so long after the meeting."

"Well, I live over by Saxon Square."

"That's not far. I'd be happy to see you home. I hope your parents won't mind that we don't have a chaperone."

As they left the office and Leopold locked the door, Regina felt her mind go blank. She was curious about Leopold. From what she understood when she first joined the Bund, he wasn't married, which made him a bit older than most unmarried men.

I wonder why.

He traveled a lot for work, so that was one possible reason, but Regina would never ask him such an invasive question.

I wonder if he's promised.

Regina wondered if walking her home meant that Leopold was interested in her or if it was nothing more than him just being polite and protective as a gentleman and co-worker.

I hope it's more, but how could it be?

No gentleman would allow a young woman to walk home alone when it was getting dark. That was why their meetings were always scheduled early enough so that people could get home before dusk.

As they drew closer to her home, Regina wondered if she should introduce Leopold to her family.

Maybe they will see that my Bund group has a reputable leader.

"I greatly appreciate this, Leopold, but it will be quite dark for you going home. Surely someone will be waiting for you and concerned when you don't get home at your usual time."

This was Regina's way of fishing for information.

"I'm fine. No one is waiting on me. As you probably know, organizing meetings and groups doesn't fit neatly into regular office hours, so there is often something that keeps me from a regular schedule."

Regina held her breath and was relieved to know that Leopold wasn't married. That still didn't answer the question of whether he was spoken for by anyone.

I should not get my hopes up. He probably feels I am too young for him or that I am already spoken for myself.

It would not have been unusual for a woman her age to still be available. Regina had worked hard to avoid making Gita, the shadchanit, aware of her. There were still many men and women of marrying age to keep her busy. And everyone was focused on Chaja Fajga and Aron, so it was a bit easier for Regina to stay out of sight.

As they approached Saxon Square, they could see the Anuszewicz home nestled in a small community of houses. It was a wood framed, single-story structure with a sleeping room for the parents, one for the girls, and a separate one for the boys. The dining room had a large table that could seat all eight of them, and there was room to add four guests. The kitchen had a double wood-burning stove and a large prep table where Lena rolled out the dough to make the weekly challah. They had a modern bathroom with indoor plumbing, with a basin they could fill with water and a flushing toilet.

It was a respectable abode, a bit upscale from many of the middle-class neighbors. Yosef had inherited it from his father, who was the best-known furrier in town. When the house caught fire one day, his clients, friends and the local synagogue came together to rebuild the house even nicer and larger than the original.

Regina was proud of her home and glad she could show it to Leopold. As they approached the front door, she invited him to join her family for dinner as a courtesy, a tradition her mother had taught her. Regina knew that Lena always fed Zelman's friends when they came around.

"They have heard so much about you, Leopold, so I know it would assure them to meet the person who has been running our meetings. Please just say 'hi,' would you?"

Leopold said he would be happy to meet Regina's family. She knew they would be as impressed with him as she was.

Regina opened the front door wide enough so the family could see her and Leopold at the same time. It was dark by then, and she knew her parents were worried. She also knew they would be pleased that this young man had escorted their daughter home to be sure she was safe.

"Where have you been?" Lena said. "We have been worried about you."

"I'm fine. Leopold made sure I got home safely."

Regina noticed the silence as she observed how surprised her family looked to see a young man standing next to her.

"Oh, thank you so much, young man. We were worried, as Regina always gets home way before dark. Thank you. What is your name again?"

"Leopold Frenk, Mrs. Anuszewicz."

"Regina is an important part of our group, and I would never let anything happen to her. It is my fault she is late. She was telling me about her experience in Bialystok and I kept asking her more questions and it got later than normal when we left our meeting."

Lena shot a glance at Regina, hoping she didn't tell him what really happened. Judging by Leopold's comment, she guessed that Regina had whitewashed the story.

Regina was thrilled.

This is going better than I hoped.

Leopold was impressing her family and she felt giddy, knowing what would happen next.

"We would be so pleased to learn more about the Jewish Bund," said Lena. "You must stay for dinner, Leopold, and please tell us more. Regina is always trying to explain what your group does, so this is a chance to learn from one of its leaders."

"That is so nice of you, Mrs. Anuszewicz, but I don't want to intrude."

"No, you are not intruding. Fortunately, we always have enough to eat. Unless of course, you need to get home for your meal?"

"Sadly, no one is waiting for me. My parents, who moved to Kiev for business in 1904, were killed in the pogrom there a year later. It's because of my parents that I'm so committed to the Bund."

Regina had never heard this story. She wondered if anyone in the group knew about Leopold's background.

This explains why Leopold is so dedicated, and his concern for safety.

"Let me introduce our family," Regina said. "This is Chaja Fajga, my older sister, who will become a rebbetzin next year. My younger sisters, Kejla and Dina, and my younger brothers, Zelman, and Aleksander."

"Nice to meet you all. Thank you for inviting me to share your table."

"Please, come. Sit with us," Lena said.

Regina made sure she sat next to Leopold. There was lots of conversation about the coming wedding, as well as a brief mention of the increasing number of antisemitic incidents.

Here he is in my home, not married, but I don't know if he is promised.

Regina was happy that she was the woman at Leopold's side and that her family could now see how special he was. After dinner, she took Leopold's plate with hers as if he was her guest alone. She knew the evening was coming to an end, and she was sure Leopold would not want to hang around after dinner. He didn't disappoint her, as he made a gracious gesture to Lena.

"That was an amazing meal. Thank you so much. I don't think I've eaten this well in months."

"Thank you. You are welcome anytime," Lena said. "And now that I know you, I'm not as worried about Regina's activities with your group."

"It's not my group. We are part of the larger Jewish Labor Bund party. It's all over Poland. We are a socialist party that promotes the political, cultural, and social autonomy of Jewish workers. In fact, we are a secular group within the Bund with many women who occupy important roles. The non-Jews with us have been very active campaigning against antisemitism, defending Jewish civil and cultural rights and rejecting assimilation."

Leopold shifted his focus for a moment.

"As you know, I am completing my three-month assignment here in two days, finishing my work in the Mokotów office with our student group. I leave next for Belarus, where I will organize the Bund group in Minsk. Happily, things in the office here are now running smoothly. In fact, Regina is proving to be a great asset to our branch, with her wonderful translation skills. I don't know what we would do without her. There aren't too many people who are as fluent and able to express meaning in multiple languages as your daughter."

Regina blushed as she looked around the table.

"She fits in so well. All our women are valuable, and they provide a lot of important support for everyone. They are not just there to help make things better for women. They help everyone."

"Your kind words about Regina are greatly appreciated," Lena said, "as she has worked very hard at her studies. And thank you for explaining these things to me. I'm not as up to date on political events as I would like. Your explanation of plans for the organization helps me understand the Bund's work much better."

Leopold thanked Lena again for her gracious hospitality and wished the entire family a good night. As soon as he was out the door, Regina waited to hear her family's opinion of him. Chaja Fajga was the first to speak.

"Wow, Leopold is really something! So, he is the person you have been meeting with weekly in that Bund party you keep talking about! He's impressive, Regina. No wonder you don't like to miss the meetings."

As she smiled, Regina made sure she didn't appear as smitten as she was for fear the family would tease her.

I hope it's not obvious.

"Leopold is very good at what he does, and he is well respected by the leaders of the General Jewish Labor Bund in Russia. We are doing good things, especially for women."

Now, instead of being on the defensive, Regina was suddenly the center of attention and she thought she detected a new respect for her involvement with something so meaningful outside the home.

Mokotów, Poland
1907

14

Leopold Returns

It had been quite a long time since Leopold left Mokotów for Russia and Belarus, beginning with six months in the Moscow office, training with the manager there. Finally, he was re-assigned to Mokotów to run the office. He was happy to be back near the center of Warsaw, with a community he knew.

While Leopold was away, Regina's language skills became the envy of other Bund offices, and sometimes they sent their documents to the Mokotów office for her to translate.

She knew that Leopold would be back, so on the day he was supposed to return, she picked a dress she normally wore for special occasions.

Today really is *a special occasion.*

Her dress had special bone buttons up the front that Chaja Fajga had made for her to wear at Zelman's Bar Mitzvah. She pulled her hair back and made a braid at the back, something she rarely did for work. Regina wanted to appear relaxed and not show how excited she really was. For weeks, anticipating Leopold's return, she had relived the last time they were together when he walked her home and he stayed for dinner.

Are any of the other women in the Bund as taken with Leopold as me?

No one ever talked about their lives outside the Bund. It wasn't that kind of office, where everything going on outside was shared the next day.

Who wouldn't be taken with Leopold?

He was tall, had a strong build, green eyes, and thick brown hair that often curled just above his eyebrows. It was easy to feel how passionate he was about the Bund and the community. It didn't make sense that he was not married or at least spoken for. He was so nice to everyone, and they all liked working for him. It wasn't like anyone made a lot of money working there, but Leopold was so warm and supportive, which made everyone comfortable.

But he's had plenty of time to marry.

Regina felt foolish in her fancy dress.

Why didn't I think of that?

Leopold had not announced anything about being married or having children. Chaim did tease Leopold, asking him how he managed to leave Belarus without a wife. Leopold said he had been too busy working to have time to see the ladies.

Regina didn't know what to do. It was not her place to pursue him, and Leopold hadn't seen her in a while.

If it's meant to be, it's meant to be.

The first of May fell on a Sunday. Leopold told everyone in the office that they could take Friday off. May Day had come to symbolize an annual recognition of the fight for workers' rights, inspired years earlier by an enormous strike in Chicago by 400,000 workers on that date, so May 1st became known as International Workers Day at the International Socialist Conference in 1889.

Regina didn't want to take the day off, and she wondered if she could find an excuse to go by the office on the pretense of taking home some materials to translate.

Will that seem odd? I've never done something like this before, but I want to find a way to see Leopold before the weekend. Even if I go to the office, there is no guarantee he will even be there.

The walk to the office near Belgijska Street was a few blocks from the bakery downtown where her parents shopped. As Regina headed that way, she wondered what she would say if Leopold was there, and how disappointed she would be if he was not around.

At that time in Poland, social customs dictated that an unmarried man would not meet an unmarried woman in private without a chaperone. But in the working world, these meetings were considered much more casual.

As Regina approached the Bund office, Leopold was just leaving. The abrupt encounter caught them both off guard, so they stuttered their hellos, which embarrassed Regina.

"Cześć."

"Regina, hi, did we have a meeting I forgot about?"

"No, no, I forgot some materials I planned to work on over the weekend."

"Oh, then it's good you caught me because I always lock the door when I leave. It's so good of you to work on your free time. You know we greatly appreciate it. The whole Jewish Bund organization knows about you. I'm afraid they will try to take you away from our little group here."

"That is very nice of you to say. But I like working with the people here and can't imagine going anywhere else. I also like that I can just walk to the office. I was given a key when you left for Belarus so I could open or close the office as necessary."

"Oh, I'm glad you told me. I didn't know that."

Regina was just making conversation. She didn't know what else to say to Leopold. She just wanted to be around him. Then, she remembered that she had to go inside the office and find some files she could take.

Leopold waited outside as Regina looked for documents in Polish that needed to be in Yiddish, as well as files in Yiddish that needed to be in Polish. Finally, she took two files and came back out.

"Find what you needed?"

Still flustered, Regina nodded.

Now, what?

She stood still, looking at the ground.

"The weather is nice and it's still early," said Leopold. "Would you like to walk over to the Promenade? It's just around the corner."

"Oh, yes, that would be nice. What a great idea."

That was a little too enthusiastic.

She walked slowly, not wanting to appear awkward. She slowed down and swung her arms casually.

What a great stroke of luck. If I had come a minute later, I would have missed Leopold!

Regina suspected that a shadchanit had approached him about finding a wife because he was a desirable man and would make a good husband and father. She also suspected there were many young women who would like to be his wife . . . including her.

Regina walked in silence, wondering what Leopold was thinking.

He's an orphan, but very eligible.

"Regina, I can't walk you home tonight because your family will think I am just looking for another free meal."

Leopold laughed.

"My mother would be more than happy to feed you, but I think that would put you in an awkward position. Don't you agree?"

Leopold knew exactly what Regina was talking about. If he came over again, it would be interpreted that he was interested in making Regina his wife and he wasn't ready for that.

"I know what you mean, but I do like talking with you, you know."

What is he saying? He likes to talk to me?

Things were happening so fast that Regina didn't know what to make of it all.

What am I supposed to say?

"I like talking to you as well, Leopold. Everyone in the group has so much respect for you."

When they reached the Promenade, Leopold found a bench and offered Regina a seat.

"Okay, can I be honest with you, Regina?"

"Of course."

"I have never met a woman so bright and fun to be with as you, Regina." He looked into her eyes as he spoke.

"We have just discovered each other after all this time working together. But this is different, and I'd like to be able to call on you more formally. What do you think?"

Regina held her breath, pursed her lips, and swallowed.

"Leopold. I don't know what to say. But, yes, I would like that, too. I'm a bit shocked as I was not expecting this, but I do enjoy your company, and I greatly enjoy working with you."

Am I stuttering?

Reality set in when she realized that she needed permission from her parents to spend time with Leopold.

I'm not as independent as I thought.

"I need to ask my parents if they will allow it. If they agree, you will need to come to my home and ask them formally."

"Yes, of course. But how will I know unless we wait until next week?"

She knew she should wait until then so as not to seem too anxious. Her face flushed.

Can I wait that long?

"I have an idea, Leopold. Why don't you come by tomorrow on Shabbos afternoon after we get home from synagogue and ask my parents then?"

"Great idea. See. You are so clever. That is one of the things I find so impressive about you. It's settled. Expect me in the afternoon, but don't tell your parents I'm coming because they may not be happy to learn that I am already taking you on walks."

"You forget. I was the one who came by the office."

"Yes, but you are still their darling daughter. I can't compete with that."

He laughed.

Regina stood, smoothed her skirt, and said goodbye, tickled by their secret plan. She was not sure she could keep it a secret but knew she had to. She didn't want to do anything that would sabotage her friendship with Leopold. She was also hopeful her parents would agree to this arrangement.

He doesn't have parents to conduct a formal match if it should come to that. But he's stable and I've never heard anything untoward about him.

She couldn't stop herself from thinking about what it would be like to be Leopold's wife and what it would mean to *not* be just a housewife and mother.

We could be partners in the Bund and live in the world together.

Regina realized she was getting ahead of herself by thinking so fast about becoming Leopold's wife, which she knew may not happen.

What if he gets to know me better and decides I'm not who he thought I was? Am I too simple, and not the smart translator he thinks I am?

It was all she could do to not jump in the air after she and Leopold said goodbye and went their separate ways.

15

The Visit That Never Happened

Regina couldn't think of anything else as she counted down the hours until Saturday. She was amazed at her good fortune, living at a time when customs were changing from never being allowed to talk to an adult male without having parents around, and only marrying someone the shadkin arranged, to being able to request that a boy or girl you know from school or work be considered for marriage, like Chaja Fajga and Aron.

She knew she was projecting something farfetched. She and Leopold didn't know each other that well yet, and she had to admit that at least part of her attraction to him was about his leadership in the Bund. The fact that he was so good-looking didn't hurt. Not a lot of Jewish boys were as tall as Leopold, and he seemed so comfortable functioning in the adult world. She also remembered how relaxed he seemed at dinner with her family.

How could any other boy ever catch my fancy?

She still found it a bit odd that someone his age was not already married or at least spoken for, but then she remembered that he'd been constantly moving from city to city over the past four years.

Could I be the woman he's been waiting for?

Regina was not like her former school friends who spent all their time primping and talking about boys. Many of them were now married and having babies, but that was not the life Regina imagined for herself. For the time being, she was more interested in being part of stopping the antisemitic attacks that were increasing. Her friends thought her focus on those issues was boring, but she thought *they* were boring with their old-fashioned values.

She looked through her clothes and took extra care to select a dress that was a bit nicer than usual for going to synagogue the next day and hosting Leopold later that day.

Since it was already Friday afternoon, she worked with Lena to prepare the cholent, a thick stew made with onions, beef, beans, barley, and potatoes, cooked, and thickened overnight on a low flame to make a tasty meal for Saturday afternoon.

Since Chaja Fajga's wedding and departure with Aron for Paris, where he became the assistant rabbi at the Synagogue de la Victoire, or as some called it, the Grand Synagogue of Paris, Regina had become the oldest daughter, which brought extra responsibility.

She recalled the excitement when it was announced that Aron, having finished at the top of his class, had been honored with the assignment in Paris. Their departure two days after the wedding was not for a honeymoon, but a move to another country, at a great distance from the family.

Regina and Lena had cried about this family separation, but they did nothing publicly to take away from the excitement of the wedding and the challenging assignment for the new rabbi and rebbetzin.

All I can think about now is tomorrow!

Chaja Fajga had added a decorative ruffle to Regina's favorite dress, and she was anxious to see if Leopold would like it.

"Mama, I'm sweaty from making the cholent, so I will take a bath now, if you don't mind."

Normally, she took her weekly bath on Saturday night. Lena was a bit surprised but didn't question her daughter.

The next day, Regina sat in synagogue thinking about Leopold stopping by their house. While she mumbled the prayers, her thoughts were elsewhere. Every time they sang another prayer, Regina tried to pay attention.

Finally, the service ended, and the family greeted the rabbi and wished him well. Regina shifted her feet as he asked her what news they had from Chaja Fajga and Aron, and if Yosef and Lena's grandchild was on the way.

Walking home, Regina tried to relax, but her heart was beating fast.

It won't be long before Leopold comes calling.

After they finished their meal, Regina waited for Leopold as the afternoon dragged on. She grew concerned when he had still not appeared by late in the day, as they had agreed.

Maybe he changed his mind and will come at dinner time?

By sundown, her chest was tight, and she had a lump in her throat. It was all Regina could do to not break down and cry. She didn't know what to think.

Did he not care? Did he forget?

She could hardly focus on reading her book and she tried to stop feeling abandoned. Since she had to keep her secret, Regina was alone in her distress.

Dinner was served, and still no Leopold.

I feel like a fool for agreeing to such a plan. Maybe I am just a silly girl with a crush on someone older and more experienced. Is he playing with me, laughing behind my back because I believed someone like him would be interested in someone like me?

Regina had no idea what to do or how she could face Leopold on Monday morning. She felt embarrassed and closed her eyes to keep the tears from dripping down her cheeks.

On Sunday, Regina woke up still hoping that Leopold would come by and apologize, telling her that something had come up on Saturday, which is why he didn't call on her. That would have made her feel better, but he never showed up or sent word.

Regina contemplated staying home from the office on Monday, but she didn't want to appear weak and afraid of a confrontation. When she arrived, everyone was talking furiously about what had happened to Leopold on Saturday as he was leaving his home.

Regina was confused.

"What's going on?"

"Didn't you hear? Where have you been? Leopold was attacked. Some thugs beat him up on his front steps. Cowards. Three against one. Fortunately, someone chased them away before they did too much damage or killed him."

Regina stood still, trying to comprehend what she had just heard, which explained why Leopold never showed up. She felt relieved to know that he didn't decide to play a joke on her. But the attack was an awful reason. She felt compelled to go to his side and comfort him, but she didn't know where he lived.

"How is he? Who is taking care of him? You know he lives alone, that both of his parents were killed."

"Yes, of course, we know his circumstances. We heard that the neighbors who saw the attack took him to one of their homes and are keeping him until he can be on his own. It was very lucky someone happened to be outside at the same time because they scared those goons away. Fortunately, Leopold did not get seriously beat up."

Regina wanted to run to be at his side, but she knew that kind of special attention would look overly attentive and inappropriate.

"What can we do for him? Where is he staying? Perhaps it would be nice for us to visit him, and maybe bring something to the people who are caring for him."

"Oh, we never thought of that, but we are grateful to the Czerniakow family," said Amiel, one of the student workers. "They live near me, so I know the neighborhood."

I must see Leopold and tell him I understand why he didn't come by.

Regina was angry and frightened about the antisemitic attack right there in their own community, a place where Jews had always been safe. For her, the attack was one more reason to be more vigilant, to not feel so safe, and maybe to even leave before the attacks came too often.

Amiel, Regina, and the other Bund workers stayed for most of the day before closing early. Rachel, who lived nearby, stopped by her home, and asked her mother if she had anything she could share with the family taking care of Leopold.

Regina was having a difficult time not lashing out about the violence she had been talking about for months. She hated to be right. She wanted to get even. She wanted to know who the cowards were who ganged up on a man with no way to protect himself being so outnumbered.

He could have been killed.

Regina and her co-workers made their way to the home of Ceira and Herszel Czerniaków. Herszel was a local physician, so it was a good place for Leopold to recover.

When they reached their home, Ceira greeted them warmly and thanked them for the pirogi, saying it wasn't necessary, but they appreciated the tradition of never going to someone's house empty-handed.

"You must be Leopold's office friends."

"Is it okay for us to visit? We don't want to cause Leopold any distress."

"Oh, no. It will do him good to see your faces. He kept saying he needed to go into the offices to be sure everyone had what they needed for the day. I assured him you would all be fine without him babysitting."

Regina looked past Ceira to see if she could spot Leopold, anxious to see him and afraid of how badly he was hurt.

"It was lucky that Herszel and two neighbors, who we always walk with on Shabbos, left at the same time as Leopold and we saw him get attacked. Our men ran over and chased them away."

Regina was grateful and knew she was keeping a secret that the others didn't know about their plan for Saturday afternoon.

I feel special, but terrible, too.

Ceira directed the group to Leopold. Regina tried to prepare herself for what she was about to see, so she was relieved when she discovered that Leopold's injuries were not as bad as she thought they would be.

"Hey, you didn't need to come by."

"We wanted to be sure you were not just taking a holiday," said Amiel.

Just then, Regina's eyes caught Leopold's. She felt a special connection, as part of the secret they shared.

"Really, I'm okay. I was lucky that Herszel and his neighbors walked out just as these punks attacked me,"

"Did you recognize any of them?"

"No, only that they called me a dirty Jew and to go back to Russia, where all dirty Jews belong."

Leopold coughed.

Leopold's words made Regina stiffen, as it brought back memories of the pogrom in Bialystok and the attack at the old synagogue in Krakow

Another attack against Jews. It's getting worse each day.

Things were supposed to be safe in Poland, certainly in their city and especially in their neighborhood. Warsaw was supposed to be a welcoming place for Jewish communities. Jews served in the local government and were physicians, musicians, artists, scientists, many of them highly respected. Antisemitic attacks were not supposed to happen there.

Everyone stood around Leopold's bed making jokes. Regina was relieved that his injuries were not as bad as she anticipated. His left eye was swollen and dark blue around the edges. He also had a large lump on his forehead with a small cut that was covered in a light cloth. There was also a cut on his mouth, but he didn't lose any teeth.

Finally, Regina couldn't keep quiet about her concerns.

"Did you recognize them? Do you know if they belong to a group? What can we do to stop this? This is a growing problem. We need to do something. Maybe we need to create a mob of our own to patrol the neighborhood."

Amiel was startled by her outburst and her passion.

"Regina, I admit this is bad, but it was isolated. I'll bet these guys don't even live here, but they picked on Leopold because he is well-known, and he lives alone. He was an easy target."

Regina shrugged.

"What does it matter whether they live here or not? It happened here. Before the parishioners were attacked outside the synagogue in Krakow, they never had any problems. These attacks are growing because of the pogroms in Russia, and they are getting closer. Remember, we had one in Bialystok."

Leopold knew about Regina's history even though she never shared it with the others.

"I think it's important that we don't over-react because that could make things worse," said Amiel.

Regina was no longer the quiet and shy girl she had been in school. She was alarmed and felt the others were not taking the event seriously.

85

"I think we need to act now before they think we are easy to overtake. We won't be prepared, and they will take advantage of that. These thugs need to know we are not going to pretend that these attacks didn't happen, or we think they won't happen here again."

"I think Regina is right," said Ceira. "We saw those guys and they didn't look like your typical neighborhood ruffians. They were older and bigger. They also had a big stick with them. If we hadn't interfered, I hate to think what they would have done to Leopold. I think we may need to create some kind of patrol. We need to show them we are prepared."

"But don't you think by doing that they will think we are frightened of them?" Amiel said. "Shouldn't we act as though they can't scare us?"

Leopold listened to the argument and spoke up:

"I think Regina may be right. Ignoring them makes them think we don't know how to protect ourselves. Tomorrow, we need to meet and talk about how we can protect our Jewish community here in Mokotów. They think we have no resources. We will show them they can't just come in here and do whatever they want to us."

Regina nodded.

Finally!

"I will come back into the office tomorrow," said Leopold. "We can work on a plan."

16

First Kiss

Regina was glad to hear that Leopold agreed with her about the Jewish community needing to become more diligent in combating the increase in antisemitic violence that was taking hold in Mokotów. She knew his family had been killed in a pogrom, and he knew about her experience in Bialystok. Their personal experiences only enhanced their anger, and more and more people in their community were becoming fearful and angry, too. Many of them came to the Bund office to express their concerns.

If thugs think they can get away with this without any repercussions, then the situation will only get worse.

They had to figure out how to engage the Jewish community. Regina had been trying to convince her parents and their friends of the deepening problems the Jewish community faced, but whenever she proposed moving to a country that didn't have such violence, they said she was overreacting. Since they wouldn't listen to her, Regina thought that Leopold might be able to help her organize a group of community street patrols.

Back at the office, the Bund members met to develop a new strategy to protect their members.

"It's not safe for Leopold to walk alone to the office," Amiel said. "I'll walk with him, but other men should, too. I don't trust that those people won't try and finish what they started."

The group agreed to have one of the men escort Leopold to the office each morning. The new rule was to try to let no one walk alone if possible, and the women needed to have at least one male escort during the day. They also agreed to close the office early enough for everyone to get home before dark, and those plans took hold immediately.

On that first day back, Regina was pleased when Leopold found a few minutes to explain how frustrated he had felt when he couldn't come by on Saturday, and how bad he felt when he realized he hadn't had the presence of mind to send someone to explain what happened. At the same time, he didn't want to cause her any embarrassment with her family. He asked if he could come by on the Saturday coming up.

Regina sighed with relief that Leopold's absence was not due to something she said or that he was teasing her. When she snuck a look at Leopold after the meeting, she was shocked to see him looking right back at her. She blushed and quickly looked away. This happened several times throughout the day.

The fact that Leopold had escaped a horrible fate only enhanced what Regina felt was a growing mutual attraction, and the next several days made her palms sweaty as her anxiety and excitement grew.

I love our secret looks.

On Thursday, Leopold had a two-hour lunch meeting for himself and five other members of the staff with the mayor and deputy mayor of Mokotów to share what they had learned about the antisemitic gangs and their concern about the growing surge of violence toward local Jews.

The Bund members' concerns seemed to be taken seriously, and they were told that the Mokotów City Council would pay attention to their issues, but Mayor Bartkiewicz said the situation was not bad enough to require teams of men patrolling the streets. Deputy Mayor Czajkowski expressed his opinion that the thugs coming into Mokotów were from next door in Warsaw.

"I have worked on several committees with Wiktor Litwinski, who was the President of Warsaw until last year," he said. "He is a good man, forward thinking and concerned about Polish independence. One project we worked on together set the stage for merging several Warsaw suburbs into one city. I would be happy to arrange a meeting for you with him so we can look at the problem and see if it should become a regional concern."

"That would be very helpful, thank you," said Leopold.

After the meeting, Leopold said he had paperwork to complete in the office. He suggested that Amiel and the others take the rest of the day off, and he would see them the next day, on Friday.

Regina didn't want to go home yet, as she enjoyed spending as much time as possible around Leopold. So, she said,

"Leopold, I need to get some pages from the office before I go home."

"Then in keeping with our policy, I will escort you back to the office, so you can collect the documents you need."

Regina felt flush at the idea of being alone with Leopold.

It feels like my whole body is shaking.

She had never been alone with a boy, let alone a man, except for walking outside where others could observe them. Socially, it would be frowned upon, and she knew it, but decided she would explain this walk as part of the new safety policy at the Bund.

When Regina arrived at the office, she and Leopold stepped inside.

"Can you find what you need to take home?" he said.

Regina could barely breathe. As she stood still, Leopold stepped closer, as close as he could without touching. She looked into his eyes but said nothing, knowing she was breaking every rule.

But this is so exciting!

She broke out in a sweat as she looked into Leopold's blue eyes. He slowly placed his hand on the back of her head and gently pulled her forward. She was still looking into his eyes as he bent down and kissed her. Regina could barely stand as dizziness overwhelmed her. She allowed Leopold to take charge, as he forced her mouth open and put his tongue inside.

How am I supposed to react? Should I be angry that Leopold is taking such liberties?

She shivered, overcome by feelings she never felt before. An unfamiliar energy surged in her groin. As she put her arms around Leopold, she felt his muscles and the warmth of this chest. Finally, he stepped back and took a deep breath.

"Oh, Regina, I'm so sorry. I don't want to frighten you, but I couldn't help myself. You take my breath away, and I took advantage of you being here alone. Please don't hate me."

"No, no, I don't hate you. I've never been kissed before, so I didn't know what to do. I'm glad you kissed me. I've been thinking about it but never thought it would happen. We're breaking the rules being alone here. Do you think anyone knows?"

Leopold stepped closer to Regina and wrapped his arm around her waist.

"I'm glad you feel this way. No one knows we're here. We are safe."

He kissed her again, a long, slow kiss and pulled her closer. Then, he took her hand and walked to a couch in the corner, where Regina often sat as she read documents.

I'm not sure what is happening here, but I don't want to do or say anything that will stop this magic I feel with Leopold.

"We will be more comfortable here."

He sat down and held Regina's hand to guide her to sit next to him.

It feels like the world is rushing by. Leopold is so sure of himself.

He kissed her again as her head fell back against the couch. She felt herself sliding down almost onto her back.

I love the way he feels against me. I'd kiss him all night if I could.

"Are you okay, Regina? I don't want to make you uncomfortable, but I can't stop kissing you."

What can I say? If I tell him how I feel, he might get frightened away.

"I'm . . . okay, yes, I'm okay."

Leopold looked into Regina's eyes and traced a finger down her cheek.

"I've never known anyone as lively and smart as you, Regina. Let me hold you close. I want to feel your heartbeat."

Leopold put his arm around Regina's waist and pulled her underneath him. It happened so quickly she didn't know how to resist.

Do I even want to resist?

"Hold me, Regina. Hold me."

"Yes, yes."

The passion was new and overpowering.

Regina wasn't sure about what happened next. She suddenly felt Leopold strain against her as he pushed her legs apart, fumbled with his pants, and pulled at her underpants.

"Please," he said. "Please."

What is he asking me?

Leopold was kissing her, holding her tight, and she wanted to believe he loved her. She felt a sharp shocking pain shoot through her like a bolt, like nothing she had ever experienced. Leopold was holding her tight, moving back and forth. Then, he let out a groan and fell flat on top of her.

What just happened?

Regina didn't know if she could have been having sex. She and her friends had talked about it, although Lena had not had "the talk" with her because that usually didn't happen until close to the wedding day.

She felt excited to be with Leopold, especially that he wanted to have sex with her, but it was happening so fast, and she was confused.

A few minutes later, Leopold pulled his pants up quickly while Regina laid there with her skirt around her waist. All she understood was that Leopold was strong and she could feel his weight on top of her. Then, she realized that her underpants had been ripped apart.

Oh my God.

"Regina, I couldn't help myself. I'm sorry. You are so beautiful, and I care for you so much. You are all I think about. I was more upset about not seeing you Saturday than being beaten up. Please forgive me. I hope I didn't embarrass you with your family. Did you tell them I was coming by?"

Regina was confused.

He's talking about my family after he just made love to me?

"No, Leopold, I didn't say anything. I think of you all the time, too. I feel overwhelmed right now."

"Can you forgive me? I just had to make love to you."

I don't know what to feel.

Her face got flushed and her hands felt clammy. She couldn't look at him. She didn't know how to behave.

How should I act after having sex?

She was confused but also thrilled that Leopold wanted her.

I couldn't control his passion for me, but I don't want to say anything that might hurt his feelings.

Regina wondered how she would be able to hide her torn underwear. She knew she needed to look as casual as she did when she left that morning. That's when it occurred to her that it was getting late in the afternoon, and she needed to get home.

"Leopold, I need to go home. I don't want my family to get suspicious."

"We need to keep this to ourselves, Regina."

She nodded.

"I wouldn't want your family to get the wrong impression of me if we are to become close friends, right?"

Regina was relieved that Leopold wanted to see more of her after what just happened. She knew that they had to act casual. She didn't want to tell him that she wanted to marry him and not to get fixed up with a man she didn't know.

Could that happen now?

Regina kept that thought to herself. For now, nothing mattered as she was still sailing on a cloud after making love with Leopold.

17

A Bored Chaperone

Regina bathed earlier than usual for Shabbos. She wanted to look clean and fresh for Leopold's visit later that day. In the morning, she donned her best dress for services. This time, she knew he would come, finally, and they could make their friendship known to the family.

After the morning prayers, the family took a leisurely walk home to enjoy their midday meal.

"Regina, you look too dressed up to help get the food ready," said Dina. Why don't you put on your everyday clothes?"

"Oh, I'm fine. I don't need to change clothes."

Regina noticed her mother's curious look, but she just shrugged and set the table as the boys carried in platters of food and Kejla and Dina filled sherry goblets with wine for the adults and mugs of juice for the children.

As the family sat down together, Regina clenched her hands in her lap and squeezed them tight. She moved the food around on her plate and took a few bites, hoping no one would notice that she was not eating.

"Regina, my love, are you okay?" said her mother. "You haven't eaten."
Try to be casual.

"I'm fine, Mama. I just don't have much of an appetite."

After the meal, Regina cleared the table and swept the floor. She froze when she heard a knock on the door. Everyone stood still, wondering who would be calling in the middle of Shabbos.

"I'll answer," Aleksander said.

The family stood by, curious about the caller.

"Leopold!" he said. "What a pleasant surprise. Is everything okay? No one has been hurt again, have they?"

"Oh, no. I didn't mean to frighten you. I'm sorry. I came by to see your parents if that is okay with them."

"Of course, come in. I will get them. They are in the other room. We just finished our meal, but I'm sure we have some kugel left. Mama always makes too much for one meal. Have a seat."

Regina scuttled into the kitchen to cut a piece of kugel and put it on a plate. She grabbed a clean fork from the cupboard.

Lena and Yosef were surprised when they stepped into the parlor and saw Leopold eating kugel with relish. Regina sat nearby, watching anxiously.

"Why, Leopold, what a pleasant surprise. You look recovered from that horrible incident last week. How are you?"

"Thank you so much, Mrs. Anuszewicz. I'm much better, and this kugel is delicious. I don't think I have ever had kugel this good."

"Lena is an excellent cook," said Yosef, "and she has taught our daughters all her secrets."

As Yosef sat down, he hoped he had gotten his point across to Leopold.

"I'm guessing your visit has something to do with Regina. She is the only political one in our family."

"Yes, Sir, Mr. Anuszewicz. But it has nothing to do with politics. I would like to call on Regina socially, with someone as a chaperone, of course."

I hadn't thought about chaperones. That will be annoying.

Regina was pleased that Leopold brought it up, because that was the only way that would be allowed. She was impressed with Leopold's confidence and smooth manner.

"Well, this is unexpected. We know you lost both of your parents a few years ago and you have been mostly on your own. So, you don't have parents to make this call for you."

"I hope that won't influence your decision. I only mean the best for Regina. We have a lot in common and we would like to see each other outside of the office."

That declaration answered a lot of questions Lena had about Regina's behavior that day.

She and Yosef excused themselves and went into their bedroom to talk privately about this new situation.

Regina felt sweat dripping down her back.

They have to say yes.

Her little brothers stood by, smiling, and nudging each other, teasing about who would be the chaperone each time Regina and Leopold wanted to go out for a walk.

A few minutes later, Lena and Yosef were smiling as they came back.

"Of course, we are okay with you and Regina spending time together. You can visit here with the family, and if you want to take a walk, one of the boys will go with you. We find you mature and responsible, Leopold. You are a lovely and well-mannered young man, who has had his share of heartache."

Regina and Leopold were all smiles at the announcement.

"Well, then, is Regina available to take a walk now, as the afternoon is warm and pleasant?"

"Why not?" said Lena. "Zelman, go and get some proper clothes on to join Leopold and Regina for a walk. Leopold, when you come back, you will have tea with us, won't you?"

Zelman groaned, but he went to find his outdoor shoes and a jacket. Then, he went over to Yosef to ask what a chaperone does.

"You are now a shomer, Zelman. That means you are a watchman, and you always keep them in sight. You can walk behind them, but not so close that they can't talk. You are not to be part of their conversation unless they ask you, okay?"

Zelman shrugged and rolled his eyes at Aleksander

"It's your turn next time."

Regina focused on Leopold, unaware of what was going on around her. She expected they could arrange time alone again if they wanted.

I crave Leopold's kisses and I want to learn how to kiss better.

"You have about an hour to walk and talk," said Yosef.

"Thank you so much, Mr. and Mrs. Anuszewicz. I appreciate your trust. I will have Regina back in an hour."

"That's fine. Have a nice walk."

As they left the house, with Zelman following behind, Regina was careful not to stand too close to Leopold. He nodded, a signal that they needed to watch what they did with her brother so nearby.

"We can't seem too familiar, Regina. Otherwise, this could blow up for us. You understand?"

"Yes. I'm so impressed with how you act with my parents. You are very sophisticated, but of course you are not a child at twenty-three years old. I guess you had to grow up fast after your parents died."

Leopold sighed.

"Yes, I was old enough to be on my own. My brothers and sisters were also killed in that pogrom in Kiev. I lost everyone. I wonder if people who have never experienced what happens in a pogrom really understand how barbaric it is. These people who join the soldiers tear people apart and cut off the heads of men, women, and children. No one is spared."

Regina shuddered and remembered what she heard in the boarding house, the sounds of her sister being raped, and the sight of murdered women and children in the street. They both knew how lucky she was that her life had been spared.

I will never share what happened to Chaja Fajga, not even with Leopold.

"I wasn't with them at the time, so I don't exactly know what they did with my brothers and sisters and my parents. All I was told was that they died. It's probably better I don't know. But you are right, Regina. Unless people see the viciousness, they can't possibly understand why we react so strongly about antisemitic acts."

Regin a nodded.

"So, yes, I was left on my own when I was eighteen and considered an adult. My colleagues in the Bund and the Kiev community took care of me. They made all my food, sewed clothes for me and checked in on me every day. I was fortunate."

"I can't imagine my life without my parents and my brothers and sisters. That had to be so difficult."

"It was at first. I didn't leave the house for weeks. Then, Ukraine's chief rabbi, who lived in Kiev, came over one afternoon with his wife. They sat with me for hours, asking me to tell them everything that was on my mind. I think they thought that if I could talk about my feelings it would help, and they were right. It did. I owe them so much."

Leopold and Regina strolled in silence for a while, looking back to check on Zelman, to be sure he was still with them.

"You know we will meet with Wiktor Litwinski sometime in the next couple weeks," Leopold said. "Even though he is now out of office, he is still widely respected in the city. I'm not sure about how his successor, Aleksander Müller, feels about Jews. He is a Russian who came here from St. Petersburg."

"As soon as that meeting is scheduled, I'll get train tickets for our group, and we will go into town together. It's a short ride, but too long to walk. Once that is scheduled, can you plan to meet me at the office early?"

Regina was anxious about the meeting.

"Of course, Leopold. I will come early. I'm already nervous. What will we talk about?"

"He is progressive, and he has worked with our Bund. We need his advice about fighting the rise in these incidents. I don't know if he will support a police patrol, but we need to at least make him aware that we are concerned."

"We must do that!"

"Yes, Regina, and I want you to help us prepare for the meeting, including information about our history in Poland. Make it interesting so we don't bore him. It needs to be well focused, not just a dry history list, so try to point out how bad things have gotten."

"Yes, I will do that."

Regina's took a deep breath. Her admiration for Leopold continued to grow, but she didn't have anyone to talk to about him. She was bursting to tell her friends about their relationship.

I don't think they would approve if they knew the real story.

On their way back, Leopold and Regina checked in with Zelman to see how he was doing.

"I'm bored. That's how I'm doing. This a boring job. Is it okay if next time Aleksander comes with me?"

"Fine with me," said Regina. "I don't care."

18

When the Office Door Closes

First thing Monday morning, Regina got a message that her group had an appointment to meet with Wiktor Litwinski in two weeks, which meant she would be extra busy beyond her regular translating work.

I'm doing what I'm supposed to do, but all I can think about is Leopold.

As she spread out her Russian and Polish documents, Regina thought she felt Leopold's eyes on her. She looked up and saw that she was right. He was at his desk, with papers in front of him, but he was not looking at them.

Regina worked hard to keep their frequent glances as private as possible, and their Saturday afternoon walks were not discussed with other members of the staff. But she and Leopold grabbed hugs and kisses any time when no one else was around, which fed Regina's thoughts about being together long-term.

On the Monday morning of their meeting, Leopold, Regina, Rachel, Chaim, and Emiel assembled in Mokotów and took the train into the city center. Wiktor Litwinski's office was in a new 11-story skyscraper, the tallest building in Warsaw, two blocks from City Hall. After waiting almost an hour, they were finally escorted in.

"I'm sorry to keep you waiting," Litwinski said. "You never know what is going to happen on Mondays."

He didn't shake hands with anyone and apologized that he didn't have chairs for all of them. He didn't ask for more either, which Leopold recognized as a tactic to keep the meeting short.

"So, what brings you all the way from Mokotów? Nice town. Lots of parks and greenery."

Leopold spoke first.

"Thank you for seeing us. We know you have a lot of influence in Warsaw and in Poland, and that your time is valuable. Thank you for seeing us. We are here because of the growing number of antisemitic activities here in Poland. In fact, I was brutally attacked just three weeks ago and could have been killed, except my neighbors happened to come outside just as the thugs grabbed me. Jews have a long history here in Poland, more than a thousand years. We asked Regina to talk a bit about that, to provide a perspective on these current happenings."

Regina dried her hands on her skirt and fumbled the pages she prepared.

"As we all know, Poland was founded in 550 A.D., and Jews began to settle here in the eighth century. Over time, they became merchants, bankers, and members of the intelligentsia. Jews have held high office, and a large part of the healing community is Jewish physicians, nurses, and midwives. Many professionals, such as those who practice law, teachers, merchants, butchers, bakers, and greengrocers, are Jewish. My point is that the Jewish community is an important part of Poland. Not just in Mokotów or here in Warsaw, but all over Poland."

Litwinski nodded.

"In short, there were thirty pogroms in one year during the first wave, including in Kiev and Warsaw, and they continued for another three years. A second wave erupted in 1902, starting with a conflict in a marketplace in Czestochowa, which escalated when a Cossack troop ravaged a Jewish neighborhood there. Kishinev happened in 1903, and a string of pogroms persisted until 1906 that followed the Kishinev model. You may not know that Leopold's parents and siblings died in that pogrom, and I experienced the Bialystok pogrom."

Litwinski nodded again.

"May I ask if you have ever witnessed a pogrom?"

Regina knew that Leopold did not know this would be part of her talk.

Litwinski didn't answer.

"I'm guessing you haven't, which is fortunate, because no one should see what really happens in a pogrom. But please, Mr. Litwinski, you must try to understand what we, and my colleagues are dealing with, not to mention many other Jews in our communities."

"I'm not sure that is relevant, Regina, is it?"

Without waiting, Regina quickly listed the violence that took place.

"Oh, but it is."

She glanced at Leopold before she went on.

"Beheading, pulling limbs off children and babies, rape, stabbings, burning homes and businesses, poking eyes out, slicing people up. I could go on, but this is what takes place in a pogrom."

Litwinski sat up straight as Regina continued.

"If we just look at one of these, the 1903 pogrom in Kishinev in Moldova, in Southern Russia, not far from Odessa, we can see the same factors that seem to appear again and again."

Regina felt beads of sweat break out on her forehead. She took a breath.

"And that brings us to today. We have continued to see attacks on Jews in our own streets in Mokotów, so close to Warsaw, and in Krakow at the Alte Synagogue. It seems that we need to involve our government, our police, and perhaps armed Jewish patrols in the streets to protect us."

Regina looked around, nodded to each person, and sat down.

Litwinski spoke slowly.

"Most of the attacks in Russia are in the Pale of Settlement. It's terrible, I admit, but I wonder if those attacks will come outside of there. However, your point is well taken about Krakow, and your own attack. I'm so sorry about that and glad your neighbors showed such good timing. I want you to know I'm sympathetic to this issue and I'm not one of those politicians who just says nice things and then does nothing. We have a very large Jewish population in Poland. I know what is going on in Ukraine and Belarus, so don't think I'm not aware or don't care. However, at this time I'm unsure how to take a stand."

Regina and Leopold looked at each other.

"Leopold, perhaps the attack on you was from some guys who have a grudge against you. Do you know them, and did you do something to make them angry?"

I'm not surprised that Litwinski is trying to whitewash the issue.

"Sir, I assure you I didn't know them," said Leopold, "and I guarantee that the attack was purely antisemitic. I'm known in our community for leading the local Jewish Labor Bund, as you know from our appointment. We see these events growing and would like your support to create a team of men to patrol our streets in Mokotów during the days and evenings. We can't do it officially without your signature."

Litwinski nodded twice before he spoke.

"I see. Yes, you need government support to make it official. Otherwise, I'm afraid, it would appear to be vigilantes, and of course, that won't do. I'm not sure I can recommend such a move without more concrete evidence that this is becoming more prevalent. What I can do is share this with President Miller, to watch and see if things get worse. I understand your concern and it probably feels like we are waiting until something bad happens before we can do something about it, but in fact that is the case. If you and the other Bund offices in the area are having the same problem, then you can join forces and come back to me, and we can figure out how to help you further."

Litwinski took a deep breath.

"I can't talk about all the details, but I want you to know I am working hard to support Józef Piłsudski and his work with the Polish Socialist Party. So, while I will alert our city leaders to keep an eye on antisemitic incidents, I encourage your Bund to support Pilsudski's political efforts because he can lead us to enjoy a better country for all of us."

We need to reach out to all the other Bund offices around Warsaw and Poland and see if they also have problems.

"Thank you, Sir," Leopold said. "We appreciate your willingness to meet with us and we will take your advice, both to write to the others and to support our socialist brother, Josef Pilsudski."

Litwinski stood and shook hands with everyone.

"Let me know what you find out. And be careful."

Once the group got outside, they walked the few blocks to the train station in silence. As they reached the train, Leopold passed out the tickets and they headed back to Mokotów. As the train pulled into the station, Leopold spoke.

"Why don't we go home. It's been a long day. I'll see you tomorrow. Thanks for coming along."

"Leopold, we appreciate everything you are doing for us. We'll see you tomorrow," Emile said.

He and Rachel grabbed their coats and headed out.

I hope Leopold won't leave so soon.

As Regina took her time to gather her things, she noticed Leopold watching her.

"Hey, do you have to rush off, my pretty Regina?"

Regina's hands were sweaty, and she could hardly catch her breath. Leopold locked the office door.

Oh my God.

"Do you think anyone knows we are in here alone?"

Regina was concerned because if they were caught it would not only ruin her relationship with Leopold. Her reputation in the Jewish community would be ruined, possibly making her undesirable for marriage because of bad morals. None of that mattered, though, as she wet her lips and took a breath.

"If you want to go, I'll understand. I never want you to feel like you have to stay here with me."

"Oh, no, hardly. I was hoping we could sneak a few minutes alone, Leopold."

I wish I felt as confident as I might sound.

Leopold approached Regina and slipped his hand behind her neck. Softly and gently, he pulled her head to his and kissed her lips lightly and tenderly. Soon, his energy became more urgent, and he pushed his tongue into her mouth, urging her to do the same.

As they stood in the middle of the room, holding each other, Leopold rubbed her breasts, breathing harder with every swirl of his hands.

"Regina, I constantly want to be close to you. To kiss you and make love to you. I'm so sorry."

Did I hear him right? Did he just say "love?"

She held onto Leopold as dizziness overwhelmed her.

I'll lose my balance if I let go.

"I feel the same way, Leopold. I want to kiss you, too."

"Hold me, Regina. Just hold me tight."

To Regina, what was happening did not seem real. She was dizzy with desire that she didn't understand. But nothing mattered. All that she wanted in life was happening right now. She wasn't even worried about being caught.

"Let's sit down before we fall down," Leopold said.

He laughed and guided her toward the couch, where he had made love to her for the first time.

He can't tear my underpants again because Mama will surely notice.

As Leopold moved his hand under her skirt, Regina pulled her underpants off before Leopold was aware of what happened. He fumbled with his pants, freeing himself and guiding his cock to its destination.

Regina felt a sharp, hot jolt inside her and held Leopold as he moved on top of her. Just like last time, after one last thrust, he let out a moan and then fell silent.

19

Deaf Ears

Over the next few weeks, the Bund staff tried to establish security routines based on information Leopold gathered about incidents in other parts of Poland. He suggested they meet to talk about how they could stop the attacks. Regina needed to translate several relevant documents, along with reports about more incidents in response to Leopold's inquiries.

Each Saturday, he came to Regina's home for lunch, and when they walked together each weekend, her brothers tagged along, joking, and laughing several feet behind. She felt herself falling more and more in love with Leopold, but she kept her feelings to herself other than telling the family how much she continued to admire him.

Regina was so pleased when Leopold bragged to her family about the presentation she had prepared and delivered when they met Litwinski, who supported Piłsudski and his Polish Socialist Party. At the same time, the right-wing National Democracy Party, led by Dmowski, seemed to be growing its core of strong support.

Regina thought that the recent low-profile incidents had been organized or at least condoned by the authorities.

How else could they be so well-timed and organized?

She couldn't avoid the continuing friction she felt with her family and friends when it came to her push for action against the increasing antisemitism they were hearing about in the nearby towns and districts of Warsaw.

As the news came in, Regina felt increasingly uneasy about everyone's safety. She felt particularly vulnerable since the attack on Leopold was probably triggered by his work at the Bund.

So, what about me, Eda and Emiel, Chaim, and the others? Have we also become potential targets?

Her arguments for patrol groups taking up arms against the gangs fell on deaf ears. The prevailing sentiment in the office, as well as in the community, was that Regina was overreacting and that the patrols would anger the locals and cause more problems.

She decided that even without support from politicians in Warsaw, her group should print up flyers and distribute them all over Mokotów. On Friday, when the office closed early to allow everyone to get home for Shabbos, Regina had her first disagreement with Leopold about taking more action.

After everyone left, Regina stayed at her desk instead of moving to the couch, where she and Leopold normally came together.

"You look so serious, my Regina. Is something wrong?"

Leopold was teasing, almost to the point of mocking.

"You know what is wrong. We are so vulnerable here. Just because that dummkopf in Warsaw refuses to see what is right in front of his face doesn't mean we can ignore what is so obvious to us."

Leopold held Regina's gaze.

"I'm not sure that acting on our own would be wise without the approval of the Bund office in Warsaw, and without support from the city government here in Mokotów and in Warsaw. I'm sure we will invite trouble if we create a flyer warning people against antisemitic attacks."

"I don't agree, Leopold. Why is sitting here waiting for something to happen a smart idea? We know it's just a matter of time before more attacks come and acting now could save lives."

Regina was frustrated. She didn't know how to argue with Leopold about politics while also dealing with her growing feelings for him. She was not in the mood to be romantic at that moment, but she knew that Leopold had it on his mind. Besides, she felt more tired than usual and just wanted to go home and take a nap before dinner.

"I can see you are upset," Leopold said, "and it's been a busy day. Maybe we can talk more about it tomorrow afternoon when we walk after lunch."

Regina agreed. She gathered her jacket and a cloth bag she used to bring her lunch to the office. She gave Leopold a kiss on the cheek and walked out unaccompanied into a late afternoon breeze.

When she arrived home, everyone was busy preparing the table for dinner, which included Shabbos candles and platters for the challah, gefilte fish, matzo ball soup, roast chicken, and cinnamon noodle kugel.

When everyone was seated, Lena stood with a cloth napkin over her head and lit the two candlesticks she and Yosef had received as a wedding present. She placed her hands over the flame and recited a prayer.

Baruch Atah Adonai, Eloheinu Melech haolam, asher kid'shanu b'mitzvosav v'zivanu l'hadlik ner shel Shabbos.

May the presence of God be with you and give you peace. Blessed are You, our Eternal God, Sovereign of the universe. You hallow us with Your commandments and command us to kindle the lights of Shabbos.

After dinner, Regina said her goodnights and went to bed immediately. Lena and Yosef looked at each other with concern because Regina seemed more tired than usual for a healthy young woman. Lena went to see her.

"Schatzeleh, are you all right? You seem to be tired all the time these days. Are you working too hard? Maybe you need to cut back your schedule."

"Thank you, mother of mine. I'm fine. I've been working hard, but no more than usual. I'm just frustrated because I think Warsaw is not taking these attacks seriously. It feels to me like we are just waiting for something worse to happen before we do what is needed to keep people safe. Am I the only one who sees what is happening?"

Lena sat and looked at Regina and then put her arms around her daughter, who was clearly distraught.

"Schatzeleh, I know you want to keep people safe, and I also know you had a terrible experience in Bialystok that has stayed with you, but you can't let that one time dictate your future. Is it really so bad here? I know Leopold had a scare, but that was the only one."

"A scare? You call that a scare? Mama, he could have been killed if his neighbors hadn't saved him from those thugs. They were ready to clobber him with a big stick. That's not a scare. That's an attack that could have been fatal. And that was not the only one. We get reports from other Bund offices about incidents like that all over Poland."

Lena sighed. Her friends thought the attack on Leopold was not primarily because he was Jewish, but because of what he was doing as the head of the Jewish Bund Party in Mokotów. Some people didn't like what they stood for and the changes they were trying to make with labor laws.

"Sleep, my love. Things will look better in the morning."

Regina rolled over and fell asleep within minutes.

An Unexpected Pregnancy

As soon as Regina woke, she felt a rise in her stomach. She rushed to the bathroom, quickly bent over, and retched.

Is it something I ate?

Dina rushed to her side.

"Regina. Are you ill?"

Regina took a big breath and bent over the sink, vomiting once again as her hair fell across her face.

"I don't know. I felt fine last night, but I was extremely tired. Maybe I am ill. I think I should stay home this morning. I don't want to get sick at shul."

Lena was slightly alarmed. She agreed that Regina had been very tired lately and that maybe she was ill.

"Maybe I should stay at home with you, Darling. I don't think you should be here alone."

"Mama, I don't want you to miss hearing the rabbi. I'll rest all morning until you come back, okay?"

"Yes, but don't do anything about the meal. Just rest."

After the family left to attend services, Regina retched again but she had nothing in her stomach.

What could be wrong? It can't be Mama's food. Maybe it's my nerves from all the conflict about the attacks. Yes, that must be it. I'm having serious issues with my nerves.

Regina laid down, rolled onto her side, and fell asleep. She was still sleeping when the family returned from synagogue. Lena went to her bedside.

"Regina, what is ailing you? I've never seen you so tired! I'm worried about you. Maybe we should call for the doctor."

Regina rubbed her eyes and tried to assuage Lena's concerns.

"It's just tension, Mama, I'm sure. I don't need the doctor. I'm okay, and I'm hungry. Let's just eat first."

"Are you sure? I'm glad you are hungry. Okay, let's eat."

Lena got up from the bed and gave orders to the children to get the table ready. She checked on the cholent, and as soon as the table was set, Lena dished out heaping ladles of what she called a "one dish" meal.

"I love Saturdays when you make cholent," Zelman said.

"Yeah, it is so good, Mama," said Dina.

Everyone at the table agreed as they dug into the hearty meal.

The sounds of everyone enjoying their meal were broken when Lena suddenly remembered that Saturday was when Leopold called on Regina.

"Regina, Leopold usually joins us for lunch and to take you for a walk. I wonder where he is today. But I don't think you should go walking today. You need to rest."

Regina agreed with her mother that she should stay home and rest for the weekend. Yet, she wanted to see Leopold, to hold hands and be close as they walked, and to talk about creating flyers to warn Jewish families to be cautious and walk in pairs or even three and four people at a time. But she couldn't deny that she felt tired, and she wanted to be sure she didn't get ill in front of him.

"Maybe so, Mama, but I think it was just nerves."

Regina still felt tired at the table, though, so she went back to bed as soon as she finished eating. As the rest of the family cleaning up from lunch, there was a knock at the door, as Lena expected. Regina heard it, but she stayed in bed, allowing her mother to manage the moment.

"Leopold! We were wondering if you were coming today. How are you?"

Lena sounded more cordial than she felt because she was sure that Regina's fatigue had to do with her workload at the Bund offices.

"Hello Mrs. Anuszewicz. How are you today?"

"I'm well, Leopold, but I'm afraid Regina is not. She returned home yesterday quite tired. She has not been well today, and she was ill last night and this morning. She didn't even go to the synagogue this morning and she's in bed, so obviously she will not go for a walk with you today or even tomorrow. We hope her fatigue is nothing more than tension, which does not please me at all."

Leopold's face reddened. He apologized that her ailments were due to her activities at the Bund and assured Lena he would keep an eye on her.

After Leopold left, Lena went to see Regina, who had heard some of the tense conversation between Lena and Leopold.

Will that frighten Leopold away?

She hoped their bond was strong enough to withstand two days of rest on the weekend.

By that evening, Regina felt much better and joined her family in the large sitting room. Zelman, Aleksander, and Dina were reading. Kejla was sewing herself a dress the way Chaja Fajga had taught her, and Yosef and Lena were ecstatic about a letter they had received from Chaja Fajga, talking about how well Aron was doing as the assistant rabbi in Paris, and how excited they both were about her being halfway through her second pregnancy.

Regina had brought home some work from the Bund and went about reading the documents in Yiddish and Russian to prepare them for translation. She felt like her old self for the moment, making jokes and sharing some of her work with the family.

Seeing Regina eating and joking made her mother more relaxed. She was sure that whatever had ailed her was gone, and it was probably just fatigue.

Her relief was short-lived, however. On Sunday morning, Regina was bent over the kitchen sink again, retching once again.

As Lena watched her daughter, she knew she wasn't ill.

"Regina, I don't think you are ill. Have you been alone with Leopold?"

Regina stiffened, feeling immediately hot and confused, as she guessed what her mother was referring to and had no idea how to respond.

Lena stood over Regina with a stern face.

"So, those walks you go on were a ruse to reduce any possible suspicion about misbehavior."

Lena almost spit. Regina was devastated.

I've brought shame on my family.

110

She suspected that Leopold would not want to get married, but unless he left town, Yosef would not give him a choice.

Lena stood over Regina, her face flush with anger.

Regina was afraid that her father would go to Leopold's home and hit him hard for taking advantage of his young, naïve daughter. Leopold was older, had lived on his own for five years, and was more worldly than Regina. She had never thought about how having sex could make her pregnant. She was so madly in love, and it never occurred to her to take precautions.

Did Leopold take advantage of my naiveté?

Regina stood up and held a cloth to her face.

"I'm sorry, Mama. I was feeling so much better last night."

"Come with me, my daughter."

Lena took Regina by the hand, and they walked outside. She looked her daughter squarely in the eyes and sighed.

"Regina, you are not ill. You are pregnant. I can see it in your breasts and your morning illness tells me all I need to know. Don't deny it. When did you and Leopold lay together?"

Regina broke down in tears. She had not paid any attention to the dangers of being intimate because she felt that Leopold would have kept anything bad from happening. When she thought about it more, she believed that he was so overcome with love that he couldn't help himself.

"It's past my monthly, I know, but I haven't paid attention. Are you sure, Mama? How could this be? What am I going to do?"

"This isn't just about you, Regina. It affects our entire family. Do you realize what you have done? How could you and Leopold be so selfish and irresponsible? When did this happen?"

Oh my God. I must tell her. It's too late now to hide anything.

"At the office when the others left. We have a small settee that we sit on sometimes. Leopold loves me. I love him. We couldn't help ourselves!"

"You will say nothing to no one. Do you understand?"

Regina nodded.

Oh my God. What have I done?

"We will see how you feel tomorrow, but I am very sure you are pregnant. You will stay home today. I told Leopold not to come for you this weekend."

Lena looked around the garden and picked some radishes, so they had a reason for being outside. A few minutes later, Lena and Regina re-entered the house, where the others were wondering where they had gone.

"Where did the two of you go?"

"We saw some nice ripe radishes," said Lena, "and I wanted to pick them before the animals ate them. Regina wanted to come because you know how she loves radishes."

Regina smiled and popped one in her mouth, hoping that no one would suspect anything.

21

A Sudden Change of Plans

As the day dragged on, Regina tried to be as inconspicuous as possible, but she couldn't stop thinking about the possibility of being pregnant.

What if I am? What will Leopold do? We will have to get married, and he will hate me.

She questioned his responsibility, remembering that he was older and should be wiser about these things. She hoped she would feel better in the morning and that missing her monthly might just be a bad calculation.

Regina lay in bed, staring at the ceiling, consumed with worry about the next morning.

Can I keep myself from getting sick and show Mama I am not pregnant? Would it make a difference? Maybe I'm just late with my monthly and it will come soon. That will prove I'm not pregnant.

First thing the next morning, Regina sprinted into the kitchen and retched again. The only person up that early was Lena, who purposely got up to keep an eye on Regina. Lena grabbed her daughter's shoulders and looked directly into her eyes. Regina couldn't stop sobbing.

"I'm so sorry, Mama, I'm so sorry. I've disappointed you and Papa. I'm so ashamed."

"I know you are, my sweet daughter. But crying won't help. We need to make plans and I must tell your father. You will not go into work today. In fact, you will never go back there. You have other things to do."

"What about Leopold? What will he do? They need me there. Who will do the translating? No one knows Yiddish and Russian like I do."

"That is not your problem now. Don't you worry about Leopold. He is the father, and he must take responsibility."

Regina tried to stop crying. Lena whispered so no one could hear her.

"He should have thought of that before he took advantage of you, Regina. We will deal with him later."

Regina crawled back into her bed and rolled on her side, huddling with her arms around her knees. Life as she knew it was over, and now she was about to become a mother.

What about if I take the same medication Chaja Fajga used to end her pregnancy? Why not me, too?

Lena watched her daughter curl up on her bed.

"Mama, what if I take the same medicine Chaja Fajga took? Would that resolve this problem?"

"Regina, that was less than a week after your sister was raped. How long has this been going on? Over a month? Even I know it is too late."

As the day dragged on, Regina wondered what went on at the Bund office when she didn't show up.

Will Leopold come by later to check on me? Does he know I am pregnant? Does he care? Is he suspicious after Lena said I wasn't feeling well and needed to rest?

Multiple thoughts raced through her mind, but Regina didn't know how to improve her situation. As the hours ticked by, Lena carried on with her normal chores and ignored Regina. While her siblings were in school, Lena sat with Regina and told her what would happen over the next few days.

"When your father gets home, I will tell him about you. He will be very upset, but mostly with Leopold because he is old enough to know better, especially the consequences of his behavior. It doesn't help, though, that you also allowed this to happen."

Regina felt foolish and out of control.

Maybe I was fooling myself that Leopold really cares about me. Maybe he just took advantage of a silly girl. But didn't he know the consequences? Did he assume I knew about taking precautions with a sponge? How would I? It was never discussed.

"Mama, what will happen with Leopold?"

"I will tell your father not to beat him up because that won't help your relationship, but he must marry you immediately. I'm sure this is not how you pictured this, but it is exactly what will happen. You will live together with Leopold as husband and wife."

Later that afternoon, Regina was still frozen in bed, knowing her father would come see her at any minute, angry and heartbroken at what his daughter had done to herself and the family.

She didn't have to wait long. The look on Yosef's face told her everything she needed to know.

"Regina. How could you be so stupid? How could you allow Leopold to take advantage of you this way? I don't totally blame him because you have the strength and the willpower to say no. Don't you? Or did he force you? Did he hit you or threaten you? If not, why did you let this happen?"

Regina was in tears.

"No, Papa, Leopold didn't force me at all."

"Where does he live? You must know that."

As soon as Regina told him, Yosef was out the door. Lena came back and sat on the edge of the bed.

"Your father will sort out everything. We will make the announcement at shul on Saturday, and you and Leopold will be married there the following week. It won't be a grand function like we had for Aron and Chaja Fajga, but we will make honey and sponge cakes and provide wine for the congregation for the oneg. Then, you will move into Leopold's home."

They have my life all planned out.

Regina had no choice. Her dream of working at the Bund full-time was over. She was shocked by how fast her life was changing.

Sad or glad? I'm not sure. Trapping Leopold into marriage is not what I wanted, even if we got married the formal way.

Regina couldn't have the baby without getting married to the father. It would be a shanda, terrible for her and for her family as well as the child.

She was more nervous about the proposal than being pregnant. She decided to wear her best dress, which luckily still fit.

115

22

The Proposal

After her morning sickness passed, Regina drank tea and ate some scrambled eggs and a slice of bread. She filled her bathing bowl with water and ran it over her body to feel as clean as possible. It was an important day, and she wanted to look and feel her best.

She could only imagine what went on when her father went to see Leopold. What did he say? Did he blame Regina? Did he fight with her father? No one said anything except that Leopold would be coming by today.

I guess he was convinced to marry me.

Throughout the day, Regina felt nervous about seeing Leopold under these new circumstances. It wasn't the same as when she was at work or when they took their walks. Life was casual then.

How did I let this happen?

Regina was in denial, and she knew it. This was not how she wanted to be married and become a parent. She closed her eyes and felt his kiss on her cheek. It was magical even as she remembered it.

Will Leopold even want to kiss me now? What does he think of me? Does he blame me?

Her carefree life seemed to be over. She and Leopold had to prepare to be parents, long before either of them anticipated such a life change.

When she heard a knock at the door, Regina knew what was about to happen next. She stood back as Yosef answered the door, revealing a nervous Leopold, looking anything but confident and casual as usual.

"Come in Leopold," her father said.

He sounded friendly. Leopold handed Yosef a bowl of fruit he apparently bought along the way.

"Why, thank you. This looks delicious."

Regina was impressed by Leopold's gesture. That small expression made a big difference to her. She watched her father let go of some of the tension and anger he had been feeling.

As Yosef and Lena welcomed Leopold into the house, Regina noticed how awkward everyone appeared.

"I guess you and Regina have something to discuss," said Yosef, "so we will be in the kitchen if you need us. Lena has made one of her sweet noodle kugels, which I imagine you will enjoy after your talk."

"Thank you, Mr. Anuszewicz, but I'd like it if you and Mrs. Anuszewicz would stay for a moment."

Yosef and Lena were not sure what was going to happen next. As Regina looked at Leopold and her parents, beads of sweat appeared on her forehead. Leopold walked over to her and took both of her hands in his.

"Regina, we both know we are having a baby, and a lot sooner than either of us planned. But that doesn't make it any less wanted and we must do what is right. So, Regina, would you marry me and give our child a proper home?"

Yosef stood quietly and Lena began to cry.

Regina was stunned.

Leopold is acting so boldly, having my parents witness his proposal.

She was smiling and crying at the same time.

"Leopold, yes. Yes! Of course, I will marry you."

Regina and Lena hugged and cried together.

Thank God Mama will be close by during my pregnancy.

Chaja Fajga had not been so lucky during the difficult months she spent in Paris without her mother nearby.

Regina felt confident that she and Leopold would make a good home.

This solution makes the best out of this terrible problem.

Their next challenge was deciding what to tell the rest of the family and people in the community. Regina's siblings had to be told that their sister was pregnant and getting married very soon. Aleksander and Zelman would be relieved not to have to follow Regina and Leopold anymore on their walks.

Yosef told Regina and Leopold that he would find a rabbi to marry them as soon as possible.

I need to sit down. This is all happening so fast.

Leopold sat next to her. Regina wondered what he was feeling.

"Thank you, Leopold," said Yosef. That was a lovely proposal."

Leopold looked at Regina and sighed. They both smiled, relieved to still be together but obviously anxious about what was to come.

What about all the gossip? People in our community will figure out soon enough that I was already pregnant before we got married. Well, it's not the first time a young couple married quickly. I just wish it didn't happen to me.

She knew that Leopold had not planned for his life to take a turn like this so soon. She heard that the shadchanit had told him about some "lovely" young women who would make a good wife. He told Regina that he told Gita politely that he was not ready, that he knew the women, but while they were lovely and he was sure they would make good wives, for the time being he was enjoying his freedom.

Regina respected her father for confronting Leopold and demanding that he marry her.

That's what a father does for his daughter.

Regina knew her father would respect Leopold for asking him and her mother to be present when he asked her to marry him. She suspected that Leopold wanted her parents to witness his proposal to diffuse Yosef's anger. If he was going to be his father-in-law, it would be better to ease any undertone of anger.

It was a ploy, but a good one.

Regina realized that she and Leopold needed to start thinking like parents. Life wasn't just about the two of them any longer. She needed to gently guide him to stop thinking only about himself and start considering what their baby will need.

Keeping Regina's parents close was a good strategy. She knew that their new son-in-law would have to create a man-to-man bond with Yosef and in another way with Lena. She thought it would also be wise to let them know, or let at least let them think, that Leopold had planned all along to propose marriage to Regina, just not so fast.

But it will take a lot more than minor machinations to make things right with my family. We will have to let them see Leopold being a good husband and father.

Regina knew it would be a long time, if ever, before she could go back to work at the Bund office. For now, and for the next several months, Leopold would need to learn how to prepare a household for his new family.

Leopold's House
1908

23

Baby!

As Regina's belly grew, a new reality set in. She would no longer be just one person. Now, she was living for two. She already missed her carefree days when all she had to do was focus on herself and her work. Leopold brought home documents that needed to be translated, and Regina kept up as much as she could, but she knew that all that translation work would soon stop.

Will I ever have a chance to do it again?

She knew her group at the Bund missed her contributions, and she longed to be part of their activities.

How will I cope?

Regina wasn't the only one trying to manage such a big change in her life. Her mother was struggling with mixed feelings about her two daughters. Chaja Fajga was far away in Paris with her lovely husband and pregnant with their second child, while Regina, still obsessed with politics, was eight months pregnant with no idea how to be a wife or mother.

Married life had been a huge adjustment for her. She was not used to getting up every morning and making breakfast for someone else, along with lunches he took to work. She had rarely shopped alone for the daily meals. Fortunately, Lena helped with the transition, teaching Regina how to shop, what to prepare for dinner, how to make cholent, and how to keep house.

Some young women already knew these things, but Regina had never been one to prepare herself for marriage and motherhood. She lived as a casual observer of these things, and while she always helped her mother to take care of her younger siblings, she never paid much attention to developing any homemaking skills.

Life is changing quickly, and not like I expected.

She even saw Leopold differently now.

"How are you, Regina? Do you feel okay today?"

Her husband's daily inquiries seemed weak to her. He was no longer the self-confident hero she fell in love with. But they were married.

Regina still felt hurt by some of the hateful things people said about her getting pregnant so quickly. She heard about it from her co-workers at the Bund, who came by to see her sometimes.

"Some people say you did this on purpose to trap Leopold into marrying you. We told them that was not your plan, that both of you knew what you were doing."

The friends who cared for Regina and her family defended them, or they were no longer friends. It surprised Regina that some of her friends had turned on her and her family over something that was out of her control. She soon discovered that several women acted out of jealousy because they wanted to make a shiddach for themselves with Leopold.

Even though she was hurt by some of the remarks and accusations, she felt heartened by those who defended her and her family.

They should know that we don't lie when life doesn't go as planned.

As her ninth month of pregnancy began, Regina woke with a cramp in her stomach, followed by another one after that.

This must be what Mama described as the baby getting ready to be born.

She tried not to panic but she sent Leopold to get her mother. While he was gone, she held her abdomen and cried. She only calmed down a little when she heard Leopold and Lena entering the house.

"Calm down, Regina. The baby will be fine. They don't drop so quickly. Leopold, please go to Ceira Czerniakow's home and ask her to come."

Ceira, Leopold's neighbor, came quickly to be with Regina. She held a cold cloth to her forehead and squeezed her hand.

"Oh, Ceira, thank you for being here," said Lena.

After the two women made plans for the early arrival of Regina's baby. Lena went to her daughter's side to calm down.

"My lovely Regina, it looks like you will be a mother a little sooner than you thought, but that is all right. You are almost at the end of your term, so everything will be fine. Not to worry, we will be here to help you."

"Mama, I'm scared. What if the baby isn't ready?"

"The baby is saying it's time to come out and it doesn't want to wait a few more weeks. It's all going to be fine."

Lena turned to Leopold.

"Show me where you keep the blankets and towels we will need. Then go find Stanistawa the midwife. Hopefully, she is available."

Regina held her mother's hand, terrified of letting go.

"Don't leave me, Mama. Please stay right here."

"Ciera and I will not abandon you. We'll help you have this baby."

Regina cried out with a new contraction. Then, they started to come faster and faster. She let out another cry and her breathing intensified.

It feels like my entire body is tearing apart!

Just when her contractions seemed to ease up, another one stabbed her.

Where is Leopold? Doesn't he know the baby is coming?

As Regina leaned forward, another crushing contraction took hold. She closed her eyes and screamed. Just then, Leopold appeared with the midwife.

"Well, what do have we here?" she said. "Looks like it's time to have a baby. Leopold, you can go outside now and wait."

It's the same woman I went to for Chaja Fajga's medicine.

Stanistawa was highly regarded within the community. If there was ever a problem, she would know how to take care of it. With the baby coming a month early, her presence was particularly appreciated.

"Let me look."

As she lifted the blanket covering Regina, she poked her head down, pushed Regina's legs apart, and put two fingers inside her.

"Aha! You are doing quite well. Soon, I will ask you to push hard to get the baby out. In the meantime, you might be more comfortable on your side."

As soon as Regina turned, she felt better. But when another contraction came, she let out another cry.

She was able to relax for a few minutes before the next contraction, when Stanistawa put her hands on Regina's swollen stomach and declared it was time to get the baby out into the world.

"Okay, Regina, I want you to sit up as much as you can, and Lena and Ceira will put some pillows and blankets behind you to lean on. Pull your legs up to your chest."

With great effort, Regina did as she was told.

"Regina, I'm going to tell you to push the baby out. When I say stop, you stop. When I say push, I want you to give me the biggest push you can."

It seemed like only seconds before the next contraction when Regina was told to push. She squeezed her eyes shut and let out a wail, pushing as hard as she could.

"Good job. It won't be long now."

Regina lay back exhausted between contractions, unsure if she could get through such an enormous ordeal. Not long ago, when she was a carefree young woman fighting for the safety of Jews in Mokotów, she never imagined being married or giving birth.

Now look at me. I'm forcing a child out of my body.

She bent over and pushed as hard as she could.

"That's it, Regina, almost there. I can see the baby's head. Now push again! Here it comes!"

Stanistawa knelt beside the bed, arms buried under the covers, her head down as she watched a new life appear. As she lifted the baby, he whimpered and then cried out. She held him for Regina to see before placing him on Regina's stomach so she could hold him.

"He's gorgeous!" said Lena. "A healthy boy. You did it! Hold him close and put a blanket over him so he doesn't get chilled."

Lena was crying tears of joy.

"He's wonderful, Regina," said Ceira. "Mazel Tov. You did a great job. I must head home now, but I'm so glad I was here. Now, get some rest."

Ceira smiled as she headed for the door.

"I'm going to cut the cord now," said Stanistawa. "You need to put the baby by your breast."

Regina wasn't sure what to do. She knew about breastfeeding but felt awkward. She pulled the blanket away while Lena helped her position the baby's head and gently pushing Regina's nipple into his mouth.

"It might be a bit too soon, but see what happens," Stanistawa said.

She twisted the umbilical cord and pulled the rest from Regina. Just then, Leopold came rushing in the house, looking wildly around until his eyes fell on Regina and the baby.

"You have given me a son! Let me see him."

He was practically yelling with joy as he sat next to Regina and looked at his new child.

"Don't touch him until you wash up," Stanistawa said. "Everything must be very clean around him. He's just a baby, Leopold, and he could get sick easily, so please be careful."

Leopold stood up, a sheepish smile on his face and went to the wash basin and scrubbed his hands with soap before drying them with a towel.

"Is this what you mean?"

He showed everyone his hands.

"Yes. That will do. Just be sure you always wash up before you handle the baby. And make sure all the blankets and baby clothes are clean. Babies are susceptible to germs. They can get infections and die."

Stanistawa wiped away the blood and tissue from Regina's womb and cleaned the baby's body. She pressed firmly on Regina's abdomen several times, wiping up more discharge until nothing was left. Then, she wrapped up the sheets and towels and bundled them together.

"You won't be using these any longer. I will dispose of them on my way home. You are all fine now, and I wish you all the best. I'll drop by again tomorrow to see how you are coming along."

Lena went over to Leopold and whispered in his ear.

"You need to pay Stanistawa before she leaves. Do you have money?"

Leopold was stunned, as if he had no idea what was expected.

"Don't worry about that now," Stanistawa said. "You have plenty to think about right now. I'd be happy if you pay me tomorrow."

"Thank you. I assure you I will show my appreciation tomorrow."

Regina held her new baby son in her arms and gently encouraged him to nurse. But he seemed to have other things on his mind as he looked around his new world.

"Look at his eyes. He is looking at me, Mama."

"Keep him warm, my daughter. He is so delicate right now."

Lena encouraged Regina to drink some water and eat something. Leopold stood by the wall in the kitchen, watching Regina and his new son.

"Your mother says to eat, so let me see what we have."

Leopold investigated the ice box.

"We have the potato latkes you made the other day. I will heat them up for all three of us."

"Let me help you, Leopold," said Lena. "I'm sure you want to sit with your wife. I can get the food ready."

"Oh, he's sucking now. Mama. He's nursing!"

Lena stopped what she was doing and looked at Regina and the baby.

"You won't have milk until tomorrow," she said. "So, what are you going to name him? Have you thought about it?"

Leopold had discussed it with Regina and felt strongly about naming their new child after his father or mother. Most Jewish families never named a new baby after a living relative. Instead, they named the child in honor of a loved one who had passed away. There were no "juniors" in the Jewish tradition.

"I would like to name him Louis," said Leopold, "after my father, and Regina is okay with that."

"I think that is a lovely name. Now we have little Louis."

As Lena and Leopold talked, Regina's eyes started to close. Lena sat down on the bed next to her daughter.

"Schatzeleh, it's time for me to go home and get dinner for the family. You have your husband with you now, so I'll leave you two alone with your new son and stop by in the morning to see how you are getting along and let Leopold go to work."

At first, Regina looked upset and didn't want Lena to leave.

Mama is right. Leopold is the man of the house and I know he will take good care of me.

"Thank you, Mama. Please stop by before Leopold goes to work. I'm so tired and Louis and I need our rest."

"You sure do."

"We had a busy day."

Regina's joke made Lena feel comfortable about leaving. She kissed her son-in-law, her daughter, and her new grandson before heading home.

"Mazel Tov to all of us!"

24

Louis' Future

Regina enjoyed her new life as a mother. She never anticipated feeling such an immediate and deep love for her little boy.

At ten days old, Louis was an easy baby. He slept for several hours at a time and cooed and murmured when he was awake. He nursed voraciously, making up for the nourishment he missed by arriving a bit early.

Just as Regina was getting him ready for a nap on Tuesday afternoon, putting a blanket around his little body so he would feel secure, she heard a noise that disturbed her tranquility.

She didn't recognize the loud voices coming from outside. It sounded like an argument, but it didn't make sense to her in her neighborhood.

Maybe someone needs help?

She crouched behind the settee to peak out the window and see what the fuss was about. Her neighbor, Herschel Czerniaków, an elderly physician with white hair and a mustache, was in the middle of an argument with a man she didn't recognize. He was yelling at the doctor and shaking his fist.

Regina felt unsafe and a sense of terror washed over her.

Is this the start of another pogrom? Will others join in and then go house to house?

She shuttered all the windows and made sure the door was locked. Then, she peeked through a small opening and listened. It was difficult to make out exactly what the man was saying but she could tell clearly that his demeanor was threatening, and his face grew red as he yelled at Herschel.

He's wearing dirty pants and a filthy jacket. Maybe he works in the mill.

Regina's heart pumped faster. She felt powerless to do anything to help her neighbor, and she felt tears on her cheeks witnessing such an event.

He called Herschel a dirty Jew! He's calling him a thief, and now he's saying something about pogroms.

At one-point, Regina heard the man say that all Jews are cheaters, that they should go back to Russia, and the Russians should get rid of all the Jews.

Herschel stood his ground, but it was clear he was upset and tried to make the man calm down.

"I did not cheat you. You brought your wife to me, and I treated her the best I could. Why are you saying I did nothing and that is why she didn't get better? I told you she should have seen me sooner. She had a bad infection in her hand and there was only so much I could do."

"You didn't do anything, you dirty Jew. You just wanted money and you took two of her fingers as revenge because you hate Christians. It's what you unscrupulous Jews do, and then you say it isn't your fault. You made that up, and now my wife has only three fingers on her left hand."

The man spit at Herschel.

"Why won't you understand? The fact that I saved those other three fingers is a miracle. You're lucky she didn't lose her whole hand. You should be thanking me instead of being angry. I don't know anyone who could have done more. Your wife waited too long to get help."

"Liar! Crafty Jew thief. You stole money from me because you knew you couldn't help her."

"What do you want from me? No doctor could have done anything else. Why don't you take your wife to another physician and see what they say? Will that help you feel better about what I did?"

"Yeah, another dirty Jew doctor who will also cheat me because that is what you people do. You live off the problems of others. All you Jews work together at night to see how you can cheat the rest of the world the next day. This isn't over!"

As Regina watched the man walk away, she saw that Herschel was clearly shaken, but only after the man was a few blocks away did several neighbors who heard the commotion come outside.

"What happened? Clearly the man was upset with you," said one of them.

Regina stood just outside her front door with Louis in her arms.

Herschel sat on the stairs in front of his house with his head in his hands.

"There was nothing I could do. This woman's hand was so infected, I wasn't sure I could save it at all. She waited too long. It was a wonder I could save those three fingers. Obviously, it didn't matter to that man."

It was late afternoon, the sun was setting, and the temperature grew chilly, so Regina went back inside her house. She was shaken by what she had seen, so she sat down and rocked Louis back and forth, trying to calm herself down as much as the baby.

This was the kind of incident she had been hearing about at the Bund, the same ones she and Leopold had been arguing about. Antisemitic remarks and attacks were becoming more and more prevalent.

But this one was right here on our own quiet street in Mokotów.

She put Louis into his little bed and sat down to think. She had tried to ignore her anxiety and listen to those who told her she was over-reacting, but inside she knew she wasn't.

Regina remembered the heated discussion she and Leopold had just a week before Louis was born after an incident in downtown Warsaw, when a Jewish man and his wife were beaten badly on their way home from Shabbos services. The man eventually died, but Leopold refused to listen to Regina when she insisted that they needed to think about leaving Poland, for the sake of their entire family.

"What kind of future will Louis have here?"

"That's ridiculous, Regina. Are you going to let a few local confrontations drive you out of the country? You are probably overly sensitive because you are pregnant."

Regina remembered the exchange well. She had taken a deep breath and worked to keep her voice calm.

"Leopold. You know I love and respect you, but I don't think you are giving enough weight to the rise in these antisemitic incidents. What has been happening in Russia and Lithuania and other countries is spreading here to Poland now. You of all people should know this better than anyone. I don't understand how you can keep acting like it's not happening."

"That is always your answer, Regina. Leave Poland. That is too much!"

"Okay then, how about this? Has the Council reconsidered agreeing to let the Bund pass out flyers that we are willing to fund, warning Jews not to go out alone at night? We all know that the incident in Warsaw was an attack and not a robbery."

Leopold threw his hands up in the air.

"Regina, not every act or argument is because someone is antisemitic. Sometimes, it's just a difference of opinion, and sometimes it's just ordinary street crime."

"Leopold, if they are calling people dirty Jews, that sounds clear to me. What is it going to take to make you see what is going on all around you?"

"Regina, I don't hear other people in your family or people I work with raising the same degree of alarm that you are."

"Could it be that they simply choose *not* to see what is going on around them? Because if they are honest, they would have to do something about it. Like fight back or move away."

Leopold said nothing.

"So, do you think the politicians in Warsaw care at all about what is happening to us? You know that Dmowski's National Democracy Party is only getting stronger, and they are pushing a boycott of Jewish businesses. They are beginning to mobilize in the industrial centers of Poland. They have even announced it as a nationalist-led Christian boycott of Jews in Warsaw."

Their argument had finished at that point, at least for the moment, as each of them walked away deep in thought.

Regina knew, based on what she learned when she was still active at the Bund, that the socialist movement was struggling with its own failures and was now vulnerable and led mostly by people inside the Russian government. That made it even more threatening, which appealed to many Poles who found labor issues to be a reason to form mass organizations and get attention.

Now, sitting in the rocking chair, as the afternoon light turned to dusk, Regina realized that for her, the threats to the doctor were the last straw. The changing political climate in Warsaw only made her more anxious.

There is deeper trouble in our future.

Her heart raced as she considered what it would mean to leave.

Am I ready to undertake the complicated journey to America with Louis? What about Leopold? What about my family?

She wanted her parents to come, but she did not think they would, and she knew that parting would be terribly difficult for her. She believed that Leopold loved her and Louis enough to join her, and that the three of them could make the trip together as a family and have a life free of discrimination.

We could be much happier without all the stress we have now.

25

It's Only Getting Worse

Louis grew to be an active toddler and kept Regina busy. She enjoyed getting together with other women and their children to have picnics and watch their kids play and scream, hopefully using up enough energy that they would fall asleep easily in the evening.

While life with Leopold and Louis was pleasant, it took all of Regina's strength not to scream whenever she heard news about another personal attack or a demonstration against a Jewish owned business.

What kind of life will this become for Louis, my schatzeleh?

On a mild spring afternoon, Regina took Louis to meet some of their new friends at a local square to play and share treats. She was looking forward to visiting with the other mothers and enjoying their children, too. As she held Louis' hand and walked the few blocks to Mokotów Square, she thought she heard loud voices, but there were always kids playing ball or racing around.

This is different. There is no laughter. No joy.

Then she saw one of the mothers standing off to the side.

She looks frightened.

Regina approached her.

"What is going on?"

"A demonstration against Jewish businesses."

A man stood in the center of the square, his arm raised high, screeching about how Jews cheat their customers and must be shut down.

"Don't shop at Jew owned stores. They cheat. Shop with Christians only!"

Others yelled in agreement.

"Shut them down. Shut them down."

One man with a bat said he would go shut them down. As he moved, some other men followed him.

Regina and her friend quickly turned back and left the square.

Too many of these to count anymore.

Regina had instigated repeated conversations with Leopold about the continuous attacks on Jews and their businesses over the past two years. They were escalating, and while Regina took no pleasure in being right, there was no disputing the facts. Events were getting more frequent and violent.

It's getting worse, not better.

The scare she felt at the square pushed Regina a step further over the edge.

We must leave Poland.

It seemed like every day brought more demonstrations, stories of people being beaten, and then someone tried to burn down the synagogue.

Enough. I will not raise my son in a world that hates him. Dayenu.

Regina knew it was time for them to go to America, where she thought they could start a new life. She hoped she could convince her who family to leave with them as well. After the fire, they could no longer say she was overreacting. Everyone knew what was happening in Poland.

As Regina sorted through her clothes, she was sure that Leopold would not let her leave without him. He insisted that she was not departing, and that she certainly was not going anywhere without him.

Regina realized what a huge adjustment it would be for Leopold to start a new life somewhere else. After all, his work and commitments had been starting new Bund offices in countries throughout the Russian sphere.

What could Leopold do in America to support his family? Do they have Bund offices there?

Despite Leopold's arguments and her parents' refusal to see what was going on in Poland, Regina would not change her mind about leaving Poland and emigrating to America. She told her husband that they needed to leave so they could give their son a better life.

"Leopold, our first responsibility is to fight for our family's safety now that we are parents.

"I know you are right about the increasing antisemitism here, Regina, and it is my mission to combat it on a broad scale."

"How can this whole terrible battle be your responsibility? What are your priorities, Leopold? To strangers or to your wife and son?"

Every few days they had the same conversation, and Regina was getting worn out. She had fallen in love with Leopold's passion and commitment to the cause, but that focus was becoming troublesome for her, and it got in the way of their intimacy.

I miss feeling close to my husband.

When Leopold came home from work the next day, the first thing he saw on the table were documents he didn't recognize. One read: VISA America.

"What is this, Regina? What does this mean? You applied for a visa to America without me? What is going on?"

Leopold was close to tears.

"Regina! What are you doing? Do you really plan to leave Poland without me? How do you expect me to agree to you taking Louis with you? You can't just take my child away from me."

"I've asked you repeatedly to go with me. How can you be so blind about what is happening all around us? You talk every day about your commitment to fighting antisemitism, but you don't seem to want that fight to include taking care of your own family."

"Regina, that's not true."

"Leopold, Jews all over Europe are leaving, especially those in Russia. It isn't just me who wants to go. Thousands are leaving. At least they see what is happening. Why can't you?"

Leopold stared at his wife.

"And no, I don't want to take Louis from his father. If you'd look, you'd see that I have papers for the three of us."

Leopold was shaking with anger and the shock he felt from Regina's resolve to leave. He was already fatigued from fighting with her each time she brought up another antisemitic event as a reason to leave.

Why can't he see what I am seeing?

Jews in Poland and across the Pale of Settlement were escaping religious, racial, and political persecution as they sought relief from a lack of economic opportunity. Famine in some areas was pushing more and more Polish Jews out of their homes. They believed that America offered jobs that Poland did not, and they hoped to find prosperity, acceptance, and peace across the ocean.

Finally, Leopold acknowledged life was becoming more difficult for Jews in Poland.

"But did you forget that I made a commitment to fight antisemitism here? You stood by my side! Have you forgotten our life back then? Just because you are now a mother, that doesn't change your responsibility to the Bund and its mission."

Leopold was crying and said no more. Regina turned away as the fight left, at least for the moment.

Would leaving Leopold and taking his son away be cruel?

When she organized the papers, she thought he would relent, agree that she was right, and make plans to join her. She had not anticipated such a sorrowful exchange.

Have I thought this through? I know what I believe, but I didn't anticipate Leopold's response. I was sure he would see things my way.

Regina decided to leave the fight for another day. She fed Louis and went to bed, leaving the documents on the table where Leopold could inspect them.

The next day, she took Louis in his stroller to do some shopping, but she felt detached, as if she was moving through a sea of thick fog.

Am I seriously about to leave my home and move to a brand-new country? I have no idea what I am doing! I love my life with Leopold and my family. How could I possibly live without them? Going to America is unthinkable. I need to step back.

When Leopold returned from work, he said nothing about what had happened the day before. Regina was relieved because she wasn't sure she could face his anguish again.

Two days later, the fog lifted, and she felt renewed energy to move forward toward achieving her goal.

Maybe when he sees more documents he will realize I am serious and come around to the right decision.

She had heard of the Hebrew Immigration Aid Society (HIAS), a Jewish-American group that helped immigrants from Russia and central Europe settle successfully in America by providing meals, transportation, and jobs.

They will help Leopold find work in this great new land.

The increasing clarity of Regina's plan generated an army of friends and family who fought to keep her in Poland. In response, she tried her best to bring them around to her side, to see what she was seeing.

Lena was not convinced at all.

"This is not the daughter I know. I can't imagine how you can even think about doing this.

Yosef took a different stance.

"Besides the fact that you would even consider leaving the country and your husband, I'm not sure it is even legal to take Louis with you, to take him away from his father. Regina, have you thought through the consequences of your actions?"

The barrage from friends and family was an intervention she had not anticipated because she viewed the situation so differently from them.

I'm stuck on an island where only Louis and I live.

As she continued to rebuff her family and friends, Regina built a wall around her and Louis. Every argument increased her defense. The family life she and Leopold had built together did not return to normal after weeks of relentless arguments designed to make her change her mind.

Leopold's random kisses on my neck have stopped and he never pinches me anymore. Where has my loving husband gone?

Their conversation carefully avoided any talk of antisemitic events. On the surface, their life was peaceful, but Regina knew it was an illusion.

After such a long time sounding the alarm of antisemitism marching its way into Poland, not to mention the growing attacks in Lithuania, Belarus and Russia, Regina closed herself off from any discussion.

I don't know who I am any longer. It feels like I am standing outside of myself, looking at a woman I don't recognize.

Over the next few months, Regina lived inside a bubble that protected her from outside influence. Her life revolved around Leopold and Louis, and nothing else.

Until the unthinkable happened.

One morning, as Leopold was getting ready to leave for work, they heard pounding on their front door.

"Leopold, come quickly! We need you! Chaim's been attacked!"

It was Amos from the Bund and two others he didn't recognize. They implored him to go to the hospital to see Chaim, whose face was covered in blood after one of his eyes was gouged out. He couldn't speak. His jaw was broken, and his front teeth were missing.

Two of Chaim's neighbors had heard a disturbance, but they couldn't stop the attackers from pushing Chaim into his home where they beat him brutally and quickly before leaving his house, laughing as they ran down the street.

Regina grabbed Louis, and she joined Leopold as they rushed to Chaim's bedside. Leopold said nothing as he held Chaim's hand. Regina handed Louis to Amos so she could sit next to Chaim.

"Chaim, we are here by your side."

She was careful not to say they would find his attackers. She wondered if they were the same thugs who had attacked Leopold, and if they had figured out a new way to demonstrate their fury by pushing their victim into their home before they could alert their neighbors with cries for help.

As the news traveled through the Jewish community of Mokotów, the visits to Chaim's bedside soon stopped. His parents, who lived in Warsaw, contacted the Bund to say that Chaim died two days after the attack.

A pall settled over the office. Some members stayed home, and others went to synagogue to try and find comfort, even if they were not particularly religious. Amos took charge of finding a minyan to have services at Chaim's home. Leopold orchestrated a collection for the family. Even though they didn't need Chaim's salary, Leopold felt it was the right thing to do. The entire Jewish community rallied in support of the family and cooked meals they delivered daily.

Regina said little, except to express sadness about the attack and the death of such a wonderful young man. Lena, Yosef, and Leopold were keenly aware that this incident would embolden Regina to grab Louis and flee Poland.

They were not wrong. A week later, when the shiva (mourning period) ended, Leopold returned home from saying prayers at Chaim's and saw Regina waiting for him in the kitchen.

"You realize that Chaim's attack was not isolated. So far, we have seen the beginnings of an antisemitic war on Jews in Poland. Leopold, if not for you, think of our son. Do you want him raised in a place where he is not safe to walk down the street?"

Leopold took a deep breath as he threw his arms in the air. He turned and walked out the door, closing it behind him. Regina stood still and blinked.

My husband just walked out of his home, leaving his wife and son. Is there anything more to say? Is this his way of declaring defeat?

A sadness spread over her body like thick syrup as she put her head in her hands, sighed and sat on the floor.

That's it. I've decided. I am leaving Poland with our son. The question, is, will Leopold leave with us?

Leopold returned the next day after work and found Regina making dinner. He made her turn away from the burners to face him.

"I'm through fighting with you about this, Regina. You know my position and I will not try to stop you. If you continue down this path, so be it. But know this. I'm divorcing you, and you will get no help from me. And after I get a legal divorce from the government, I'm going to see Rabbi Simcha about obtaining a gett so I can remarry."

Leopold walked out of the house because he needed to be away from Regina and stay somewhere else until she left. He accepted that she would take Louis with her, and this hurt him deeply. However, after more than a year of enduring the same arguments, he needed to move on to a new life.

On the Train
1908

26

Into the Unknown

Regina couldn't hold back her tears as she held Louis in her arms. They were both bundled up wearing multiple coats, even though it was a mild June day, because of a one-bag limit for train passengers to Paris, France.

Leopold was not at the station, which came as no surprise to Regina. He had been clear that he would not go, and he had already filed divorce papers.

Why should I expect him?

However, her parents, brothers and sisters waited for the train with her, still beseeching her to stay. Regina's decision to leave Poland had driven a great wedge in the family, especially since she was taking Louis, too.

In some ways, Regina didn't recognize herself.

Who have I become, and is all this real?

She felt like she was living in a different world, but she remained stubborn in her belief that she was doing the right thing. The Poland she remembered and loved was changing, and not in a good way. The government was doing nothing to protect their Jewish citizens. They had turned their backs on them and allowed more and more abuse and violence to go unchecked. Regina could not understand why others didn't see it. Yet, she was not alone, as other Jews were also leaving Poland.

Her family could not understand why Leopold allowed her to take Louis, but they couldn't stop her. There was speculation in the community that the marriage was never legalized, due to the circumstances that triggered it, when Regina got pregnant so soon after she and Leopold had met.

The family shared few words about visiting or wishes of good luck. They cried and begged Regina to change her mind, but she was resolute in her determination to leave a country she no longer recognized.

"You will join me sooner than you think. Just don't wait too long before it becomes too difficult to leave. There are already some difficult hurdles to jump over to get permission."

No one answered Regina's pleas.

One bright spot for Regina was that she would see Chaja Fajga very soon. Her heart swelled every time she thought about seeing her favorite sibling. She was also excited to meet her new niece and nephew and introduce her sister and her husband to Louis.

Chaja Fajga had sent all the information Regina needed to find her house in Le Marais, the Jewish section inside the Fourth arrondissement of Paris.

The train horn blasted for final boarding and the smell of oil filled her chest. It was a signal that her life would be changing dramatically as soon as she put her foot on the train steps.

Life will never be the same. This is a final statement.

She couldn't stop herself from letting out a huge cry, making one last plea for her family to follow soon. As she boarded the train, her thinking moved from what she was leaving behind to what was ahead. The train would pass through Germany, which was a concern. Even though Jews had been mostly welcomed in Germany for 1,500 years, they were experiencing increased levels of active antisemitism, and documents Regina had seen at the Bund showed that such incidents were on the rise.

I will be happy to leave all of this behind and get out of Central Europe.

The trip took 40 hours and four trains to go from Warsaw to Paris. The first stop was in Poznan, before she changed to a new train to enter Germany. The train would stop in Berlin and continue to Frankfurt, where she would change trains again for Luxemburg before a final change took her to Paris.

This 1,400-kilometer trip will be difficult enough with a toddler, but at least it will get us out of Poland and closer to America.

Regina didn't want to draw attention to herself, but since she spoke Polish, Russian and Yiddish, and was traveling alone with a toddler, it was probably enough to get noticed. She did her best to blend into the crowd by keeping her head down and not making idle chat with other passengers.

At the first stop, Regina needed to feed Louis, so she bought sandwiches and milk for Louis and tea for herself. She had booked second-class seating, which offered a bit more privacy than coach, yet not as much as first class. It was the best she could do with the money she had squirreled away. Her parents reluctantly gave her what money they could spare, so she could book safe passage and get by in Paris until she left for America.

At each stop, Regina changed Louis' diapers, bought sandwiches and tea, and found a private place to feed him if he was awake. All she wanted to do was keep him calm during such a long trip.

When they finally reached Luxembourg, Regina felt she could relax. It felt like a big load has been lifted and she felt lighter, eager to begin her new life. Still, when she reflected on the past few months, she squeezed her eyes tight and struggled to even consider what was ahead.

Is this what I envisioned? I became a wife and mother and now I am alone, divorced, and single. I've left behind a man I thought I loved, so what now?

Leopold had been a good husband and father, except for his blind spot about the world around him. Regina would have been happy to spend the rest of her life with him and have several more children.

Sadly, the world got in the way of my plans.

As she boarded the train for the final leg of the journey, she felt a new burst of energy and renewed hope, knowing she had almost reached her first destination. Suddenly she didn't feel as tired and even said hello to another woman sitting across the aisle.

"Pardon me," Regina said in Polish. "Where are you traveling to?"

Regina thought she recognized the woman from the platform in Warsaw. "Paris."

"We are going there as well. My sister lives there. I haven't seen her in a while, but I will be traveling to America."

They talked about their new lives until Regina felt a sudden surge of exhaustion. She fell deeply asleep with Louis bundled in her arms. It seemed to her like just a few minutes until she heard a whistle and an announcement that they had reached Paris.

It was just barely five in the evening. Regina grabbed her suitcase, bundled Louis up, looked for a money exchange office, and bought another sandwich and some tea. Then, she hired a carriage to take her to her sister's home just off Rue de Beauce. She had told Chaja Fajga not to meet her because she wasn't sure exactly what time she would arrive and didn't want her sister to hang around too long.

As she gave the driver her sister's address, she could hardly contain her excitement and relief.

We made it!

She was exhausted when they pulled up to Chaja Fajga's home, a small two-story stone building with a lovely small garden. Judging from her letters, Chaja Fajga was very happy with her life there. Her biggest challenge was learning French, even though a good part of their congregation spoke Yiddish and some Polish.

As the driver pulled up, the front door flew open and a very excited Chaja Fajga ran down the steps, arms open wide as she squealed with excitement.

"Regina, Regina! Oh my God, you are really here. I've missed you so much. And look at little Louis. He's beautiful. Come, my little schatzeleh. Let me hold you."

She kissed Regina's cheeks. The two sisters held each other and cried with joy. Little Louis was stuck between them and started to cry with all the emotion around him. The girls separated and laughed and soothed Louis.

Oh my God, we made it.

"Come in, my dear sister. You must be hungry and exhausted. I've set up a corner for you to stay for your first few nights."

Chaja Fajga took Regina's sack and led her inside.

Fatigue overwhelmed Regina again. All she wanted to do was lay down and sleep and she hoped Louis would do the same.

I've met my first goal on my journey to America.

27

Welcome to Paris

After sleeping nearly 12 hours, Regina woke up disoriented. The turmoil of the past few days had caught up to her and it took her some time to process her current surroundings. She could hear Louis in another room and found him in the kitchen with Chaja Fajga, who was waiting for her with a breakfast of eggs, sliced meats, croissants, and tea.

Oh my God, it smells so good in this house.

"I'm sorry I slept so long. I hope I didn't cause you any problems. You've got your own kids and I'm sure you must be busy with your rebbetzin duties."

"Not to worry, Regina. I told people you were coming, so unless it's an emergency, I'm free. Fortunately, several women in the congregation can help me with all sorts of things, even shopping. This support allows me to spend time with my family. After all, once you move to America, I don't know when I'll see you again. By the way, it's still not too late to change your mind."

"Oh no, not you too? You've been away from Poland almost four years. You have no idea how bad things have gotten. But people still deny what is happening, even when they see attacks on Jews right in front of them. One of my colleagues at the Bund was murdered in his own home! What does it take? It's not safe and I made my decision. I'm not going to sit around any longer, waiting to be slaughtered."

"All right. Let's not discuss it anymore and enjoy our visit. I don't want to spend our time arguing."

"Thank you. I want the same thing."

Regina fed Louis and enjoyed her own big meal. Chaja Fajga suggested they take a walk with the children. Her son was about to turn two and her daughter was nine months. A neighbor had given them a stroller for Louis so they could walk with their children comfortably.

"Let me show you the neighborhood. I found a wonderful boarding house where you can stay. It's well known for welcoming Polish Jews, those who live here and others passing through on their way to other countries. I spoke with the owner, Madame Suzanne. She's lovely, and, best of all, it's not far from here. We can walk to each other."

Regina was grateful that Chaja Fajga found her a good place to stay for a while. She knew that her sister didn't have enough space to host her and Louis for very long, especially with her busy life. This way, they would still be close enough to spend time together.

As Chaja Fajga led Regina on a stroll along Rue de Beauce toward Rue de Bretagne, she told her about a nice park where Regina could take Louis. Chaja Fajga was lucky to have space behind her house where her children could play.

The park, Chaja Fajga's house, and the boarding house were all located in Le Marais, a Jewish district in Paris. The neighborhood was also known as the "Pletzl," a Yiddish word for "Little Place."

Three days later, after catching up on family matters, it was time for Regina to move into Madame Suzanne's boarding house on Rue Portefoin. She knew the Madame was originally from Poland and Jews there knew this was a welcoming place for them to stay in Paris.

Regina rang the bell a couple of times, eager to get inside. A pleasant looking plump woman in her 40s appeared with long, braided brown hair pinned over the top of her head. Her bright smile was inviting.

"Oui? Madame Regina? Je suis Madame Suzanne."

I think she recognizes who I am.

"I'm sorry. I don't speak French."

Madame Suzanne switched to Polish.

"That's fine. We can communicate in Polish or in Yiddish if you prefer. You are welcome here. I recognize Madame Chaja Fajga because she already came here and paid for your first week."

Regina was not surprised because that is something she would have done for her sister if the roles were reversed.

She looked at Chaja Fajga.

"Thank you, my dear, but it wasn't necessary."

"You are my little sister. It's my job to take care of you the best I can. I just wish you and Louis could stay in our home while you are here. If we had one more sleeping room, you would be with us."

"I know, but I also never expected it, and we are still close by."

"I have some duties tomorrow," said Chaja Fajga, "so I won't be around for most of the day but come for dinner so you can tell me and Aron about the boarding house."

They kissed and hugged goodbye.

Now, I'm on my own. Again.

Regina's room was on the second floor at the back of the building. It had a large window overlooking the street. The bathroom was down the hall and shared with two other boarders. Her room had a bed, a sink, and a closet, and a ceramic plate warmer. Madame Suzanne had a kettle to heat water for tea in the dining room.

Regina sat down on the bed and sobbed. This was the first time she was totally alone since she had left home.

Am I crying for the rest of my family back home, or is this gratitude for finally getting out of Poland? Probably both.

As she settled in, Regina checked her finances. She needed to pay rent and save money for the crossing to America.

Things will be tight, but I have enough to manage.

She couldn't help second guess her decision.

It's not too late to turn around and go back to Poland. If Leopold would have me, I could go back to him, too. Is this the right thing to do? I've shown everyone I could really leave, but were they right? Was it really so bad?

Regina planned to stay at the boarding house until she could book passage on a ship to New York. Even though she was thrilled to see her sister and meet her niece and nephew, she wanted time to just do nothing for a few days.

I am in Paris! What next?

She put Louis on the floor in a jumble of blankets and went down the hall to use the bathroom, trying to be as quick as possible.

When she returned, Regina played with Louis for an hour before going to see Madame Suzanne and ask where she could buy food and snacks.

For the moment, her journey to America felt like too much to consider.

Should I just stay here? I don't speak French, or English, either so what difference does it make?

It was too much to think about. Regina told herself to put those thoughts aside and deal with her life one day at a time.

Ghosts of the Past

Regina woke the next morning in another unfamiliar room. Her life had been a jumble of train rides, crowded stations, a few days jammed into her sister's house and now a private room in a boarding house in Paris.

Is this real?

When she opened her eyes, it took a moment for her to recognize new surroundings. So much had changed in such a short time. She was slow to rise from an unfamiliar bed and it took her a second to adjust to the height of the bed as she placed her feet on the floor.

She still had moments when she felt unsure of her decision.

Who have I become? Is this my destiny?

She felt a familiar anxiety creep in as she thought about her friends and family facing impending doom. She squeezed her eyes shut and sat quietly as Louis fiddled with a toy Chaja Fajga had given him.

Enough. I am far away from Poland. I made my decision and I acted on it. I can always change my mind and return to my family. Leopold will probably not take me back but at least he could be with his son. Wait. Enough!

Regina changed Louis' diaper and went downstairs for breakfast.

She quickly developed a comfortable routine. First thing in the morning, after waking to the light shining through her window, she found Louis already awake, thankfully playing by himself on his makeshift bed on the floor.

She took him to eat a breakfast of tea, milk, pastry, and fruit and enjoyed some conversation with some of the other residents before taking a pleasant walk down the tree-lined Rue des Archives to Rue de Bretagne, where the park was located at Square du Temple. She usually sat on a bench to watch the birds and the young children at play.

This is lovely and inspiring.

Tall leafy trees lined the surrounding streets. The homes were painted different shades of blue, lilac and lemon. It was like something Regina had seen in photos. The sameness had a calming effect, which Regina sorely needed after the past several months.

Over the next few weeks, Regina learned more about the neighborhood. She found shops to buy what she needed and tried to chat with the store owners and employees, even though she didn't speak much French at all. It provided a sense of place, which she sorely needed after such a chaotic year.

When Chaja Fajga wasn't busy, she joined Regina at the park, and they walked to the corner store for treats. Chaja Fajga always paid when they were together, and she often gave Regina some extra francs.

On more than one occasion, Chaja Fajga brought up Regina's decision to leave home and her husband and how she took their son away from him.

"I know you don't want to talk about this, but I need to understand your decision. I'm not taking sides. I'm just trying to understand. Please, help me. I love you, Regina, but this is such a huge thing to do!"

Regina threw her hands in the air.

"You can't understand because you don't live in Poland. You don't know what it's like. Every day means another antisemitic attack or an anti-Jewish demonstration. Even the government is against our businesses. It's not safe, and it's getting worse. People pretend it isn't bad, but it is."

I can't believe I have to keep explaining this.

"You of all people should understand. You were lucky that Aron was assigned out of Poland."

She looked at her sister.

"Yes, Regina, you are right. I must admit it. That was one of the reasons I agreed to marry him."

I knew it. And thank God she did.

As they walked, neither one of them continued the conversation.

Over the next weeks, the weather grew warmer and by mid-July, Regina and Louis went to the park every day.

One sunny Wednesday, as Regina was reading and Louis was crawling around, a man sat down on the same bench, seemingly to also enjoy the sun.

"Excuse me, Madame," the man said in Polish, "but I have seen you here several times, so please allow me to introduce myself. My name is Morris Butlaw. I hope you don't think I am being rude."

Is he Polish, too?

Regina found him attractive, with his hazel eyes, black hair, strong jaw, and solid build, but she was not ready to engage with a stranger in the park. His approach had caught her off guard, as she had not enjoyed any interactions with a man outside of a boarder or at the grocery store and bakery.

Regina was impressed that he seemed so quietly sure of himself. He appeared to be clean and decently dressed, and he was certainly not bad to look at.

"Thank you for introducing yourself. I don't think you are being rude. It is a lovely day, isn't it?"

"I've seen you here with another mother and children. Are you related?"

What an odd question.

"Yes. She is my sister, and her husband is the assistant rabbi for the Synagogue de la Victoire."

"Oh my, that is wonderful. What an excellent post for a new rabbi."

Regina nodded and smiled.

"How old is your son? He is a boy, right?"

"Yes, all boy! He's barely a year old and getting quite rambunctious. We will move over to the grass lawn soon so he can move around with a ball we brought. Children need room!"

Then, it was Regina's turn to ask about this stranger.

"Do you come here often, Mr. Butlaw? I don't recall seeing you here."

"Usually on the weekends, but on the other side of the square. This side has more sun, I've discovered, so I came over to this bench as it is well suited for sun and shade, if necessary."

Regina began to feel more comfortable chatting with this stranger.

I've been yearning for this kind of interaction.

She loved that she could see her sister and her family, but they had their own lives. While the boarders were nice people, most seemed to have known each other a long time and Regina was the newcomer and who knew how long she would be there.

"You are Polish, obviously," he said. "How long have you lived here?"

"Not long. I'm planning to go to America, but I'm taking some time here before continuing my journey, as life is quite rigorous with a little boy. My sister is here, too, and I want to spend time with her."

"Yes, travel can be exhausting, no matter what the reason."

I'm glad it's not just me who feels the rigors of such big changes.

"I'm staying at a boarding house. It's convenient and the Madame is quite nice and an excellent cook."

As they talked, Regina and Morris looked straight ahead, careful not to appear too pushy or rudely invasive.

"I was able to rent a small flat here in the neighborhood for not much more than a boarding house would have cost, and it gives me my own space and privacy."

I get the message that Mr. Butlaw lives alone.

"So, Mr. Butlaw, do you practice a profession here in France?"

"I didn't get your name, I'm afraid. May I be so bold as to ask?"

"Oh, you are correct, I did not introduce myself. I'm Regina Anuszewicz, from Mokotów, a suburb of Warsaw."

She did not give him her married name.

"Oh, yes. I know Mokotów. It's a lovely town and so close to the center of Warsaw. I worked there in the city, coming in by train each day from the shtetl. I'm a jeweler by trade."

Regina was happy for the conversation but careful not to sound too eager to talk to a stranger. She excused herself to move on to the grass and let little Louis move around with a ball she brought from her sister.

Morris didn't ask if there is a Mr. Anuszewicz, and I will never ask if there is a Mrs. Butlaw. That would be much too forward, and what does it matter, anyway?

"It was lovely chatting with you. Mr. Butlaw. I'm going to take Louis over to the grass now and let him get some sun. A good day to you."

Regina and Louis walked to the grass and spread out a blanket. Louis played with the ball. Regina laughed at his enthusiasm and determination.

When she got back to the boarding house, Louis became fussy, and he cried as they entered the dining room. It wasn't long before they left, and Regina struggled not to yell at her son in frustration. All she wanted to do was enjoy a nice meal and talk to the other residents.

Why can't I do that? Why do I have to deal with a fussy child?

It wasn't long before she heard a knock on her door.

"Madame Anuszewicz? Are you and the little one okay? I have a meal for you."

Madame Suzanne! What a welcoming voice. Just what I needed to hear.

Regina was relieved and opened the door.

"I expect you are hungry, and I want to be sure you have your meal. Forgive me. I don't know your taste, so I included a bit of everything. Please don't feel that you need to eat it all."

Regina was touched by the Madame's kindness. Regina was even more surprised by her next offer, which nearly brought her to tears.

"Madame, I am a mother as well, although I'm quite a bit older than you, but I remember taking care of children and how stressful it can be. Since you are alone, without a husband to share responsibilities, I see that everything is on you. I would be happy to watch Louis for a bit while you eat and take some time to breathe."

I'm not sure I can take all this generosity. Did I hear Madame correctly? Did she just offer to watch Louis while I eat?

As Regina stared at Madame Suzanne, she broke down in tears and covered her face with her hands.

"Oh, my goodness, my dear. I didn't mean to upset you. I only offered to help, but if I've overstepped my bounds, I'm sorry."

Regina regained her composure.

"Oh, Madame! No, not at all. You have not overstepped your bounds. I'm so grateful for the offer, you have no idea. I love my little boy, but I have no one to share the day to day caring with, as you know, and sometimes I just get so tired or frustrated, so I welcome your offers with open arms."

Madame Suzanne smiled.

"My sister is wonderful, don't get me wrong, but she has her own family and lots of duties. We get together, but not for childcare."

Regina threw her arms around Madame and hugged her.

"There, there, my dear. I know you are going through a difficult time. I'm happy to enjoy your little boy from time to time."

Regina let go and stepped back.

"I hope I didn't offend you. I'm just so overwhelmed at your kindness."

"Regina, women need to take care of each other."

Regina nodded. As Madame Suzanne took Louis' hand, he looked from his mother to Madame Suzanne to be sure it was okay. Regina nodded.

"Louis, I have some special treats for you and even a toy. It's okay with your mama for you to come with me. Is it okay with you?"

Regina nodded again and held her breath as Louis walked away with Madame Suzanne. She immediately took the tray of food, put it on the warming tray and began to eat. She suddenly felt much less tired. Madame's kindness was more than she could have imagined, and she was thrilled for her willingness to take Louis.

After Regina finished eating, she took the tray downstairs and went to get Louis from Madame Suzanne.

"Get a good night's sleep, Regina, and I'll see you in the morning. We can make plans for the day."

The next day, Regina took Louis to the park. Then, she walked to Chaja Fajga's house to leave a message, hoping they could get together soon.

I hope Chaja Fajga is home and cooking dinner.

"I'm so glad I'm home. You must stay for dinner."

"I would love to, of course, but are you sure Aron won't get sick of me?"

"Aron loves you! He's happy my sister is here. He only wishes that his family would come see us so his parents can meet their new grandchildren."

"If only it was that easy. You must tell them they need to make plans now because the future does not look good."

155

Chaja Fajga sighed.

"I love you, Regina, but every time we talk of Poland, you bring up the antisemitic attacks as if they happen every day. It gets tiresome. I'm sure if there was an imminent threat, they would leave."

Regina knew she could get tiresome, but she felt it was her responsibility to carry the message about what she had seen in Poland.

I don't want to risk my relationship with Chaja Fajga and Aron, so I better back off. For now, let's just enjoy each other.

Regina was grateful that Chaja Fajga was in Paris and that they had renewed their special relationship as the two oldest siblings in the family.

She left Louis in the family room to play with his cousins as she joined her sister in the kitchen to help with the evening meal.

29

American Dream

During the following weeks, Regina began to feel more and more at home in Paris. One evening just after dinner, she found a comfortable chair in the drawing room and settled Louis at her feet, hoping another boarder would join her. The majority were permanent residents, while a few like her were passing through. She was trying to expand her social interactions because she didn't want to depend on seeing Chaja Fajga every day.

She felt more comfortable chatting with Morris Butlaw, her new friend at the park. On a rare occasion, Madame Suzanne offered to watch Louis so Regina could shop or spend a few minutes alone, chatting with Morris.

How does a jeweler have time to sit in a park?

She remained a bit cautious about getting too familiar with this stranger.

"Mr. Butlaw, as you said, you are from Poland, so what do you hear from your family there? I'm sure they miss you, but you traveled alone. They didn't want to join you here?"

"I'm afraid they don't see the situation like I do, how antisemitism keeps growing in our country."

They agreed that their relatives were in denial and hoped that they would soon be realistic and make plans to leave.

No matter what, I will never return.

"Do you think your family will change their minds, Regina?"

"I hope so, but if they don't I hope things do not get as bad as I expect. It's confusing. On the one hand, I want to be proven right, but at the same time, I want them to be safe, even if they don't go to America."

Regina sighed and rubbed her eyes. As much as she enjoyed Morris' company, she was tired of talking about the rise of antisemitism. There was nothing she could do about it, and constantly talking about it didn't help, and she did feel that maybe she had been successful in leaving it behind her.

I would like to think I've left that behind me.

"Morris, I need to go back to the boarding house. Madame Suzanne is watching Louis, and I don't want to take advantage of her good will."

"Of course. It is exhausting talking about Poland. I apologize if I have become a bore."

Regina was surprised at his insightfulness.

"Please don't feel that you need to apologize. I also contributed to this conversation. We have similar opinions. I talk about it more than you. Maybe promise that the next time we see each other we will not talk about the problems back home."

"Fair enough."

Before she left, Regina remembered that she wanted to arrange for Chaja Fajga to meet Morris and get her opinion of him.

"You have never met my sister, Chaja Fajga, and I've talked about her so much. Let me see when I can introduce you two."

"That would be nice. I'd like to meet your sister."

"I will see her tomorrow."

Maybe Morris could join them for dinner, but I don't want to say anything until I speak with Chaja Fajga.

The next day, Regina and Louis went to see Chaja Fajga immediately after breakfast. She was interested in her sister's assessment of this stranger she met in the park.

"Tante Regina!" her nephew squealed.

He jumped up and down as Chaja Fajga appeared.

"Tante Regina!" said Chaja Fajga.

She smiled as she mimicked her son. "It's so nice to hear you called that, Regina. How are you this fine morning?"

"I'm glad you are home. I have a favor to ask my older and wiser sister."

"Oh, my, this sounds interesting."

"I told you I met a gentleman at the park. His name is Morris Butlaw, and he is also from our part of Poland. He is a jeweler and works in a store as well as from his flat, so his schedule is flexible. That's why he can take time to go to the park."

"He sounds a bit mysterious. What do you know about him other than he says he's a jeweler?"

"Nothing. He is a stranger, but very charming. He has walked me home to the boarding house and Madame Suzanne met him."

"So, why are you bringing this up now?"

Chaja Fajga laughed.

"Would you have us over for dinner? I'd like you and Aron to meet him and see what you think."

"Of course! Let me check Aron's schedule and see what we can do."

Chaja Fajga arranged for Morris to join everyone for Shabbos dinner on Friday the following week. Regina was excited and anxious about what Chaja Fajga and Aron would think of Morris.

He's very gracious with me, but what about with others? Madame Suzanne thought he was nice, but those interactions were minimal.

Morris said he would come by and walk with Regina and Louis to Chaja Fajga's home. He showed up with a bottle of kosher wine to give his hosts.

As soon as they arrived, Aron greeted them, and Louis ran to play with his cousins. Morris put a kippah on his head before entering the house. Regina was impressed with his awareness. Aron thanked him for the wine and suggested they open it for dinner. He invited Morris to join him on the couch while waiting for Chaja Fajga and Regina to bring food to the table.

After everyone sat down, Chaja Fajga went to the sideboard to say the Shabbos prayers. She put a small covering over her head and waved her hands over her eyes three times, then held her hands there while she said the blessing over the candles.

Morris sat attentively as the rituals were performed. Along with the challah, Chaja Fajga served matzo ball soup, followed by roast chicken, glazed carrots, and baked potatoes. For dessert, she had made apple cake, a Polish favorite, using Lena's recipe.

Morris offered his compliments for the meal and almost thanked Chaja Fajga and Aron too much for the invitation.

Regina tried to catch Chaja Fajga's eye to see if she indicated any reaction to Morris, but her sister was too busy managing the dinner.

"Tomorrow," she whispered.

Aron made conversation by asking Morris about his work as a jeweler. Morris asked Aron about his role as the assistant rabbi at such a well-known and historic synagogue.

The next day, Regina stopped by to hear what Chaja Fajga and Aron had to say about their dinner guest.

Chaja Fajga and Aron were wondering about why a 26-year-old man who had worked in Warsaw was not married and living alone so far from home. That's what bothered them most because it seemed to challenge the tradition they were raised to believe.

"What is he hiding, and why did he leave his family? You don't know anything about his family?"

Regina shrugged.

"You two have something in common: You both left Poland alone, but did he ever tell you why? Did he also say it was about politics, like you?"

He never said why, but I never asked him.

Chaja Fajga and Aron thought Morris had nice manners and was easy to talk to, but that wasn't enough for them to tell what kind of values he had. They wondered if he had left something bad behind in Poland.

"Morris said there was little opportunity for him to build the kind of life he wanted in his small shtetl. I admire him for having the chutzpah to take such a big step in leaving Poland for Paris."

Chaga Fajga probably can't understand why that is attractive to me.

"Just be careful, Regina," said Aron. "That's all we're trying to say."

As the warm summer days waned and the days grew shorter, Regina kept those words in mind as she took her walks after breakfast and returned to the boarding house before lunch. Louis was a growing boy.

It's time to book passage on a ship that will take us to America.

Regina realized that getting to Glasgow and boarding the ship that would take them to New York was complicated.

It would be easier to stay here in Paris, but my goal is to go to America.

The next day, she asked Madame Suzanne about finding the ticket office.

"I know you were planning to go to America, but I was hoping you would change your mind after living in our beautiful city."

"Thank you, you have been so kind to me and Louis, and I have enjoyed my stay here, but my dream is to live in America."

To reach Glasgow, Scotland, she, and Louis would need to take a train to the northern coast of France, a ferry to England, and several trains through Northern England, Edinburgh, and finally Glasgow. There, they would take a ferry up the River Clyde to a port where they could board the ship to America.

The SS California was built in Glasgow in 1907 as a replacement for the aging ocean liner Astoria, which had been in continuous service since 1884.

Regina booked a second-class cabin, even though it did cost a bit more than she anticipated, but third class meant steerage and that wouldn't do with a child, and first class was too expensive.

The next day, Regina bundled up Louis against the cool October weather and headed to the park to meet Morris.

Maybe I'm looking forward to our daily connections more than I should.

She knew that she was leaving for America in a month. Morris wanted to get together as much as she did, and he encouraged their meetings.

"Morris, I must tell you something. I have booked my voyage to America. I need to leave soon because I can't use up all my money in Paris, as much as I like it here. I will leave in late December to reach Glasgow in time to sail on January 13th to New York City."

For several moments, neither one said a word. Regina was uncomfortable as she waited to hear what Morris would say. He appeared deep in thought before he finally spoke.

"I don't know what to say, Regina. I must confess my feelings for you have grown immensely since we first met months ago, and I've grown very fond of Louis as well. I'm distressed beyond words. I was hoping you had changed your mind about leaving because you haven't spoken about it lately."

Regina was a bit shocked but flattered by his words and feelings.

"I don't know what to say, Morris. I have grown fond of you, too. It's mostly because of you that I have stayed this long. But I must go to America. It's been my dream for so long now."

"Even before Louis's father said he wouldn't leave with you?"

"He knew of my wishes even before Louis was born. Things are not good in Poland. Warsaw will not be safe, just you wait and see."

Morris went silent again, brows furrowed, which made Regina feel sad about her decision, at least for the moment.

If I don't go, I will regret it forever. I've given up so much already to do this, so I can't let a nice acquaintance keep me from leaving.

"Morris, I know this is sad news, for both of us. I'm going to go back to my boarding house now, as it's getting too cold. Will you meet me here again tomorrow so we can continue our lovely visits?"

"Yes, yes, of course. I will be here. I look forward to it."

When Regina returned to the boarding house, she shared her conversation with Madame Suzanne, who had become a genuine friend.

"I'm not surprised at his response, Regina. It's been obvious to me from the few times I've met Morris that he is smitten with you."

"Really? I am very fond of him, but I didn't assume he felt the same about me. That is lovely to hear because I'm so impressed with Morris. I'm going to be sorry to say goodbye to him as well as you. You both have made Paris wonderful for me. But I must follow my dream of living in America."

"Why don't you invite Morris for dinner here tomorrow night?"

"Thank you. I will."

The next evening, Morris knocked on Madame Suzanne's door at exactly eight p.m. for dinner.

"So lovely you can join us, Morris," Suzanne said.

Throughout their meal, as Morris's elbow grazed Regina's arm in a secret game between them, she recalled little things she had felt long ago when she first came close to Leopold.

That all seems so immature now. My connection with Morris feels much more grown up.

After dinner, Suzanne offered to watch Louis while Regina and Morris took some time together. Regina was thrilled as they moved to the privacy of an anteroom near the outside door.

"I'm so glad you came to dinner, Morris."

Morris shuffled his feet and put his hand on Regina's arm and stroked it lightly, looking into her face. She felt dizzy from his touch.

I haven't felt like this since I fell in love with Leopold. What is happening? Where have these feelings come from?

She felt a familiar warmth come up from her stomach. She took in a deep breath, and then remembered her plans to leave.

"Regina, you know I have strong feelings for you. I am heartbroken that you will leave Paris after the wonderful time we have spent together. Is it too late to ask you to change your mind and make a life with me here?"

Regina couldn't think straight. She loved being with Morris, but staying in Paris went against her dream.

How can I change now and stay for one person?

"Morris. I'm confused. I'd love to have you in my life, but I've bought my passage to America. I'm finally going to realize my dream!"

Tears fell down Regina's cheeks. Morris wiped one away with his finger.

"We must have dinner together someplace nice before you leave. Can you arrange for Madame Suzanne to watch Louis so we can dine at our leisure?"

"That would be lovely. I know she has obligations, so let me check and I will let you know at the park tomorrow."

"Of course."

Then Morris said something that caught Regina by surprise.

"May I kiss you?"

"Oh, uh, yes."

Regina was flustered. She was not used to a man being so formal.

Leopold never asked before he kissed me. He just took what he wanted.

Morris bent his head down to reach Regina, took her head in his hands and gently kissed her on the mouth. She swayed and took a step back.

His kiss is sweet and tender.

As she opened her eyes, she saw Morris looking at her with what she wanted to believe was a loving expression.

"I don't know what to say, Morris, except keep warm out there on your way home."

Why did I say something so silly?

"Yes, I'll be warm enough, Regina. Please don't forget to ask Madame if she can watch Louis."

"Of course. First thing in the morning. Good night, Morris. See you tomorrow at the park."

She walked back inside, her face flushed and a bit out of breath.

30

Dazzled By a Kiss

Regina's thoughts bounced from kissing Morris to sailing to America, a mission she had fought to accomplish for years. As she pictured herself on a ship making her way across the ocean to a new life, she also remembered what she felt when Morris kissed her.

Morris is elegant. I've never been around a man like him. If he's trying to dazzle me, it's working.

She found Suzanne in the kitchen, clearing dishes while Louis played on the floor playing with the toy truck Chaja Fajga had given him.

"Thank you so much for allowing me to give Morris a proper goodbye."

"I was happy to do so. Louis is so delightful and easy."

"Thank you. I feel terrible if I'm taking advantage of you, but can I make another request?"

Suzanne smiled and nodded.

"Morris wants to take me out to dinner before I leave, and he would like to go to an elegant restaurant. Can I impose upon you to watch Louis one night next week for an hour or so?"

"Only if you go for more than an hour! That is not enough time to spend at an elegant restaurant."

"You are wonderful. I'm going to miss you, Suzanne. You have me feel so welcome here and I appreciate your support. How can I ever repay you?"

Regina couldn't help herself as tears appeared in her eyes.

"Oh, my goodness, my dear. Don't cry. It's been my pleasure. I only wish you the best. Follow your dream, and don't let anyone change your mind,"

"Oh, I won't. As much as I have loved it here and you know I have, it has been my dream for a long time to go to America."

"Remember what I said. So, how about Tuesday for your dinner?"

"Thank you so much. I'll take the little man upstairs now and we will have a good night's sleep."

The next day Regina went to her sister's house to ask another favor.

"Chaja Fajga, I hope I can impose upon you for something special. Morris wants to take me out to an elegant restaurant before I leave, and I have nothing to wear. Do you still have any of those dresses you made back home?"

"Are you still seeing Morris? If you are leaving, why is he still seeing you? Don't you think that is odd, Regina?"

I didn't expect such a pointed observation.

"You are right. All I know is that I enjoy his company and he has always been a gentleman and a friend to me. He has never done anything to make me uncomfortable. I would like to go to dinner with him before I depart."

"That's up to you, and of course I will find a dress for you."

The day before the dinner, Regina went to her sister's house for a fitting. She was surprised to see that Chaja Fajga had altered a conservative dress she brought from Warsaw to reflect the latest styles in Paris. It was made of silk with a brocade on the top, and a long skirt with chiffon. According to the fashion of the time, the dress had red beading on the top to match the red fabric and a sheer layer over the skirt. The sleeves were short, exposing a bit of shoulder.

"Oh, this is wonderful. Thank you so much."

When the special night came, Morris appeared with a carriage at Madame Suzanne's front door at precisely 7:40 p.m., as he had made a reservation at Maxim's de Paris for eight. The restaurant was the epitome of Art Nouveau design and very elegant.

"Regina, you look so elegant. Your dress is magnificent."

Regina smiled.

I do feel elegant, indeed.

Some of her self-confidence slipped away as she realized she was not familiar with restaurant culture in Paris and felt self-conscious. She knew this meal was partially Morris' attempt to change her mind about leaving Paris.

166

Maxims decorated its dining room with an expensive carpet of red, green, and gold and chandeliers hung from the ceiling. The walls were painted in rich reds and gold, which were reflected around the room with mirrors.

When they were seated at their table, Regina couldn't believe the array of utensils, dishes, and glasses in front of them.

Maybe I should faint right now, so I won't embarrass myself or Morris.

The table setting had more types of plates, glasses, and utensils than Regina had ever seen.

What are all these for?

"Morris, I'm not used to seeing so many dishes at dinner."

As Regina stood behind her chair, sweat beaded on her forehead. She didn't want to embarrass Morris, but she was terrified of making a fool of herself. The only "restaurant" experience she had was ordering lunch from the local baker back home, who served sandwiches to neighborhood workers.

I've never even seen a menu.

Morris calmly puts his hand on Regina's arm and guided her to her seat.

"We will work through the meal together. I know all these plates and glasses are confusing, but don't worry."

The waiter handed Regina a menu first, then gave one to Morris. She was overwhelmed and grew pale as she surveyed the menu. Fortunately, Morris stepped in.

"Would you rather have beef or chicken, or do you fancy fish?"

I have no idea!

She decided to play it safe with chicken. It turned out to be their farmer poultry with vegetables and Périgueux sauce. For dessert, they had traditional raspberry Charlotte with a red fruit sauce. Morris offered Regina wine, which she happily accepted as she wanted to do anything she could to reduce the knot in her stomach from feeling so out of place.

At least I am dressed for the occasion and Morris likes it.

Several glasses of wine later, dessert was finished, and it was time to go. Regina was sure she might lose her balance. She had indulged more than she ever had before and was afraid to stand up. She shot a look at Morris, who went to her chair and offered his arm.

Regina was relieved and grateful that he was paying attention, even though he was the one who had kept filling her glass. Regina felt tipsy and awkward, especially when so many people acknowledged their presence at the restaurant.

Morris seems used to this lifestyle. I think I admire him even more now.

Outside on the sidewalk, he slipped an arm around Regina's waist and suggested they go back to his flat for some tea.

"The night is too young to call it an evening, Regina, especially if I am going to lose you in just a few weeks."

"I guess that would be nice. I could use some tea right now."

Morris flagged down a carriage. As he helped Regina step inside, she lost her balance and he quickly put a hand on her back to keep her from falling. Regina felt dizzy and closed her eyes to feel the cool evening breeze.

Regina tried to keep herself steady while they walked up two flights of stairs. With one arm around her, Morris opened the door. His apartment had a large sitting room, a small kitchen, and a bedroom. It was nicely furnished, and neatly kept. The bathroom was down the hall.

Morris guided Regina to a chair, then put on the kettle for tea.

"Are you comfortable, Regina? Would you like me to walk you to the bathroom down the hall?"

"Oh, yes, that would be good. Thank you."

Morris steered her down the hall and waited outside.

Back in the apartment, he poured two glasses of tea.

"You look beautiful this evening, Regina. I can't take my eyes off you."

As he stroked her hair, Regina's breath quickened. She closed her eyes to enjoy his touch but struggled with her feelings.

I can't let my feelings influence my ultimate decision.

Morris turned Regina's face to his and ran his thumb down her cheek.

"I don't know what to say, Morris. Why don't you come with me to America? You will find work there as a jeweler. We could be together."

"I'm tempted because I don't know what I will do without you."

Regina suddenly felt lighter and less unsteady. Morris gently pulled her to her feet and wrapped his arms around her.

"I've never felt this way about anyone. You have captivated me, sweet Regina."

The next thing she knew, they were on his bed. Morris was on top of her, his hands under her dress as he kissed her neck. Regina was surprised but didn't object. She was intoxicated with desire and felt a yearning in her groin she never had with Leopold after they were married.

Morris engulfed her and she felt enraptured in his arms. He began to explore her more intimately, moving his hands underneath her lingerie, gently pulling her bloomers down until she was free of them.

Regina let herself go, unwilling to stop Morris.

What if I get pregnant?

In a haze of wine and lust, she didn't do anything about prevention, and didn't ask Morris about it either.

He pulled his pants down and freed his erection. He pulled at his cock, found his target, and thrust himself inside her. Regina arched her back to let him in. Then, she pulled him closer and hugged him tighter. After several thrusts, Morris relaxed on top of Regina.

"Am I too heavy on you, my darling?"

Regina rejoiced in his new name for her.

"My darling" sounds beautiful.

The evening felt magical, and she was floating on air.

When they were ready to leave, Regina reassembled her dress so she would not embarrass Madame Suzanne. Before she went inside the boarding house, Morris pulled Regina close.

"This was a magical evening, my love. I'll come by to see you tomorrow and we can walk to the park together."

Did I hear what Morris just said or am I dreaming?

As Regina opened the front door, she had to push back on letting such a magical evening change her mind.

Yes, it was lovely, but is it enough for me to stay in Paris?

The next morning, Regina had no appetite for breakfast, but she went downstairs for tea and to get food for Louis.

She remembered each detail of her magical evening with Morris and looked forward to sharing her dinner experience with Suzanne and some of the borders who had never been to Maxim's and wanted to know everything.

As promised, Morris came by to take Regina and Louis to the park, but she begged off because she had a headache.

"Tomorrow, please. I'm just not up to it today."

"I'm so sorry. It was a magical evening, but maybe we had too much wine, so I'm not surprised you are tired today."

"I'll be fine, Morris, thank you. See you tomorrow."

31

A New Life Awaits

A week later, as rain fell in Paris, Morris and Regina sat and talked in the boarding house drawing room. She reminded him that she was leaving in two weeks and begged him to reconsider coming with her to America.

Morris took Regina's hands in his

"Why don't you stay in Paris? You can get your money back for your passage. Please say you will stay."

Regina took a deep breath.

Be careful not to sound indifferent.

"No, Morris, I'm sorry. As much as I love you, going to America is my dream. Come with me, and we will make a wonderful life there."

Morris sighed and stood up.

"I need to think about it."

After he left, Regina sat without moving.

Am I making the wrong decision to leave such a lovely man who clearly loves me? How many other chances will I have to meet a man so wonderful to me and Louis?

Regina sipped her tea, and reminded herself that living in America was her plan and she had come too far to turn back now. She was afraid she would regret staying in Paris, and she knew that the longer she remained, the more difficult it would be to leave.

I have no interest in ending up divorced again.

The next day, Morris returned and said he had changed his mind.

"I can't live without you, Regina. If you will have me, I'll go to America with you."

Regina was overjoyed and threw her arms around his neck.

How can I be so lucky?

"We must go to the train station and get your tickets for the train, and we can buy your boat passage there, too."

Two days later, Morris arranged to share Regina's cabin. She went to tell Chaja Fajga that Morris had changed his mind and was going with her. She felt anxious about having the conversation because she knew they might never see each other again, or at least for many years.

How could I say goodbye all over again?

Even before the door opened, Regina was crying. Chaja Fajga stood still, wondering why her little sister was crying.

"Has something happened?"

"I'm leaving for America, and Morris is coming with me. I don't know if I will ever see you again. I'm going to miss you horribly, but I must go."

They hugged for a very long time until Chaja Fajga took Regina's face in her hands.

"I know this has been something you've wanted for years. Be sure to tell Morris that I expect him to take care of you. Write to me as well as Mama and Papa so we all know you are okay. I will miss you horribly, too, but I want you to fulfill your dream."

They planned a family goodbye dinner for Regina and Morris for the following week to say their loving "au revoirs."

Regina and Morris also made a tearful goodbye to Madame Suzanne and her boarders, as they loaded their luggage onto a carriage for the ride to the Gare du Nord station. Their train took them to Calais Maritime, where they walked two blocks to the ferry, which took them to the Dover Western Docks to begin their journey north to Scotland.

Regina's mood lightened. This time, she wasn't alone with Louis, and she could share her excitement with Morris.

The SS California carried 1,214 passengers, with 232 in first class, 248 in second, and 734 in third class or steerage. It was outfitted with electric lights and refrigeration. They were told to expect to be at sea for two weeks.

The passengers from Italy, Ireland, Poland, Russia, and France were all anxious and excited about their new beginnings. Some had family and friends waiting for them in America, while some knew no one.

We all share a feeling of hope.

Men, women, and children boarded the ship with everything they could bring from home. For some, it was no more than a blanket and orange in the pocket, while others had trunks of finery and expensive leather shoes.

Elite first-class passengers and those in second-class were placed in cabins and staterooms, while third-class passengers were situated below deck in a section called steerage.

The dining salon was on the upper deck, furnished with a solid oak bar, and the dining room had tables with white linen tablecloths. The drawing room was on the promenade deck at the head of the stairway leading to the dining room and staterooms. A smoking lounge on the poop deck was finished in American walnut and housed the ever-popular bar.

Second-class cabins were equivalent to first-class staterooms except for storage closets. Each cabin had bunkbeds, a sink, a desk, and a sofa. The cabins had no bathroom or lavatory, so washing facilities were communal for second-class passengers.

People gathered on the dock at two p.m., ready to begin boarding at four. It was terribly crowded until Morris, Regina, and Louis finally got to their stateroom on the second level. There was barely enough room for the three of them and their luggage. Once inside, Regina and Morris stretched out while Louis curled up on top of Morris.

"This is not so bad," Regina said. "I'm guessing we should go to dinner soon. What do you think?"

"We have a set time, but I'm not sure what it is, so I'll go and find out," Morris said.

He returned to say that they were due to be seated in 15 minutes.

This is all so exotic! We're on a real ship going to America!

For Regina, nothing else mattered in the moment. Her life back in Poland felt far away and she was consumed by her new adventure.

173

The dining hall held more than 200 people. As Morris, Regina and Louis sat at a table, waiting for the meal service to begin, introductions were made. Betina and Waclaw Roman and Hershel and Zivia Kupferman were all in their mid-30's.

They're all so trim and their clothes look new.

Bettina and Hershel were siblings and had been neighbors with their respective spouses. They all grew up on poor family farms in a small rural area of Poland between Lublin and Chelm, roughly 200 kilometers southeast of Warsaw.

It's a relief to meet these Jews from Poland.

As the soup course was served, the conversation flowed easily because they had all left home, which was no surprise to Regina. Betina, who was Regina's age, addressed her and Morris.

"Now that we know we are from the same tribe, let's discuss why each of us decided to make this difficult journey."

Betina is even more outspoken than me.

Hershel explained that he and Bettina's older brother, Schlomo, and his wife, had migrated to Chicago four years ago and Schlomo had earned enough to pay for the four of them to leave Poland. They had been scraping by on the farm, working hard for no rewards, and they wanted a better life.

"For me, your question is easy to answer," said Regina. "If you didn't see what was happening back home, you must have had your head in the sand. It wasn't *so* long ago, as we entered a new century, when good things were happening for women. My job at the Bund, for example. But as progressive as we were, we couldn't fight the growing antisemitism, especially when the words we felt aimed against us started turning into weapons."

Regina's strident, outspoken response made her sound like an aggressive feminist from a new wave of Polish women taking on the establishment.

Zivia sat up straight.

"If the status of women in Warsaw was so good, then why did you leave?"

"Fair question, Zivia. Our status in Poland was improving, but the march of antisemitism from Russia got stronger every day. The strides we made as Jewish women are useless now because we can't stick around to enjoy them."

174

Zivia and Betina looked at each other and shrugged.

"It was not an easy decision for me, but ever since I experienced the pogrom in Bialystok in 1906, I felt differently about our future. Each year, I came to realize more and more that we were doomed, and I knew deep in my heart that I had to leave, no matter how hard it would be."

"Oh, Regina! I'm so sorry," said Zivia. "What happened? I don't want to get too personal, but was it as horrible as I heard?"

Be careful with your answer in front of Morris.

"It's okay, Zivia. I can imagine what you might be thinking. I went to Bialystok to visit my sister, who was working at the Lewandowski textile mill. After her work, we were going to have a picnic along the Biala River, but that never happened, of course. I was able to hide so the Russian soldiers didn't find me, but let's just say some other women were not so lucky."

"Can you tell us more?" said Betina.

"I was frozen with fear even after the stomping and shouting stopped because I didn't trust that they would just walk away. I heard my sister, Chaja Fajga, calling to me, but I didn't trust that the soldiers weren't making her call me, so I stayed in the closet for I don't know how long. Chaja Fajga kept calling me, and it sounded like she was crying, so I finally peeked out and it was only her. We hugged for a long time."

Zivia dabbed at her tears with her hanky.

"What did you do next?"

"You can imagine we didn't go on our picnic. In fact, we packed up Chaja Fajga's clothes and headed back to Mokotów as soon as we thought the coast was clear. Of course, Chaja Fajga never returned to the mill."

The entire table fell silent after hearing Regina's experience. No one wanted to be the first to talk or change the subject. Finally, Regina picked up the conversation.

"Outside the boarding house, I saw the worst carnage I could have ever imagined. Dead bodies everywhere. I'll never get over it. That event changed me forever and I became highly sensitive and aware of any antisemitic situation. While thank God we haven't seen any full-fledged pogroms in Poland since then, attacks on Jews have been growing steadily over the past few years. Soldiers are marching through Russia and attacking Jewish homes and businesses, so it's only a question of time until they arrive in Warsaw."

Morris squeezed Regina's hand.

"I think the table has probably had enough talk of antisemitism and pogroms for one evening," he said.

"Well, I don't know about you," said Waclaw, "but I'm hungry."

As he stood up to go to the buffet line, the others followed. Regina and Morris were the last to leave the table.

"Regina, my love, I think we have had enough politics for the evening," said Morris.

"Okay, okay, I hear you."

I've heard myself enough for now, too.

At the end of the meal, the Romans and the Kupfermans said goodnight and left the table. Regina sensed that they left a bit abruptly, but she didn't say anything to Morris.

"They seem like nice people, don't you think?" he said.

"Yes, but a bit skittish."

"Hardly. They are on this ship to America. That is not an easy decision to make a commitment like that."

Regina thought about Morris's comment and had to agree.

"You are right. I still think my reactions have a lot to do with Bialystok. It made me extra sensitive. They didn't have the same experience, but they left where they were to seek a better life, just like all the others on this ship."

Morris caressed Regina's back.

"Let's get to our stateroom. I think Louis has had enough for one day."

Over the next week, the three couples became fast friends. Waclaw explained that representatives from United Jewish Charities would meet them at Ellis Island and help them find their train to Chicago. Regina indicated that she had worked with the Hebrew Immigrant Aid Society in Warsaw, and she expected similar assistance when they arrived in New York.

Waclaw also explained more about opportunities Shlomo had found in Chicago. Regina and Morris had not made plans beyond getting to New York, so they were interested in what was possible in Chicago.

It sounds like a winning city with fewer immigrants than New York.

Twelve days into the journey, when they were just two days away from Ellis Island, Regina and Morris heard that when an unmarried couple were processed, they would be separated because they were not a legal family unit.

I wish this trip would last longer. I feel so comfortable on the ship, without a care in the world. All I must do is show up on time to eat and find a nice chair on the deck to enjoy the sun. Life is easy now, but soon it will all be unknown again.

Regina and Morris couldn't confirm if they had to be married when they arrived, but just in case it was true, they needed a remedy. Without much discussion at all, they sought out the ship's captain to marry them that morning because he was legally authorized to perform that ceremony at sea. He wasn't enthusiastic about their request, but he did it anyway because it was considered part of his duties.

The ceremony was short and included all the legal requirements. It meant that Morris and Regina were now husband and wife. They shared this news with their tablemates at lunch, who offered their best wishes.

Is something wrong with me? I don't feel any thrill at all about being a new wife. I guess it's just business and Morris is sweet, but we have no place to consummate our marriage.

During dinner that night, Hershel arranged for the bakery to provide a special cake and wine to toast the new couple. The others had assumed Regina and Morris were married, so they were surprised to find out they had met only recently and decided to leave Paris together.

With only one more day before they arrived in America, Regina kept questioning Morris about what they should do there. She made a list of their belongings and how much money they had. She also made lists of what they needed to do once they got off the boat.

How will we get to Chicago?

Every conversation with Morris made Regina short tempered.

"What if they refuse us? What if we don't pass the health tests? What if we don't qualify?"

"Why are you worrying about things you don't even know yet? Please stop being so nervous, Regina. It's affecting Louis, too. He's crying more and more."

Regina was somewhat calmed by Morris' steady demeanor. She rarely saw him nervous or insecure about anything, which she liked. She still worried but leaning on Morris helped her contain her anxiety.

As they sailed into New York Harbor, everyone gathered on deck to view the Statue of Liberty and pinch themselves that they had finally made it.

Oh my God, if I think about everything that led me to this point, I might faint and fall into the water.

Regina squeezed Louis' hand and hugged Morris.

"We did it!" We're here!"

Before the ship was allowed to enter New York Harbor, it stopped at a quarantine checkpoint off the coast of Staten Island, where doctors checked for contagious diseases, such as smallpox, yellow fever, plague, cholera, and leprosy. Once the ship passed inspection, immigration officers boarded the ship via rope ladders before its passengers were allowed to board the tenders.

Once cleared, the ships flat-bottomed tender ferried passengers from the ship to the processing center on Ellis Island, located at the mouth of the Hudson River between New York and New Jersey.

America
1910

32

On to Chicago

Regina scanned the crowd for someone from the Hebrew Immigrant Aid Society. People with signs from various organizations were calling out family names and announcing who they were. Everyone was jumbled together in a crush, waiting to be interviewed and allowed to disembark once the ship docked. Regina and Morris had provided their information to officials in Europe and hoped it would help them as they arrived.

This is chaos!

Since Regina and Morris were second-class passengers, they moved through the immigration checkpoints without delay. They received translation assistance, and the Hebrew Immigrant Aid Society paid their landing fees.

While Regina was grateful to finally be on American soil, she found it difficult to deal with the crowds pushing, shoving, and yelling. She was exhausted by the time they passed through all the checkpoints.

Now, we must make our way to Chicago.

They were stuck in a jumble of people and organizations all scrambling to find each other. Louis put his hands over his ears because the noise was overwhelming, and Regina saw many passengers with no family or connections with a group just looking around with no idea what to do.

"Jewish Family Services!"

"United States Rescue Committee!"

"United Jewish Charities!"

We're lucky to have the Hebrew Immigrant Aid Society helping us. We'd be lost without them.

The pushing and shoving only increased as they waited their turn to get through the final step of their intake process. Babies were crying and the odor of some the steerage passengers who had not bathed in two weeks was quite strong. Everyone was trying to get to the front of the line for their medical inspection. Regina, Morris, and Louis were finally checked and approved, so it was time for them to say goodbye to the friends they had made onboard.

Saying goodbye was bittersweet after getting to know each other as they did, but all of them had their next destination on their mind.

"Good luck to you all," Regina said.

"We're glad you are going to Chicago," Zivia said. "It's not as crowded, and there are several Jewish charities there to help you get settled."

"We don't know anyone in New York or Chicago," said Morris, "but it sounds like there are good opportunities there."

"We appreciate your help!" said Regina. "All the best to you!"

They walked three blocks from the barge to the train that would finally take them West. A ticket master handed them train tickets and meal vouchers. Since they had not booked the trip in advance, they were relegated to a car without sleeping quarters for a trip would take a day and a half.

As the train departed, Morris made sure that Regina and Louis had a seat and could sleep. After several hours, Regina got up and insisted that Morris take the seat and get some sleep himself.

When they finally arrived at Chicago's Union Station, Regina held Louis while Morris gathered their belongings.

It feels like I haven't eaten in days.

She tried her best not to be irritable as they departed the train and headed upstairs into a large hallway, complete with Corinthian columns and rosettes around the ceiling. Once again, they were stuck in a mob of people, and the bitter cold of January hit them in the face.

Is this what it's always like in Chicago? It feels even colder than Warsaw.

Morris found a woman from the Hebrew Immigrant Aid Society directing other travelers and answering their questions.

"What is your name and where did you get the ship?"

Morris approached her as she shuffled through her papers.

"Oh, yes, Mr. Butlaw. We've been informed that you and your family are here in Chicago without any sponsorship. We will get you settled for the night and talk tomorrow."

Regina let out a huge sigh of relief.

Finally, a place to lie down!

The woman motioned to a man to with scruffy hair and a kind face.

"Yacob, please take them to the boarding house on California Avenue."

She turned to Morris and Regina.

"We will talk tomorrow. Go get some rest. They will feed you there."

Regina felt great relief hearing those words.

We can finally stop traveling. We're almost home, wherever that may be.

Yacob motioned to the family to follow him to his carriage on Canal Street. He loaded their bags in the back and directed the horses. It took half an hour to reach the boarding house. The streets were filled with the sounds of horse hooves, carriages vying for space, and an abundance of black Ford Model T automobiles. Throngs of people moved in all directions.

The wind was relentless. Regina snuggled Louis under her coat to keep him warm. Their winter clothes from Paris were not enough to keep them warm during a typical Chicago winter.

When they reached the boarding house, they saw a large sideboard with sandwiches, hot tea, and apple cake.

I think I'm going to cry.

She was overwhelmed from exhaustion and the charity they had received. After they ate, they were shown to their room and the bathroom down the hall. They had two regular beds and an optional folding cot, with a pitcher of water, a wash station, and pegs on the wall to hang their clothes.

Regina felt like she was encased in fog. She couldn't think or speak. All the magic of the ship life was gone and now she was just another refugee among thousands. She was not unique or special, and no one in Chicago was waiting for her. She knew that, but feeling the reality was another story.

Now, I am just another face in the crowd.

She fell onto the bed with Louis at her side. She struggled to get up, undress him, and get him comfortable on his cot. Once he was settled, she fell back on the bed in her clothes, too tired to change. All three fell into a deep sleep for the rest of the afternoon.

At six p.m., they were awakened by a knock on the door.

"Is anyone awake? We are serving dinner if you would like to join us."

Regina didn't want to miss the evening meal, as she was not sure if there would be anything to eat until the morning.

"Yes, we are up. Thank you. We will be down momentarily. Thank you for checking."

Morris rolled over and stretched.

"What do they want?"

"They are serving dinner. I don't want to miss it."

Morris stretched again and sat up wearily on the side of the bed.

"Okay, guess I need to get dressed again. My clothes are not very fresh, but they're all I've got."

"I'm guessing they are used to it if they take in travelers like us who spent two weeks sailing across the ocean. We should see if we can clean our clothes. Mine are smelly, too."

They poured water into the bowl and splashed water on their faces. Then they bundled up Louis and headed downstairs, looking forward to a home cooked meal.

The dining room table seated 14 people. A long counter had a buffet of chicken, green beans, mashed potatoes, and bowls of matzo ball soup, along with loaves of dense brown bread.

It looks like all of us are hungry!

After everyone ate like they had missed a meal or two, they sat back and began talking with each other about their journeys, where they had lived, the family members they left behind, and what brought each person to America.

The boarding house was a way station for Jewish immigrants. The Hebrew Immigrant Aid Society helped them find places to live. They were supported by contributions from the local Jewish community, but they always ask for a donation from travelers who could manage it.

The following day, after breakfast, Ben Horowitz, a short, round man with thinning hair and a warm smile, arrived from the American Jewish Joint

Distribution Committee, part of the Hebrew Immigrant Aid Society, to meet with Morris and Regina.

"Welcome," said Ben. "I hope you have gotten some rest. I know the journey is exhausting, and you have your toddler with you. That must have been challenging."

Morris and Regina just stood there, unable to respond.

"Oh, sorry, we are still a little in shock at finally being here," said Morris. "I guess you see that a lot… people at a loss for words."

"Not to worry. I totally understand, and yes, when I meet people during their first days in America, they are in the same state as you, overwhelmed and unsure where their life is going."

Regina took Louis and sat down on the couch in the entry way.

"Let's get some information to get you on your way to your new home. You are from the Warsaw area, and came here on the SS California?"

Regina and Morris nodded.

"Morris, it says here you are a jeweler, and Regina, you did some translating from Yiddish, Hebrew, and Russian to Polish?"

Regina and Morris nodded again.

"Do either of you have any leads for work?"

They looked at Ben and then at each other, unsure how to answer. They had no leads and had planned to walk the streets looking for help wanted signs. Morris had good luck that way when he was in Paris finding a jeweler who needed extra help. He had saved money from that work that helped him pay his second-class passage on the ship.

"Ben, we have no contacts here and no leads on work. When I left Warsaw and stayed in Paris, I found work easily. Everyone needs a good jeweler, and many companies need extra help. I will be looking hard once we get settled."

Regina had no idea about finding work. She did all her translating before Louis was born. After that, she stayed home.

Here, I need more to do than just be a housewife.

"Mr. Horowitz, I'm very good at translating and I will learn English. Do you know any places that can use some help translating Polish or Yiddish?"

Ben shook his head.

"Not until you learn English, I'm afraid. Then, you will have lots of work because with the large numbers of Eastern European Jews flooding in, organizations are overwhelmed and need documents translated from English to Polish, Yiddish, Russian and German. But I can't really help you until you learn English."

Ben went on, seeing Regina's disappointment.

"Let's take things one step at a time. I have a nice apartment in a small building near Maxwell Street in the Near Westside. It's much nicer than most of the tenements, and you will make friends there. It has a large bedroom, a kitchen area, and a sitting room. There are five units to a floor and two bathrooms, with one for men separate from women so you won't have any problems using the bathroom down the hall."

Ben beamed, thinking he was giving this small family good news.

All I want to do is lay my head down on a bed I can call my own.

She noticed that Morris seemed excited about the news.

"We are so grateful for all you are doing for us. But are there any stores in the neighborhood?"

"Not far, and a whole new market of small shops is opening there later this spring It's a busy place. Let's go, and you can see for yourself. The place is empty and just waiting for you."

Regina and Louis stood up to join them.

"Oh, and I forgot one of the best parts. The building owner knows that you don't have all your own linens right now so he will supply them, and you can pay him for the sheets and towels when you get work. Pretty nice, eh?"

Morris looked worried.

"We don't have much money left and it's all in Zlotys."

"We will change that for you into dollars. In terms of rent, we can help you for the first two months. We expect you will find work or sell things on the street to earn money so you can take over the rent and expenses very soon. We can help you Morris because we have an extensive list of employers."

Morris looked at Regina and shrugged.

What other choice do we have?

"Come," said Ben. "Say goodbye to these good people and let's go."

Morris and Ben carried their luggage down to the street corner where they boarded a trolley car to take them to their new apartment.

Regina felt a pounding on the side of her head. The pain overwhelmed her as she tried to absorb everything Ben was telling them.

I just need to lie down as soon as possible.

She wondered if she did the right thing.

This is America? I didn't know what to expect, but I didn't expect this. Long lines everywhere, people telling me there is no work until I learn English. I didn't think about how I would support myself and Louis. What kind of life will we have? Where is the shining light of life in America?

Morris seemed fine chatting with Ben about his jewelry skills. She knew he would get work before she did.

I don't want to depend on another person to support me.

She still had some money left to support herself and Louis for a while. Morris had money, but she didn't know how much, but judging from the dinner they had enjoyed at Maxim's, she figured he had plenty.

But who knows how long that will last?

33

The Struggles Continue

A month after their arrival, Morris and Regina began to feel settled in. Regina took care of Louis while Morris did occasional repair work for a couple of jewelers. Instead of feeling good about this, he was frustrated at not finding full-time work.

"I'm a much better jeweler than most of the others I've seen. I do better repairs in half the time, and you'd think the owners would appreciate that. Instead, I only get calls when they're backed up. I'm thinking that America may not be so welcoming to Polish Jews."

Regina didn't know how to respond to Morris' complaints.

What I thought would be a thrilling beginning, is anything but.

The stress from Morris's dissatisfaction ate into their marriage. He began to blame Regina for his problems, and as his savings ran out, even with help from the Jewish Federation, their anxiety levels continued to increase. They managed to control the discord in front of Louis, but in private they were increasingly hostile toward each other.

"You decided to come here. I didn't force you, Morris,"

"You did. You wouldn't stay in Paris, so you left me no choice."

There was no space to withdraw from one another, which only added to the stress as Morris struggled to find work and Regina studied English as she stayed home with Louis.

Two weeks later, Morris came home with good news.

"I think I found some work with a factory that uses leather skins to make book binding, luggage, and clothing."

Regina looked at Morris, not sure how to react.

Is this good news?

"Oh, that sounds like good news."

"I have to start at the bottom, but it's some money."

Regina wanted to be encouraging. She admired Morris for accepting a job that was not at all close to what he was used to.

"You will learn a new skill, Morris. That sounds like it's a good thing."

"I figured you would say something like that. You are not the one who will have to go into a smelly warehouse and work with bloody animal fur after they've been slaughtered."

"I'm doing this for you and Louis, so you should be grateful. It's not as genteel as being a jeweler, which I have done so well my whole adult life. It seems like no one in America wants to hire a poor, Polish Jewish immigrant, not like they did in Paris."

"I don't know what to say, Morris."

It feels like it doesn't matter what I say because anything I try only upsets him. I'd like to take Louis right now and go anywhere else. But without money, I have nowhere to go and no place to hide.

Finally, she found her voice.

"I'm very proud of you Morris. This process has been so difficult, and I appreciate that you are disappointed. Maybe a jewelry position will come along while you are at this factory."

Morris said nothing.

"Morris, my love, I wish I could make everything okay for you. I wish I could find you a full-time job doing what you do best. It breaks my heart that you are so frustrated."

"Easy for you to say, isn't it? Such a supportive and understanding wife."

Regina had never seen this side of Morris and didn't recognize his anger. She wondered if encouraging him to travel with her was the right thing to do. He had enjoyed a good job in Paris and here he couldn't find anything that gave him pride in his work. She also noticed that he wasn't taking care of himself, letting his hair grow long and unruly.

Other men don't have such long hair.

She offered to cut it for him, but he declined.

Morris stomped across the room and threw on his coat. He marched to the front door and slammed it shut as he walked out without a word.

34

New Job, New Life

Regina froze. She wasn't sure if Morris would come back.

What will I do without his support?

For more than an hour, she felt paralyzed, trying not to panic in front of Louis. Eventually, she changed his diaper and prepared their dinner. A few minutes later, Morris returned and sat down with them to eat.

He smiled at Regina, as if to apologize, and squeezed her hand.

"I'm sorry, my love. None of this is your fault."

Regina sighed and smiled for what felt like the first time in days. She didn't know what made Morris change so suddenly into a man she didn't recognize, but she was thankful for whatever brought him back home.

Maybe he found a jewelry job?

After dinner, as Regina tucked Louis into bed, Morris rubbed her back.

"Oh, that feels so good. But you are the one that needs a backrub.

"I am so sorry about what I did earlier. Please forgive me, Regina."

"Me, too, Morris. I wish I could help, but I must stay with Louis."

"Maybe he needs a new brother or sister."

Is he kidding? Another child now? It's all we can do to feed three of us right now. What is he thinking?

"Morris, you can't be serious! You haven't even started your new job."

Morris gave her a mysterious smile.

"It pays better than a part-time jeweler. It's full-time, so I'll make money. It's time that you and I have a child together."

Regina didn't know how to react.

"Look," said Morris. "Louis is fast asleep. We can be quiet, right?"

He moved his hand from Regina's back around to her breasts, slowly encircled them, and gently pinched her nipples.

The sex they'd had over the past several months had been quick, meeting basic needs more than feeding any romance. It had been a long time since Regina and Morris had made love back in Paris when everything was magical.

Regina sighed and lost herself as Morris wrapped his arms around her. He moved her onto their bed and unbuttoned her blouse as she wriggled out of her skirt. Morris unbuttoned his pants and slid them off as he moved on top of Regina and gently thrust himself inside her.

This is what we've needed. We need to do this more often.

She knew what to do to not get pregnant so they could enjoy making love whenever they wanted, but now that wasn't necessary. With another thrust, Morris let out a slow, low growl and relaxed.

"You know we may have to do this again to be sure you get pregnant." He laughed.

"Oh, you are wicked, my husband."

The next morning, Morris dressed in his only set of working clothes and headed out to his new job, where he would learn how to tan preserved hides and skins through a labor-intensive chemical process. Pelts were carefully scraped of connective tissues at "beam houses," and their hair and oils were rinsed with chemicals, pickled, and then safeguarded by a variety of "tanning liquors." After "currying," the finishing process workers used to remove defects, they added crucial dyes and polishes before the leather was worked into semidurable goods, such as boots, shoes, horse tack, and book bindings.

This reminds me of Papa's work.

Fortunately, the factory was on Michigan Avenue, near Chinatown, not too far from their apartment. The trolly on Roosevelt Road took him to Michigan, where he transferred to the main trolly to reach the plant at Michigan and East Cermak Road.

As Morris got more comfortable at the leather factory job, he became less angry, but he was still frustrated as he felt his years perfecting his skill as a jeweler were being wasted. He thought he was too good to be doing such menial work, but it paid the bills and was steady. He hoped to get back to jewelry making, but the demand for leather products was a lot stronger.

He insisted on still trying to find work in the jewelry world and didn't understand why it was so difficult, especially with his skills. He didn't want to think it was political.

He should be welcomed with open arms, like he was in Paris.

Morris thought that the jewelers saw him as competition rather than someone who could help their business. The customers buying jewelry were Christians who lived in wealthy districts, and they were not interested in buying from Jewish jewelers in their shtetls. That made the local jewelers more hesitant to hire anyone new.

It didn't occur to Morris that he couldn't get a jewelry job because he was Jewish. He didn't want to consider that they left antisemitism in Europe only to have it follow them to America.

Paris had been different. Jewelers there had more than enough clients and in many cases, they could barely meet the needs of their wealthy clientele.

The only thing Morris liked about his tannery job was getting paid. He suggested to Regina that she could do something to bring in money, too, like taking care of other children for families with two working parents, or for wealthier families whose wives hired help. He encouraged her to get the word out that she was available during the day.

A month later, Regina awoke feeling nauseous.

I know what this means!

She had been feeling more tired than usual. Taking Louis to the local park near Halsted Street South exhausted her, especially when the Chicago winds were cold and biting.

Because of that, Morris' wishes had fallen on deaf ears. Regina felt like she could barely take care of Louis, let alone someone else's children. It was all she could do to keep him entertained while dealing with her nausea.

Life is so stressful here. Who am I looking at in the mirror? Where is the bright, smart, political girl I once knew in Poland?

Regina didn't recognize herself and she thought her life was taking a wrong turn. She didn't know if she would be better off without Morris, especially since she had to deal with his disappointment, and the fact that she could not help him. The situation was affecting their relationship *and* her self-esteem and identity.

Their neighbors, Yankel, and Anna had a little girl a few months older than Louis. Regina had been feeling isolated and lonely, but when she met Anna and her young daughter, she was thrilled, and hoped they could all spend some time together during the day.

One day, Regina went to see her neighbor, hoping to make a new friend.

"Regina, I would love to spend time with you," said Anna. "I don't know anyone either and our children are so close in age."

The feeling is mutual. My lucky day!

Anna had similar problems, as far as Regina could tell. Yankel worked in a slaughterhouse during the day. Anna was also from a suburb of Warsaw and had arrived shortly before Regina and Morris.

"Anna, it's a sunny day outside. Why don't we take our children to see that playground we were told about?"

They bundled up the children and headed outside. As they walked, Anna asked Regina about Morris. She shared his frustration about not finding a suitable job as a jeweler. Anna had a similar story to tell about Yankel.

"Maybe he could find a job at the leather factory. I'm sure it's not as difficult as a slaughterhouse."

"Do you think Morris would put in a good word for him? After all, they have never really met except to say hello on the stairs."

"I'll speak to him tonight. I can't imagine why not. It's not as though Yankel is competition. I think they need a lot of workers because leather goods are in demand."

Maxwell Street
1910

35

New Baby!

As the contractions came faster, Regina let out a cry as each one gripped her abdomen. Anna tucked pillows behind her head.

"The midwife will be here soon, Regina, but I know what to do to get you ready."

"These pain feels stronger than when I had Louis, but maybe I'm not remembering very well."

"You're doing fine."

Two other women who lived in the building stood by to help, one holding Regina's hand while the other encouraged her to keep breathing.

"Don't worry, Regina, the midwife is wonderful."

Regina asked for help to move on her side.

"I'm having labor pains in my back like I had when Louis was born."

The midwife arrived. She was tall and angular, with a no-nonsense manner. She asked Anna to get hot and cold towels. Then, she instructed Regina to get on all fours and rock back and forth, arching her back, hoping it would cause the baby to change position to relieve some of Regina's pain.

As soon as Regina relaxed, the midwife helped her lay on her side and placed cold towels on her belly and warm towels between her legs, all to calm her down and ease the pain.

"This is much more painful than with Louis. Is something wrong? Why does it hurt so much?"

"You're fine, Regina. I felt your abdomen, and your baby is in a slightly different position, but you are both okay. When you are ready, you can push."

Just then, Regina was hit with another rush of pain. The midwife rubbed her back to ease the pressure on her lower spine.

"Does that help?"

"Yes, thank you. It's easing up a bit."

"Okay, then I want you to give me a big push."

Regina pushed as hard as she could.

"I see the baby's head, Regina. Almost there. Hang on, and rest now."

As Regina tried to breathe, she braced herself for another round of pain.

"Here we go," said the midwife. "Let's make this your last big push!"

Regina marshalled all her strength and roared loudly as she tried to get the baby out.

"Here it comes, Regina. The head is out. You're almost there. One more, Regina. Just one more. Come on. You can do it."

Regina moaned and bellowed like never before.

"It's a girl! Mazel Tov, Regina. You have a beautiful little girl."

The midwife wrapped the baby in a warm blanket and wiped her eyes with a wet cloth. Regina was still panting heavily as the midwife handed her a new baby daughter.

"Oh, my God. Let me catch my breath."

Thank God! Thank God! Thank God!

"She is beautiful, isn't she?"

The women smiled and offered their congratulations. The midwife used the wet towels to clean off Regina, and then tucked blankets around her.

"Regina, would you like some tea?" Anna said.

"That would be wonderful, thank you."

She looked around the room and enjoyed the friendly faces.

Now, I must examine my new daughter.

Regina was in awe.

What will Morris think when he gets home? Will he be happy that his first child is a girl and not a boy? It shouldn't matter what God planned for us.

"I'm sure you are exhausted, Regina," said the midwife. "You did a great job considering all the back pain you had."

"Thank you. The pressure you applied made such a big difference and the towels felt wonderful."

"You're welcome. I understand your husband is at work right now."

"Yes, but he should be home shortly, if you want to wait for your fee."

"That's fine. I need to be somewhere, so I'll come by tomorrow if you can have the fee for me then."

"Yes, of course. Thank you again for your excellent skills."

When Morris finally came home unusually late, the baby was asleep, and Regina was barely awake herself. She was partly annoyed and quite worried.

What kept him so long after he was supposed to be finished work?

He smelled of beer and his eyes were red.

This is not the man I met in Paris.

"Where have you been?"

"Well, it looks like you have been busy today. Who do have we here?"

Morris stumbled toward Regina and the new baby.

"You stink of beer, Morris. Don't come near me. Where have you been?"

"Oh, I was celebrating with a couple guys from work at a local pub. I told them we were having a new baby soon."

Regina gave Morris a disapproving look.

"How did you know we were going to have a baby today? You didn't know that when you left for work this morning. Did someone come to the factory to tell you? I don't think so."

Morris waved his arm and laughed.

"I guess I just have a good sense about these things."

"Well, we have a beautiful daughter now, and I'm going to name her Rose after one of my mother's sisters who died two years ago."

"Shouldn't I have a say in what we name our children?"

"If you had been here earlier, maybe. But since you stink of beer and come home almost at bedtime, you lost that privilege."

Oh my God, why am I so angry? I don't want to act like this, but who is this man who is supposed to be my husband?

Regina rolled over and held her breast to encourage Rose to nurse. Louis was bundled up, asleep on the floor.

Morris grunted and went down the hall to the bathroom. He returned red-eyed and lumbering into the bedroom, where he fell on the bed next to Regina and Rose and quickly began to snore.

Who is this man, and what has happened to me? I am now a mother of two children in a brand-new country where I can barely speak the language, and I am dependent on a man who appears to be very unhappy with his life.

Over the next days and weeks, Regina and Morris's relationship went from close and affectionate to distant and belligerent, especially when their conversation involved a decision about money.

36

Marauders in the Park

Morris was earning more money so he and Regina could now afford a home with more space than a typical tenement offered. It wasn't easy to find something clean and affordable that would suit a growing family. They looked for a small apartment with two bedrooms and their own bathroom.

They found a fifth-floor walk-up almost twice as large as the apartment that the Hebrew Immigrant Aid Society had initially placed them in. It had hardwood floors, glass doorknobs, and rope windows. The bathroom had hex tile with little blue squares and the tiny kitchen had a porcelain sink with a drain board and a faucet. The pantry had a small ice box to keep milk cold.

Climbing five floors was difficult, especially with a toddler and a baby, and even though Regina struggled to carry them and all their things up and down the stairs each day, she felt it was worth it to have more room, their own bathroom, and more privacy.

Finally, I can take a bath in peace.

She hoped the changes would help Morris feel better about himself now that he could provide more space and a higher level of comfort for his family.

Regina found it challenging to keep Louis entertained, as he seemed to operate at top speed all the time, which was almost impossible to manage sometimes while breastfeeding Rose. While she liked certain things about the new place, she still felt isolated with only the children to keep her company.

At least I had Anna and her daughter at the old apartment.

During this time, Regina was missing her family more than ever.

How wonderful it would be to hand Rose to Lena to hold and love? I would love to share my new baby girl with Chaja Fajga, too.

Regina wrote letters often and longed to find postmarks from Poland and Paris in her mail.

She felt unkempt most of the time, as all her energy was devoted to childcare. She used to enjoy braiding her hair or pinning it back, but now she just wrapped her dark brown hair at the nape of her neck to get it off her face.

At least we have our own bathroom so I can languish in the bathtub every now and then when the children are sleeping, especially if Morris is home and willing to cover for me in case they wake up.

Their new home had no communal place to meet the neighbors, so Regina decided to explore the local area and see if she could find a park where Louis could play, and she could meet some other mothers.

A week after moving in, Regina found the energy to carry the stroller downstairs before running back up to carry Rose and have Louis hold her hand as they walked down the five flights and out onto the street.

She stopped at a little storefront to purchase some fruit and to ask the owner if he knew of any playgrounds within walking distance. The man behind the counter, who had a short beard and curly salt and pepper hair, was loud and friendly.

"You are in luck. There is a playground a few blocks from here where mothers take their children. It's off Maxwell, two blocks past Morgan Street."

Regina was thrilled. She was eager to meet people, especially if they spoke Polish.

This is my life. Try to stay positive!

Regina took fruit and they soon found the playground, which was very close to where they lived. She smiled the first time in a long time as she stood on the sidewalk to get her bearings before locating a bench with enough room for her and Rose to sit. She noticed several women who appeared to be an immigrant like her, with at least two children in tow.

She wheeled the carriage around the crowded playground and took her place between two women. She noticed that a few women looked like they had just got off a boat at Ellis Island. Like her, they wore white cotton blouses with long sleeves, and long skirts to the ankles with heavy, black woolen skirts. Most of them had their hair twisted in a bun and fastened up high.

I must look like a Polish refugee, too.

Regina tried to sound as friendly as possible.

"Pardon me?" she said in Polish. "Is this part of the bench available?"

"Oh, yes," a young women said, also in Polish. "I'm sorry, let me move over. Anka has left, so you are welcome to join us."

Regina was relieved to hear Polish, and the woman acted like it was expected of her to use native language.

The grocery clerk spoke Polish, too. Is this a Polish enclave? It doesn't matter, but it sure would make life a lot easier.

Regina knew that she should be working harder at learning English, especially if she wanted a translating job, but at least for the meantime, she didn't mind being a Polish immigrant.

She buttoned up Louis's jacket and encouraged him to join the other children. He didn't have any sandbox toys, so she planned to get him some soon. For the moment, there were seesaws, slides, and swing sets. Although Louis was a bit younger than some of the other kids, he jumped right in.

Regina was not the only mother with an infant and an older child.

It feels good to see other mothers like me, especially Polish women.

"Thank you for making room for me. My name is Regina Butlaw."

"Pleased to meet you. My name is Bina Wojciech. Is this your first time at the playground?"

"How could you tell? I guess I look like a first timer, eh?"

Bina laughed.

"We were all first timers not long ago. There are hundreds of us coming to Chicago every day, and many Jewish people are here in this neighborhood."

Regina looked around as she listened, worried that Louis might encounter a piece of equipment too big for him.

"I hope I didn't offend you. I assumed you are Jewish, so if not, you are certainly welcome, of course."

"No, it's okay, you are correct. We are Jewish, too, and it's a comfort to meet you."

Regina smiled.

This feels good, in a way I haven't felt in a long time.

She wanted so badly to make friends, but didn't want to be pushy, as she didn't really know these women at all.

"So, which are your children Bina?"

"The one on the swing is my daughter, Golde, the daredevil, and this guy in my arms is Herschel. He's almost four months."

Regina laughed.

"We are reversed. My son is on the swings, and my daughter is an infant."

"So nice to meet you, Regina. I think we may become park friends. I also know several other moms I can introduce you to. We have an informal club. Several of us bring snacks for the older children that we share. Could you participate in that? It's okay if you can't. Money is tight, that is for sure."

Regina couldn't believe her luck.

I was hoping to make one new friend. Now, I can join a club!

She tried not to sound too desperate, but her enthusiasm was apparent. Then, just as she began to answer Bina, she heard angry yelling and saw several young teenage boys running toward the park and the swing sets.

Regina jumped up and ran to grab Louis. Before she could reach him, one of the young men ran right by her.

"Get out of our country, dirty Jew! Go back to Europe and take your rotten kids with you!"

The mothers screamed and ran for their children. The boys didn't touch any of the children or the mothers. They just ran through the playground yelling for them to get out of America.

"You don't belong here! Go away!"

As soon as the boys left, the women tried to comfort their children. Regina held Louis close. She hadn't understood everything the boys said, but she knew enough to realize it was bad.

"What was that? Has it happened before?"

Bina held her daughter and fought back tears.

"It's never happened here, but I've heard it happened at another park."

"What are you talking about?"

"There are people who think we are a different race and are here to take their jobs and cause problems. They are called White Christian Nationalists.

I read about them in the local Jewish newspaper. They say we are outsiders and threaten the nation and we are using our new religious freedom as a weapon against Christians."

Regina was shocked.

"I read that they don't fight with anyone, but they want to frighten us, so we won't come to the park. There isn't anything we can do, and it seems the police can't stop them because their attacks are random."

Oh my God.

"I also read something called "Sound the Tocsin of Alarm," which was written by some man named Orville Jones. He says that Jews practice fraud, extortion, and usury."

Regina felt the same fear she had before she left Poland.

Here it comes again in America? The antisemitism followed me here? I came here to get away from prejudice and now, it has found me all over again.

"Who are these people, and how do they find us?"

"They know about our immigrant Jewish communities. It's not a secret."

Regina suddenly realized why Morris couldn't get a job with a jeweler. It wasn't his lack of skill. It was because he was a Jew and the jewelry community in Chicago was Christian.

Now it makes sense.

"These people march down the streets and hold signs saying we are taking their jobs. They say we recruit others to take over their neighborhoods."

I never expected to run into such antisemitism in this new world. America is supposed to be much safer than Poland.

"I'm so sorry to tell you about this, Regina, but you must pay attention when you walk here. So far, we haven't had a problem at this park, but I've heard that young hooligans run into other parks where we are with our children, and they scream we are dirty Jews and push children off the swings and run through the sandbox. They have never hurt anyone, so far. It's really upsetting. We all pay attention to anyone new coming into the park."

Bina shook her head and shrugged.

"Oh no. I'm so glad you told me, Bina, and I'm so sorry to hear this. I thought all of this was behind me when I left Poland, but now it's here, too. Nothing has changed after all. What do we do?"

"What can we do? They never get caught because they run so fast and then disappear. We just hope they don't come here. It's a smaller park. They seem to like the parks in the center of town, so we try to stay small."

Regina said nothing.

What can I do? If I stay home, it means I am giving in to hoodlums, and I will not do that. I will take my chances.

"Louis, come here, my schatzeleh. It's time to go."

Regina gathered up her belongings and walked home with her children. She decided she would not be intimidated from going to the park, just like the other mothers. In that moment, Regina decided to go back the next day.

37

Sugar Cookies

"I'm glad you decided to come back," said Bina. "Some mothers have not returned to the park."

"I've been through too much to let a bunch of boys frighten me away. Besides, I would like to participate in the snack sharing. What do the kids like, and what are they permitted to eat? Is anyone kosher?"

Regina wondered what she could make for the children.

"You know, it has never come up," said Bina. "I really don't know. There are just four of us so far, and now you make five. There are other moms here who don't participate in the snack club, but they are very nice, and we don't care. It's good to have someone to talk to beyond our kids, right?"

Regina agreed.

"Are any of the moms here now?" she said.

"See that little boy climbing backwards up the slide?"

"Can't miss him."

"He belongs to Agnes. Very rambunctious kid. She can't take her eyes off him for a minute. He's fearless."

That reminded Regina to check on Louis, who seemed most interested in playing in the sand.

He's lucky another boy is sharing his bucket. That doesn't always happen.

Regina was the happiest she had been in months despite the risk of young men running through the park calling them names.

"So, is there a schedule about who brings snacks on certain days?"

"Oh no, we're not that organized. We don't want a formal arrangement, so just be sure you bring something for your son in case none of us bring any extra snacks. We don't want anyone to feel responsible or feel like they are the only ones bringing stuff. Make sense?"

"Great. I get it."

I'll bring snacks tomorrow, but what should they be?

"I have another question, if you don't mind."

Bina smiled.

"How do you know how many moms will be here on any given day?"

"Usually around eight of us show up, but not always the same ones."

"So, if I bring snacks tomorrow, how will I know who to give them to or if someone is in the group?"

"Just offer it to everyone. We don't take attendance."

"I'm so glad I met you, Bina. I look forward to getting to know everyone. And thanks for warning me about those boys. I appreciate it, and I'm glad you and the other mothers still come."

"We came here to America just like you, to get away from all that, so we are not going to let them win."

As the afternoon sun went down, Regina wanted to be sure to stop at the store before it closed so she could get what she needed to make cookies for the next day.

Lucky I have a real stove!

She greeted the grocer with a smile.

"Ah, you are back. Did you enjoy the playground?"

"Yes, thank you so much. I met many wonderful moms there."

I'm not going to mention the intruders because I don't know who might be listening here in the shop.

"I'd like to make some Polish wing cookies. I need flour, butter, oil, four eggs and frying oil, plus powdered sugar if you have it, please. If you don't have powdered, I'll take a package of regular sugar."

"Only if I get to taste them first before you take them to the park."

The grocer laughed.

"Well, we'll see, Mr. uh . . .?"

"Michnik. Like on the sign outside. You can call me Edam."

"Thank you. I will. I'll bring you some tomorrow afternoon when I come back from the playground."

Regina felt good. Despite the shock of encountering antisemitism in her own neighborhood, she hadn't felt so upbeat since long before she left Poland.

Life can be good again in ways I never thought about before.

She wondered if she should tell Morris what she learned.

Will it help him understand why he couldn't get work as a jeweler? Am I being naïve about America?

As soon as she got home, she took Louis to pee and wrapped Rose up in bed with blankets so she would stay put as Regina went downstairs to fetch the stroller. Then, she heated up the stew she had made from ingredients she bought at the butcher shop. They had brown bread with it, which Louis liked.

Next on my agenda? Sugar cookies!

Morris returned, smelling of beer again, but he was not very late or as inebriated as the night Rose was born, a month ago. Still, Regina stiffened up out of frustration.

I don't remember him ever apologizing for his behavior.

"Why are you so late again, Morris? I've kept the stew warm for over an hour now. It almost dried out before you got here."

"Stop complaining. Don't I bring home enough money for you to just sit around with the kids all day, doing nothing?"

Regina was so shocked by his accusation.

I'd like to throw the stew on the floor right now. Right at his feet.

"What are you talking about? Who do you expect to take care of our kids? Do you want to pay strangers to raise them?"

Regina knew places that watched other people's children, but she didn't consider them appropriate. They were mostly for women who didn't have a husband. Those children were often dirty, had fevers, and were not well fed.

The women who left their children in those circumstances were desperate. The only way they could earn money was to work menial jobs that barely paid for daycare. However, at least the children were fed, usually better than what the woman could provide at home.

Some mothers locked their children in their tenement apartments during the day while they worked, with food left on the kitchen table and the oldest child responsible for his younger siblings. This was not something Regina wanted to do, and she was shocked Morris would even suggest such a thing.

"You're being a snob, Regina. Those places are perfectly respectable. Some of the men I work with leave their children with caregivers. At least their wives are bringing in some money."

Regina was at a loss for words.

Even if we didn't have children, what options are available for me that pay more than the cost of daycare?

"Rose is still an infant. It's unfathomable to me to hand her over to a stranger. Who will pay attention to her like me?"

Morris grunted.

"No, it's out of the question."

Regina stopped talking and served Morris a bowl of stew and a big slice of brown bread. Then, she gathered Rose and took her into the bedroom to nurse her while Louis sat nearby, seemingly upset by the tension in the house.

The next morning, after Morris left for work, Regina prepared the dough to make sugar cookies. She hoped that the women came to the park every day because she felt so much better when she had other adults to talk to, besides Morris and Mr. Michnik.

I especially wish my family was nearby.

Regina felt tears running down her cheek as she imagined dropping Rose and Louis off at her mother's as she visited friends for lunch at their home.

I must live with the consequences of my decision to leave.

She had not anticipated the pain of separation.

Why was I so stubborn about leaving Poland? If I had known about the antisemitic marauders here, would I have still left?

Regina remembered how close her family had been. She was still trying to get them to change their minds by writing almost every week. She looked forward to letters from them as well, but they were few and far between.

I'm here now. Make the best of it.

She shook herself out of those thoughts because it was time to make cookies. She enjoyed baking and this was a fun, positive project she could do for herself, with help from Louis.

Regina grabbed a large bowl and took the butter out of the ice box.

"Louis, come here and help Mama make some yummy sugar cookies for the playground today."

She measured flour and salt into the bowl, sliced the butter into cubes and gave Louis a large spoon to mix it all up.

She let him stir it around in small circles so he would feel he was helping. Then, she separated the eggs and beat the yolks until they were foamy, added the milk, and poured it into the flour mixture before Louis mixed it again.

"What a good job you are doing, Louis. You are a great helper."

Once the combination became dough, Regina emptied it out on the table which she had spread with flour. She kneaded the dough, instructing Louis at the same time.

After dividing it into four large sections, she sliced it into thin strips. She showed Louis how to take each thin strip and "braid" it so that each cookie was made with two strips, like a bow. She wanted to be sure to have enough so that each child at the park could have two cookies, plus a couple more for Michnik the grocer.

Louis beamed as he watched his mother pour vegetable oil into a frying pan and heat it up. She dropped the dough into the pan three at a time and let them fry until they were light brown. After they cooked, she placed them onto a thin cotton cloth she used for cooking and sprinkled them with sugar. She didn't have powdered sugar, which is what she used back in Poland.

After the cookies cooled a bit, she treated Louis by letting him pick two out of the batch as his special cookies.

"I'm going to tell everyone at the park how you helped me make these."

Regina was excited that the cookies would still be warm when she and Louis got to the park. They wrapped up Rose and left earlier than usual.

They arrived before the others, as most of the mothers came after they had served lunch. Regina had brought sandwiches for her and Louis, and she had fed Rose back at the apartment. She brought the bowl and a large spoon for Louis to play with in the sand. She was determined to try and find him some real toys, so he wouldn't feel left out, although getting Morris to part with a few dollars for toys would be tricky.

I wish they would get here soon while the cookies are still warm.

Finally, Bina entered the playground and smiled when she saw Regina.

"You are here early today! So nice to see you again, I'm glad I didn't scare you away when I told you about those hooligans."

"We came here for a better life, just like you, Bina. We don't scare so easily, right?"

"Right."

"I was eager to get here and relieved to see you. I'm looking forward to meeting the other moms, too."

"I know. This is a good place to relax and have some real conversation."

"I made some cookies for snacks today."

Regina opened a cloth package to show Bina.

"Wow, these look wonderful, but you didn't have to go to so much trouble. Sometimes, just a piece of fruit is plenty."

"Oh, it was no trouble. I had an excellent helper, didn't I?"

Regina looked at Louis.

"Yes, I helped!"

"You did a great job, Louis," said Bina.

"Regina, can Louis pass around the cookies to the other children?"

"Absolutely. What an excellent idea! Would you like to, Louis?"

He looked down, not sure what to do.

"Mama, will you go with me?"

"Of course! You give out the cookies and I will be there with you."

Louis beamed with delight.

After all the cookies were distributed and some were left over, Regina decided to take them home and surprise Morris with a special dessert.

I hope he will enjoy them!

She stopped on the way home to leave two cookies with Michnik.

Back at home, Regina took the chicken she bought from the butcher, rubbed it with cooking oil to keep it moist, and put it in the oven.

This should be ready before Morris gets home from work. But will he show up before it gets late?

Morris was becoming more and more unpredictable, which only made Regina's life more difficult. She did not want to argue in front of the children, but there was no place for real privacy. Morris's voice was loud and, when he had a few beers, she couldn't reason with him. She was getting irritated with him all the time now. But she also depended on him, so she really had no choice but to try and keep things peaceful.

38

The Fever

"What is wrong with you this morning, Rose? I've fed you, diapered you, and cuddled you, and you're still fussing. I wish you could talk."

Regina was irritated that her three-month old baby kept crying and kicking her legs.

Her forehead feels a little warm, but nothing to be alarmed about.

It was getting late in the evening. The chicken had been roasted long ago, along with the potatoes and carrots, but Morris had still not arrived. Regina fed Louis and tried to keep the chicken warm without overcooking it. This scene played out most evenings as of late because Regina never knew when Morris would come home.

Regina managed to eat a little, even though Rose was still not doing well.

"What is wrong with you?"

As she looked more closely, Regina got worried. Rose's face was red, and she was sweating.

I never had this problem with Louis and I'm not sure what to do.

She began to panic. She was alone and knew no one who could help her.

I must get Rose to a doctor, but how?

Regina put the food in the oven and left a note for Morris about the chicken and where she was going. She gave Louis a warm coat and bundled Rose up in a blanket. Then, she began knocking on her neighbors' doors, looking for anyone who could tell her about a nearby hospital.

"Hello? Please can you help me? Hello?"

The first two apartments on her floor didn't answer. Finally, the third one opened, and a tall, muscular man greeted her.

"I'm sorry to bother you, but I have no place to turn. My infant daughter is burning up with a fever and I need to get her to a hospital. Do you know where it is?"

"Oh, my goodness, I can see she's bright red. Come with me. I will help you get a taxi because we don't have a car. Let me help you downstairs."

His wife grabbed a coat for him. As they made their way downstairs, the man introduced himself.

"My name is Harold. What is your name?"

"I'm Regina. My son is Louis, and my daughter is Rose. Thank you so much. I'm worried about her and don't know where the hospital is, and I've never taken a taxi."

Regina had tears in her eyes.

"Pardon my asking, but I believe I've seen your husband before. Is he out of town?"

This is embarrassing.

"Oh, no, but he isn't home from work yet and I can't wait because my baby is burning up."

He probably knows that Morris should be home by now, but what does it matter? That's my husband's problem, not mine.

As they reached the ground floor, they stepped onto the sidewalk and Harold looked for a taxi. After several attempts, he flagged down a yellow cab that had stopped taking fares for the evening. Harold explained it was an emergency, that they had to get an infant to the hospital right away. The driver agreed, and Harold climbed in with Regina and the children.

Rose continued to cry during the entire trip, which made Regina more and more fearful.

"Please, Schatzeleh, please get well."

They soon arrived at St. Luke's Hospital, a Charity of Grace Episcopal Church facility on the Near South Side at 8th and State Streets. Harold paid the driver and jumped out to find the front door and ring the bell. A woman in a white uniform opened the door and asked why they were there.

"My neighbor's baby is burning up with a fever. Please, she needs help."

As Harold described the problem, Regina ran up behind him, and Louis followed.

"Please help my baby. Please."

"Give her to me and follow me."

Louis and Harold followed her.

"Should I wait out here?" said Harold.

"Yes. Please make yourself comfortable in the lobby."

Regina thanked Harold and followed the woman into a large room with an examination table and a chair and sink. As she placed Rose on her back on the table, Regina couldn't hold back her tears because her daughter looked so tiny and helpless.

The woman identified herself as a nurse as she unwrapped Rose and put a glass thermometer into her bottom. She held it in place for a few minutes while trying to calm the baby, but with little luck.

"Is that man your husband?"

"No, he is my neighbor. My husband isn't home yet from work yet and I was too scared to wait."

"Is your husband employed?"

"Yes, he has a good job. We can pay for this care."

I must make sure Rose gets the treatment she needs.

The nurse removed the thermometer and shook her head.

"Poor little thing. She definitely has a fever. You brought her in early, which is good. We'll help her feel more comfortable. Wait here while I find the doctor. This room is drafty, so bundle her up so she doesn't get a chill."

"Thank you, thank you so much."

Minutes later, the doctor entered.

"So, what have we here? The nurse tells me you have a little girl with a fever and she's not at all happy right now."

"I've been so worried. She was burning up."

"Her temperature is high at 102, but for now, it's not life-threatening. Let's see what we can do for little Rose. That's her name, right?"

Regina nodded.

"A fever can suggest several things, but as I said, her temperature is not life-threatening at this point."

Regina did not ask the doctor what other things he was talking about, but she had heard in the park that some of the women had lost babies from something called scarlet fever.

"Here's what we are going to do. I can't tell yet why she has a fever, so I'm going to take some blood and urine from little Rose and see if it tells us anything. These tests take a couple of hours, and the laboratory is closed right now, so I'm going to ask you to stay here tonight. I know it's not comfortable, but hopefully it will just be for one night."

Oh my God.

"We will give Rose some medicine to help her feel more comfortable, and the lab results should be ready tomorrow morning."

The nurse put phenacetin solution into a baby bottle and Regina fed it to Rose, hoping she would settle down.

Harold knocked on the door after the nurse left the room.

"I'm sorry to leave you now, but I need to get home. I'll ask the nurse to help you get a taxi when it's time for you to go home."

Regina nodded.

"Do you have money?"

"No."

"Here, take this in case you need to go home on your own."

He handed Regina some money.

"I'll tell your husband where you are. I'm sure he is worried sick. He will come for you."

"That is so kind of you, Harold. I don't know what I would have done without your help."

I'm not sure if Morris will come find us. I hope he will at least show that kindness. After all, Rose is his child, too.

"Please stop by our apartment. Morris will come for us, I'm sure,"

Regina sounded more confident than she felt.

After Rose drank from the bottle, a nurse entered the room with a tray of instruments to take blood and urine from the baby.

"My name is Gladys," she said, in perfect Polish.

Regina felt anxious, but the woman's demeanor made her calm down.

"This is not going to make little Rose happy, but it only takes a second or two. I will prick her heel with a small blade and take some blood. I will need your help holding her leg, as she will try and pull away."

Gladys asked Regina to hold Rose's thigh. She held her foot in one hand and pricked Rose's heel to draw the blood she needed.

"Now, I'm going to put a little tube inside Roses urinary track and get what we need for the other test."

As Gladys put Rose on her back, she found a heavily soaked diaper.

"Good timing. She needs a diaper change."

Rose cried for a second as Gladys used the catheter.

"Done. The medicine we gave Rose should make her feel better. I'll get some blankets so all of you can try and get some sleep. Your nice young man here can bundle up on the floor."

Regina was still frightened, about Rose.

Why did they take her blood and pee? Will Morris come to be with us? What is going to happen? I barely have enough money to get home.

Gladys asked again about Morris.

"Surely when he realizes you are not home and your neighbor tells him where you are, he will come here right away. Hopefully, he can find a taxi."

Regina nodded.

I can't tell her the truth, that he may not care enough to come.

As Regina sat in a rocking chair in the examination room, she buried her face in Rose's soft hair and murmured to her to feel better. She sang her favorite Polish lullaby, Dobrej Nocy (Good Night).

Regina could not fall sleep until Rose was comfortable, which happened suddenly as she stopped screeching and felt cooler, almost like normal. Luckily, Louis also fell asleep on the floor.

As Regina closed her eyes, she heard a familiar voice.

"Is my wife here? I was told she brought in my infant daughter."

He still cares about me, and he isn't drunk.

As soon as Regina saw Morris in the doorway, she began to cry.

Here is the man I knew in Paris: strong, caring, and in control.

"Oh, my darling. What happened? Our neighbor told me you were here. What's the matter with Rose?"

Gladys explained everything to Morris, who held Regina's hand as he looked at his two children, both now sleeping peacefully.

"What do we do now?" he said.

"We are letting your wife stay in this room because we don't have any cribs available right now."

"I'm afraid you will have to go home now and come back tomorrow. Hopefully, we will know what caused Rose's fever, and we can prescribe medication for her."

Regina nodded.

"Morris, why don't you take Louis with you, so at least both of you can get some sleep and you can come back in the morning."

"Before I come back, I'll need to go by the shop in the morning to let them know why I won't be at work."

Morris kissed Regina, and then Rose's forehead before he picked up Louis and left. As soon as he did, Regina started crying again. She was a mess of emotions after fearing for Rose and full of joy seeing the Morris she knew.

Will this episode make him come back to the man I once knew and loved?

The next morning, a nurse came into the room with fresh diapers for Rose.

"Good morning, Mrs. Butlaw, my name is Ethel, and I'm your nurse for today. How are you, and how is baby Rose?"

"She slept through most of the night. I dozed off and on. She doesn't seem to have a fever now, but she still cries a little."

"We're waiting for her test results, but it's a good sign that the fever broke so easily. Let me go check."

She came back with Dr. Johnson.

"Good morning, Regina. I think Rose may have an infection because her urine is cloudy. Make sure she drinks a lot of water and put a warm pack on her tummy. We will give you some medicine to keep her fever down."

"This is all my fault," said Regina. "I've been breastfeeding her and haven't given her anything else."

218

"Don't blame yourself. We see this in infants all the time, so you didn't do anything bad. Just be sure you change her diaper more often and offer her water along with breastfeeding. I'm sure she will be fine."

Regina nodded.

"You may want to let her lay on the floor without a diaper so her bottom can get some air."

Regina felt guilty even though the doctor told her otherwise.

I'll miss the playground group for a few days, Rose's welfare is most important right now.

Ethel came back to help Regina bundle up Rose, and inquired about how she was getting home. She offered Regina a baby bottle filled with water, encouraging Rose to drink.

"Keep offering her water in addition to your breast milk. And remember to change her diaper often as the doctor said."

Regina nodded, and smiled, thankful she could understand enough English to do the right thing for her daughter.

39

Trouble Back Home

"My husband should be here shortly, and he will pay you and get a taxi to take us home. He had to stop by his work first."

Regina fed Rose the water and waited for more than an hour. As the nurses passed by, she wondered if they were irritated that she was still there.

Another hour passed by before Morris showed up without Louis.

"I'm so sorry Regina. I had to go by work to tell them about you and Rose, but my foreman wasn't in yet and I had to wait for him so I wouldn't get fired. Louis is with Harold. Anyway, here I am. What did the doctor say?"

"They think Rose has an infection, so she needs to drink more water and we should put a warm pad on her tummy and let her go without a diaper sometimes to air out her bum. They also gave me medicine to keep her fever in check."

Regina was grateful that Harold and his wife were looking after Louis.

I can't imagine how I would have managed this on my own.

She decided to make them an apple cake with her family recipe as soon as she could go shopping, which she expected might take a few days until Rose was feeling better.

Morris found Dr. Johnson and asked him about payment.

"Thank you, Morris. That will be $25 for Rose's analysis, her medication, and for Regina staying in the room overnight."

Morris pulled out several bills, but not enough to cover the hospital costs.

"I'm short four dollars, but I get paid on Friday. Can I bring you the rest?"

Dr. Johnson's expression soured.

"That would be fine. I'm counting on you to bring it on Friday."

Morris collected Regina and Rose and they found a taxi to take them home. Fortunately, Regina still had the money Harold had given her.

She couldn't wait to get home. After a meal of leftover chicken, she slept a good part of the afternoon, while Morris kept Rose in dry diapers.

The next morning, Regina fed Rose and immediately offered her a bottle of water, washed her bottom, dried her, and put her on a blanket with a diaper covering her as she was not sure it was a good idea for her to be totally naked in front of Louis.

She didn't think Rose needed any more fever medicine, and by her third day out of the hospital, Rose was her perky self again, much to Regina's relief.

Morris went back to the hospital and gave Dr. Johnson four dollars.

When Regina felt Rose was well enough, she decided to take her and Louis back to the playground. On the way out, she called on Harold and his wife to ask about their daughter, who was a year older than Louis.

She knocked on their door late that morning and a short woman with blonde hair answered.

"Hi, I think you remember me? I'm Regina, the women you and your husband helped last week. I want to thank you so much. I was so frightened, and you and your husband were so wonderful."

"Of course. I'm Sonia, and this is my daughter, Gitla. She just turned four and your Louis is three. Such a nice young man."

"Thank you. I've been wondering if you ever take Gitla to the playground on Maxwell Street."

"I've heard about it, but no. I bake most afternoons, and Edam Michnik sells my products for me."

Maybe making an apple cake for a professional baker is not a good idea.

"I usually go there each day during the week. I'd be happy to take Gitla with me so she and Louis could play together."

"How thoughtful of you. I'm sure Gitla would love not being stuck with me while I'm baking. We haven't lived here much longer than you, so as I'm always baking, I haven't had time to find the playground. I'm just waiting for Gitla to be old enough for school."

Regina suggested that on the days Sonia was not baking, she could join them at the playground. Sonia agreed and hoped to do that.

As the days grew warmer, Rose had no more symptoms. Regina kept giving her water, changed her diaper more often and made sure to air out her bottom whenever she could.

While her days were pleasant and she and the other women shared stories about their lives in Poland, Regina felt an undercurrent of concern with the growing news of increasing antisemitism in central Europe.

Dziennik Związkowy, a Polish language newspaper published in Chicago, reported on how the press and the government in Warsaw were jointly urging Poles to boycott not just Jewish shops, but Jewish doctors, lawyers, singers, and performers, encouraging all relations between Poles and Jews to cease.

This campaign was led by the new *Gazeta Poranna* newspaper, and Jan Jeleński's newspaper, *Rola*, called for strict separation between Poles and Jews and eventually an all-Catholic Poland. The *Gazeta Warszawska*, a fascist journal produced by Roman Dmowski's National Democratic party, was even more strident in its antisemitic propaganda.

Pravda, the Russian newspaper, was also part of the action. They printed a furious editorial denouncing Jews elected to local government posts who wanted to peacefully work out the differences between Poles and Jews to help them assimilate more fully into Polish society.

The situation is all too clear.

Regina wondered about her father's job with Henryk Boleslaw's leather shop in Warsaw.

Does he still have a job? Will Henryk keep him on and stand beside him? What about school for Dina and Kejla? Is it still open?

She worried about additional attacks on synagogues and rabbis.

What about Leopold, and the Jewish Bund party in Mokotów?

Regina was not one to say, "I told you so" but she wanted to remind everyone who dismissed her concerns that she was right, even though she wished she wasn't.

It was 1912, and what Regina feared most had come true. The Poles were turning on the Jews, including many of her friends and neighbors.

The election that year culminated in an anti-Jewish boycott against their workers and products, which hurt their community, but when all was said and done, the boycott consisted mainly of vitriolic antisemitic bluster and little else. It did not garner widespread support among the Polish population, which greeted the boycott with the same apathy as the earlier Duma elections.

The moral impact, however, was enormous. Relations between Poles and Jews was deeply fractured and made it possible for broad sections of Polish society to advocate radical measures, such as expelling Jews and closing their businesses. Jews of all backgrounds, religious and secular, came to be seen as "ungrateful guests," and Polish and Jewish interests were invariably viewed as mutually exclusive and antagonistic.

Signs were posted on Christian shops, urging customers to "Buy Only Among Christians" and "Buy from Your Own Kind." The posting of young ruffians in front of Jewish shops to "persuade" their customers not to trade with Jews indicated that participation in the boycott was far from voluntary. In fact, most of the violence, according to police reports, involved Poles attempting to stop other Poles from dealing with Jews. Outside Warsaw, the boycott was virtually ignored, despite the Catholic clergy's best efforts to promote it.

What Regina read in the Polish newspapers alarmed her more than ever. She was terrified and didn't understand why her family didn't see what was happening in front of their eyes.

The next day, when she went to the park, it was empty. Regina stopped at the edge of the playground. There were a few toys in the sandbox, but no children. She shuddered.

I can only guess what happened, the bike marauders were there again.
She quickly turned and left.

West 14th Street
1912

40

If Only

Regina went back to the park the next day and her friends were there. She sighed with relief. No one said anything about why the park had been empty the day before, but she thought she probably knew the answer. It felt like there was an unspoken agreement among the women not to talk about what happened, but they all knew.

She enjoyed her time with Bina and the other mothers and her neighbor, Sonia. They went to the playground together and took turns making treats for all the children.

Her enjoyment, however, was tempered by the fear and sadness she felt about her family and friends back home. Her letters went mostly unanswered, and Regina wasn't sure if her family wasn't writing back or if her letters were being intercepted by some nefarious group of people who threw them away.

I'm helpless to do anything about it. What if I get someone else to write home on my behalf? What if I write to her father's employer, Mr. Bolestaw, to ask about the family? I must know if they are safe.

Regina was also upset about Morris returning to his nightly outings with his work buddies. She had hoped those days were over after Rose got sick, but that optimism was short-lived.

Finding playmates for Louis gave her some relief, especially when she and Sonia took turns having the children play at each other's apartment and at the playground. It gave each of them some quiet time to rest and explore whatever interests they had without their kids underfoot.

If only I could find a way to connect with my relatives.

On her day to take Louis and Gitla to the playground, Regina stopped at Michnik's to see if he had any suggestions. She didn't know why he would, but something told her to ask.

When Edam saw Regina enter, he nodded hello.

"Nice to see you, Regina. What can I do for you?"

"Edam, I have a different reason for visiting you today. I'm sure you've seen the news from Poland and have read about the rise in antisemitism there."

"Unfortunately, yes. That's why I'm so glad I got my family out. It's only going to get worse. Even with the hoodlums we have here, it's still better than there. You realize that don't you?"

"Yes. That's why I'm here. Have you been writing to anyone back home? Have they answered?"

"I got my family to leave, so we don't have anyone left there to write to, *Baruch Hashem*."

"You're so lucky. I couldn't get anybody in my family to leave with me because they didn't believe there was anything to worry about. Now, we know that isn't true. None of my letters are being answered and I don't think they are getting them, and their letters back might be getting intercepted. What can I do?"

Edam shrugged.

"I'm wondering if a letter came from someone else, like from a business, maybe they would get through. What do you think?"

"I see what you are thinking. It couldn't hurt, and I would be happy to try and help you. They may intercept my letters, too, or their letters back to me, but let's try anyway. Write your letter and I'll send it from the store."

"I can't thank you enough. Toda raba. I will bring a letter tomorrow."

A month later, a letter to Regina arrived from Poland.

Writing from Edam's store worked!

Regina opened it right away. She was too excited to wait until she got home to read it. Tears streamed down her face as she read.

"Henryk had to let your father go for both of their safety. He is working from home, but his only customers are Jews. It is not enough, but we are being very frugal. The Jewish Labor Bund offices are closed. The synagogue hired a couple of local youths to stand as armed guards during Friday night and Saturday morning services, for the safety of the congregants walking to and from prayers."

Regina had to wipe her eyes before she could read further:

"Life has not been easy. The girls had to stop going to school as there are student thugs giving the Jewish students a bad time. Otherwise, we stay close to home and only visit other Jewish families. We miss you and love you. Hugs to Louis and Rose."

While it saddened her to hear the news, Regina was not surprised.

Maybe now they will listen to me and come to Chicago?

When she returned home, she wrote a letter back with a plea to leave and join her in America.

Leave while there is still time to get out!

Her pleas fell on deaf ears. The family was sure that things would get better, that these new developments would change, and that the elected officials now in power would not last.

The next day, she returned to the store and waited until the customers left to share her anxiety with Mitchnik. Regina couldn't stop what she was feeling and waved the letter in front of her.

"Edam, how can they see what is happening and not believe it's a sign of things to come? It doesn't make sense!"

I wanted to let it go and get on with my life, but how?

While Regina knew that what she did was right for her and Louis and now Rose, she was depressed that her predictions were coming true.

I need to let it go and get on with my own life here in America, but I also know that this is impossible, at least for now.

Her concern about her family faded away the next morning when she woke up feeling nauseous. It had been two years since Rose was born, and Regina feared she could be pregnant again.

I need to tell Morris. Maybe having another child will dampen his need to go out every night after work.

The days and weeks blended into each other. It felt like only a few months before Regina woke up with labor pains. She managed to get to Sonia's front door before the contractions came faster and more intense. Morris had left for work already, so he couldn't help her.

Sonia grabbed Gitla, Louis and Rose and rushed them into the other room as she settled Regina on her bed and tucked some pillows behind her.

"Let me get someone to find a midwife. I won't be long."

Regina was huffing and puffing short breaths, trying to control her labor pains as best as she could.

Sonia came back alone.

"The midwife is on her way. How are you doing?"

"Okay, I guess. At least I'm not having back pain the way I did with Louis and Rose, so this is a piece of cake."

Regina tried to laugh.

"Oof! They're coming faster now. I need to push."

"Oy gevalt. Can you wait?"

Regina let out a cry.

"No, I can't help it. They're coming faster and faster. Can you tell if the baby is crowning?"

Regina let out a large cry. Her face turned beet red as she bared down.

"It's coming!"

Sonia squeezed Regina's hand and put an arm around her back.

"Okay, Regina, do the best you can. When it stops, lay back and breathe."

The front door opened, and they heard a woman's voice.

"Where is the mom-to-be?"

"In the bedroom, right here! Her name is Regina."

"Hi Regina. Looks like Louis and Rose will have another sibling any minute. I see things are moving along quickly. Let's have a look."

She bent down to check between Regina's legs.

"You're getting there. I can see the baby's crown. When do you think you can give us a good push?"

Regina gasped for air.

"What can I do for you?" Sonia said.

"Hot compresses are good. Let's be sure Regina has good back support."

Sonia brought several hot towels and cushions from the sofa.

Seconds later, they heard a cry.

"It's a beautiful and healthy baby girl, Regina. Mazel Tov!"

The midwife laughed.

"This certainly didn't take long. Consider it my gift to you."

Regina was so preoccupied with her new infant that the midwife's offer didn't register. But Sonia heard it loud and clear.

"That is so generous of you. On behalf of the Butlaw family, I thank you so much. When Regina is less preoccupied, I'll be sure to let her know."

"I hardly did a thing. She was so far along, and everything was going well, so it was just a couple of pushes and that was it. I wish all my deliveries were so easy. I can get myself home. Good luck!"

Sonia put the kettle on for tea, checked the children, and brought in food to give them lunch. Then, she checked on Regina and her new baby girl.

"Another daughter. How are you feeling?"

"I'm exhausted. How does she look?"

"She's gorgeous and she seems to have all her fingers and toes."

Regina tried to offer her breast, but the baby wasn't interested.

"What are you going to name her?"

"I'll see when Morris gets home. I named Rose myself, so I'll see if he has any names in mind."

Regina closed her eyes and thought of her mother.

If only she could see me now.

41

Outnumbered

Morris chose the name Josephine, in memory of his aunt. Regina was pleased that he was kind to her and less grouchy around the children, but she worried that it was probably temporary.

Everyone loves a new baby, but he won't be around much to help me take care of her. That's all on me, and my life is getting more difficult.

During a visit from Sonia, she shared her frustration.

"Oy, getting three children ready to go out takes all morning. By the time I've got everyone ready, it's lunchtime, and I'm exhausted."

I didn't tell Sonia that sometimes I wish I didn't have children at all, but I can never share that with anyone. After all, it's not their fault for being born. They're helpless little children who depend on me, but it's just so trying!

Regina was still amazed that she had even gotten pregnant.

I still don't know what he does when he isn't home.

She timed her interactions with him carefully, as he always seemed to be in a bad mood at home. She went out of her way to be pleasant because she and the children needed his support.

"Morris, I'm so glad you are home for dinner. I made your favorite, stuffed cabbage with roasted potatoes. I kept it warm for you."

"I expect you to keep my dinner warm after my long day at the tannery."

When she asked for money, he gave it to her, although she was careful not to ask for much beyond the necessities, like food and clothes for the growing family and her modest weekly allowance.

Sonia gave Regina some of the baked goods she sold at Michnik's. They helped her reduce her shopping time, which had become more difficult to manage with three children.

This time around, with a new baby, Morris seemed less belligerent than he was when Rose was born.

"How are you doing with so many children about?"

Did I hear him right? He's asking me about my welfare?

"Thank you for checking on me. It's challenging, but Louis is a big help when he comes home from school. You know, he can walk back and forth by himself, now that he is six years old."

Morris' calm and gracious demeanor barely lasted a month after Rose's hospital visit. When it was clear she was no longer in danger, he went back to drinking with his co-workers, but not every night as before. He came home on Friday nights when Regina made a special Shabbos chicken.

One evening, after Morris finished his dinner, Regina tried to learn more about his work life.

"Would you like to invite one of your work friends over for dinner? We have enough room for a guest."

Regina hoped he would give her some information about his colleagues. She was curious to know if any of them were Jewish.

"Why would they want to come here with all these children about?"

"It seems like you have made some good friends, so I would like to meet them and make a nice dinner."

"They would not be interested, and they already have their own children."

Some of his buddies have families, like us. I wished I could meet them, but it won't happen. I wonder if those mothers share my disappointment.

Regina's friendship with Sonia and Bina mattered a great deal to her. If they were aware of how indifferent Morris was to her and the children, they didn't say anything. But she knew she could count on them as friends.

When the Chicago winter weather brought its typical snow and ice, going outside became prohibitive, and even walking a few blocks to another building to make new friendships became difficult. Since Regina had to rely on the people in her building for companionship, her options were limited.

She was relieved when spring came around.

Chicago
1915

42

Morris Makes a Move

Louis was now seven, Rose five, and Josephine nearly four.

Finally! No more diapers and baby bottles!

She had mornings mostly to herself once she got Louis and Rose off to school with their lunches and schoolbooks. Josephine had one more year before she would attend kindergarten.

Chicago was a city that worked hard to educate its children. Large school buildings were sprouting up all over. The kids attended John Smith Public School on 13th Street. A playground was located on the same street, which made it convenient for Regina to spend time with Josephine there.

The school was only four blocks from their apartment, so Regina would bundle up Josephine, get Louis and Rose dressed, and walk the kids to school, and then walk them home at the end of their day.

Morris was oblivious to their day-to-day activities and development. He never asked what they were learning or what their interests were.

If life is peaceful and Morris pays the bills, I can forget the rest. After all, where would I go if I left Morris? I have no choice but to stay.

Whenever Morris came home, Regina hugged him.

"How are you today, my husband?"

When she tried talking to him about his life, he brushed her off.

"Why do you want to know?"

"Because you are my husband, and we have children together. I care about you, Morris. I want to know how you are feeling. I also like to cook what you want. Is there anything special you would like?"

"Stop badgering me, will you? If I want anything from you, I'll tell you. Everything is fine, okay?"

Rebuffed and hurt, Regina reacted by backing off for at least a few days or even a week or more, before she asked him again about his life and what he would like for dinner.

One night, Morris came directly home from work in time for dinner.

"I've got this great opportunity to open a new leather shop in Houston, Texas. I'll be managing the entire project. It will mean a nice bump in pay, so I couldn't turn it down and no one else wanted to make the move."

Regina was stunned.

Move to Texas? Houston? That will mean a huge change. I will miss all my friends, who have been such a great support system for me, too.

She didn't know how to respond.

I doubt anything will be any different between us there. But will Morris be happier? Maybe that will help our marriage?

"I guess that is great news, Morris. You seem very excited. I'm so happy about this new opportunity. When do we need to be ready to move?"

At first, Morris didn't say anything.

Oh my God, did I say something wrong again?

"I guess I didn't explain that this move will be just for me. You don't have to go. I'll go myself."

Regina stopped wiping her hands on a towel she was holding and stared at Morris.

"I don't understand. You would go without me and the children? What are you saying? Are we getting divorced?"

As Regina tried to hold back her tears, Morris rolled his eyes.

"Did I say we were getting divorced? Did I? All I said is that the company is moving me to Texas, and you can stay here with the kids and your friends. They will pay for me to come back from time to time to see you."

Regina's head was swirling as she tried to comprehend what Morris had just told her.

"What will we do for money if you don't live here? How will we manage? I don't understand what this means, Morris."

This is much more than just another bump in the road.

235

"I'll tell you what this means, Regina. I am moving to Houston to head up a new leather factory for this company. It also means a raise in my salary. I will send you money every month to take care of your expenses, so you don't have to worry about that. I will come back every couple of months to check in on you and the kids."

He poured himself a glass of wine.

"So, you have already accepted this new job without even discussing it with me?"

"What is there to discuss? This is a great opportunity for both of us because I get a nice raise, which will help you, too."

As Morris settled into his favorite chair and allowed Rose to crawl onto his lap, Regina turned her attention to cleaning up the kitchen. Whenever she felt anxious, that was her way to cope.

43

Another Baby

With Morris in Texas, Regina felt guilty that she enjoyed the peace and quiet instead of the anxiety he used to bring home with him every night. She shared her thoughts with Sonia one afternoon at the park.

"So far, Morris had been good at sending money every month. I get a cable from Western Union with more than enough to cover our rent, food, and incidentals. Plus, to be honest, the apartment is more comfortable without another adult living there."

True to his promise, Morris came home every couple of months. Regina wasn't sure whether it was about missing his family or if he was his checking up on her to see how she was using his money.

She wrote to him often, hoping his new position made him feel better about his family.

"Morris, do you miss us? Could you come home more often? Surely the owner knows you have a family in Chicago. Our children miss their father."

He didn't respond right away. Then, in a stern voice, he made Regina feel even worse.

"Of course, they know I have a family here, and they offered to move you to Texas, but I knew you didn't want to leave your friends and start over in a new place where you don't know anyone."

Regina opened her mouth to say something but stopped.

Morris made this decision by himself, without consulting me.

"You told me they were only going to move you. You never told me I was expected to go or that you told them I didn't want to."

"Well, you didn't, did you?"

Regina was confused.

What is he saying? I never told him I didn't want to go to Houston.

Regina was tired of being intimidated by Morris. She put her hands on her hips and addressed him without fear.

"No, I never told you I wouldn't move to Houston with you. I never said that! This is something you decided all on your own."

Uncharacteristically, Morris backed down.

"Maybe you are right."

I could go down there with him, but I must admit I am enjoying my new circle of friends. Am I a bad wife for choosing not to go?

"You told me this move was temporary, that you were sent to open up the facility and then return, right?"

"Yes, Regina. Of course, it's taking longer than I expected to hire new men to do the work. I'm not exactly sure when or how they will get it running without me."

That sounds too convenient. But I need the money Morris sends home each month.

Louis, now almost nine years old, was getting big, and he constantly needed new clothes, especially to protect him during Chicago's freezing cold winters. Rose did, too, but Josephine could wear her hand-me-downs.

Apparently, Morris liked to brag about his kids. Regina had overheard him describing Rose, now seven, to a neighbor as a "blonde-haired, blue-eyed beauty, a real little lady," and he thought of Josephine, barely five, who had dark hair and blue eyes, as being more like a "spirited Irish lady."

I guess he can brag about his children without bothering to raise them.

On one trip home, Morris was especially affectionate with Regina and the children. He brought gifts for the kids and suggested they all go out to a restaurant for dinner. Little Italy was just a few blocks away and Morris had already picked out a nice little place.

What a huge surprise! Going out to eat is not something we ever do with the children, and it's so expensive.

Morris insisted and Regina was happy to have the night off and let someone else do the cooking and clean up.

"It's a special day being with my beautiful family tonight. It will be fun."

After returning home, Morris insisted that all three children sleep together in the main room. Regina had been allowing the girls to sleep with her in the big bed, but since Morris was home, the bedroom was for adults only.

The next morning, Regina made breakfast for everyone and kept the kids home from school so they could spend the day with their father.

Morris was pleasant, but he didn't stay long at all, insisting that he needed to check in at the factory where he used to work.

Regina had to improvise.

"Hey, my schatzelehs, how about we all go to the park together for a change? I'll send notes with you tomorrow to school to explain."

Morris left the next day on a train back to Houston, but not before he lectured the kids about getting good grades and doing their chores.

Funny that he's suddenly interested in their school and their behavior.

She decided to keep her mouth shut, kissed him good-bye, and asked him to please write, which he rarely did.

I don't want to cause any strife because so far, he has been reliable when it comes to sending money home.

One morning, about a month later, Regina woke up with an uneasy feeling in her stomach. She tried to ignore it and passed it off as something she ate. However, she knew deep down what it was.

I don't need another baby when it already takes so much work to manage these three I already have.

She went next door.

"Sonia, I'm afraid I'm pregnant again. I don't want to have another child. I can barely cope with the three I have. What can I do?"

Regina sobbed.

"I don't know what to do. What can I do?"

"My poor dear friend, I'm so sorry."

Sonia hugged Regina.

"My dear friend, I think we should contact the midwife. I've heard she has some remedies for this kind of thing. You must pay extra for those services, but I'm sure it's less expensive than having a baby."

Sonia laughed. Regina tried to smile, but it didn't come easily.

"She's a good Polish woman," said Sonia, "and she is compassionate. I only know her first name, Zofia. She doesn't live far. Why don't I go there and if she isn't home, I'll leave her a note. In the meantime, boil some water in a big pot and stand over it to let the steam go up inside you. You know what I mean. Sometimes this helps."

Regina remembered what they did when they thought Chaja Fajga might be pregnant, when the midwife gave her herbs to bring on her monthly.

"Let's see if she can come when the kids are in school."

An hour later, Sonia returned with Zofia, who was carrying her bag of tools and herbs.

"We meet again," Zofia said. "I understand that you wish to end your pregnancy if possible. Do you know how far along you might be?"

"Thank you for coming. I expect I may be four weeks. I just missed my monthly this past week. I also know the symptoms by now. I'm so sorry."

Regina teared up and shook her head.

"I used a sponge. I even coated it with olive oil because I knew Morris was going to want relations when he came back from Texas. I was prepared, but apparently it didn't work. I'm very upset. I don't want any more children. It's all I can do to manage the three I have. The medicine worked for my sister in Poland. Why won't it work here?"

Zofia and Sonia put their arms around Regina and asked her to listen carefully.

"Maybe your sister wasn't pregnant," Zofia said. "I have a remedy that pregnant women have been using for years, but it can make you feel very ill, and you should not be alone for several days. It's made with natural herbs, but I like to start with old fashioned castor oil, which will give you a cramping stomach and diarrhea. Let's start with that and a very hot bath. If you start to cramp, that's good, especially if you bleed. I also have tansy oil, pennyroyal, rue, and ergot, which I use in small amounts because it is quite strong. I must tell you that they are not my first choice because the side effects can be serious. I only use them if a woman is unmarried and may have been raped. I'd rather not use them on you, but if you tell me you are desperate and can't live with another baby, what choice do I have, even though, I don't think that is the case with you.".

Regina sat and listened.

How desperate do I really feel? What will having another baby do to my life and how will it affect my other children? Am I up for these dangerous herbs? Chaja Fajga had no other children when she was raped, so the extra risk was reasonable.

"Thank you. I've heard about the herbal remedies, that they can damage the body, but do they really work?"

"Let's try the castor oil first."

Zofia offered two tablespoons to Regina. When the bath was ready, Sonia helped Regina into it. The water was much hotter than she had ever felt, but she managed.

All I want to do is end this pregnancy! I don't want to risk my life. I have three kids who need me! And right now, I don't care if the herbs make it impossible for me to have any more children. That's not my concern.

After the bath, Regina felt some cramping and took another tablespoon of castor oil. Zofia said she would come back to check on Regina.

The next day wasn't any different. More hot baths and castor oil and more cramping and diarrhea, but no blood.

"This isn't working. What can I do? I can't imagine another baby in this house? How can that be?"

Regina couldn't accept risking her health by ingesting the herbs, even a small amount. She also wasn't willing to stick a rod into her womb and risk death. Zofia made it clear she would never do that, no matter how desperate someone might be.

After four days of castor oil and hot baths, nothing changed, and Regina continued to have morning sickness.

This baby doesn't want to go away.

Sonia stayed with Regina and Josephine until Louis and Rose came home from school. No matter what, life had to go on.

The Windy City
1916

44

A Lonely Baby

Despite Regina's best efforts, Dorothy Sandra Butlaw was born. The birth was easier than Regina's first three, and her friends were there to feed the children and distract them so Regina could get some rest.

"I don't know how I could manage without you. You are so kind. How can I thank you?"

When the weather wasn't too cold, Regina walked Louis, Rose, and Josephine to school while she pushed Dorothy in a stroller. She often bought a newspaper and read it at the playground while the baby slept.

As winter came, Regina bundled the children with extra sweaters and coats. Louis needed larger jackets and shoes as he continued to grow. Josephine and Dorothy wore hand-me-downs from Rose because clothing was expensive, even when Regina shopped at second-hand stores.

She sent letters to Morris, telling him she needed extra money to keep the children warm during the freezing Chicago winters.

"Morris, please remember that the winters here are bitter cold. Your daughters are growing and need new clothes and shoes. Louis is growing so fast he can't even wear his clothes from six months ago. I keep the jackets and shoes for the girls, but I don't have enough. Please send extra money for clothes, I beg you."

Regina dressed the children in as many layers as she could manage. Sonia and her friends offered Louis clothes and shoes from their husbands, and even though they were too large, at least he wasn't squeezing into shoes that were too small for him.

Regina went to the Western Union office to look for the next money order from Morris, but it wasn't there.

It must be lost because it's time.

She wrote again to plead with her husband, reminding him that the icy winters were dangerous without the proper attire.

Sonia stopped by with some old clothes her daughter had outgrown, and Bina brought clothes her children no longer wore. Regina was so grateful, especially when they also dropped off extra food.

Regina shared her humiliation with Morris.

"Do you know what you have done to your family? We are getting food and clothes from my friends. Are you trying to put us out on the street?"

As winter passed to spring and the weather improved, Regina was relieved that she didn't have to worry if the children were warm enough.

1917 was turning out to be a difficult year for Regina. Louis was now nine, Rose eight, Josephine six, and Dorothy was nearly one. Louis was a big help when Regina needed to go to the store, but she couldn't ask him to do much more than that.

He's my son, not my babysitter.

Morris never returned to Chicago.

The silence from Houston left Regina feeling as though she was deserted on an island in the middle of the ocean, and the waves were getting larger.

Without a boat, I will drown.

She struggled to come to terms with her husband's disappearance.

Has Morris really abandoned his family? Was I such a bad wife and mother that I don't deserve his love? What happened to the man I once knew?

Their marriage had become just a fact of Regina's personal history. She knew that she had to focus on the sheer survival of her family, which meant protecting her children at any cost.

I hate complaining to my friends. I'm sure they get tired of hearing about my problems, and I don't want them to think they have to constantly take care of me. It's humiliating. I feel like I'm barely hanging on to my dignity.

Bina told Regina about some community services available for families in need. Regina packed up the kids and found her way to the office of Family and Support Services on West Chicago Avenue to see if she could get help with rent and food. She learned she was eligible, as she had not received a check from Morris for more than two months and had four children to support.

The social worker took Morris's contact information and sent an official demand letter, but they got no response, and on the second attempt, the letter came back as undeliverable.

Why me? Why is my life being torn to shreds? Why don't I have a caring and attentive husband like Sonia and Bina? What happened to him?

Life was a constant battle. While her friends understood her frustration, Regina was no longer the fun and clever woman she used to be. Now, she was a bitter woman who blamed life for handing her such a rotten deal.

She tried not to constantly lament her circumstances, but except for the joy she felt with her children, she had nothing to be happy about.

Social services gave her some money, which she used for new clothes for Louis and Rose. Josephine and Dorothy continued to wear hand-me-downs from Rose and her friends' children.

For one last time before winter, she joined her friends at the park.

"Sonia and Bina, my dear friends. I've been thinking about moving away from Chicago since Morris is no longer around, and the winters are so bitter and difficult."

This news should not be a total shock to them. Why would I stay in a city that is so difficult? It's not like I have family here.

Regina spent all her waking hours dealing with survival. She calculated that it would be impossible for her to work and bring in her own money because she would have to pay someone to take care of Dorothy all day, and her other three after school. Louis was still too young to do that.

Pulling a meal together was getting more difficult and Regina couldn't shake herself free of the recriminations she felt, along with the worries, a lack of trust, and growing fears for her future.

She took Bina's advice and contacted HIAS to ask if they could help. She also contacted Jewish Family Services to see if they could have it officially declared that Morris had abandoned his family. A document like that would entitle her to a larger grant of public assistance.

Some people suggested to Regina that she send Louis to work in the cloak factories that hired children.

As miserable as I am, that's where I draw the line. Louis needs to get an education, so he doesn't end up working dead-end jobs and make himself unfit to take care of himself or a family someday.

The job was tempting, though, as they needed the money, but Regina never told Louis about it.

Something must change, and soon.

When she saw Bina and Sonia, she thanked them for everything they had done and begged their forgiveness for being such a burden.

"You both have been so supportive. Who could ask for more?"

Regina knew that no matter how much she tried to enjoy the friendships she had made at the playground, she couldn't avoid the frustration, fear, and disappointment that her situation had forced her to face.

Something must change.

California
1918

45

Welcome to Los Angeles

Regina's world was shrinking as she focused each day on surviving. Thanks to HAIS, Jewish Family Services (JFS) and Cook County, she received clothing and rent relief, but she knew that accepting charity was not a sensible long-term strategy.

After growing up through bone-chilling Polish winters and the biting cold of Chicago, she decided she couldn't subject herself or her children to another year of suffering.

I could save a lot of money on clothes in a warmer climate. I have lovely friends here, but we can't survive any longer like this. It's time to make a big significant change.

The organizational skills she learned at the Bund could now come in handy. She discovered there was a large Jewish community in Los Angeles, California, and JFS had suggested that they could help her move there by securing her discounted seats on the train for a sleeper room that would allow the family to stay together.

She went to her children's school to get their records, said goodbye to her landlord and friends, and headed west.

Once again, Regina was heading into the unknown without knowing a soul, and while she spoke a little English, it was still quite limited. Louis and Rose spoke the language better than she did, and she was trying to keep up with Josephine.

The train took nearly three days until they reached La Grande terminal and met a woman from Jewish Family Services.

"I hope you are looking for me. I'm Regina Butlaw, and these are my children. Thank you for helping us."

"Yes, of course. Come, you must be exhausted. Let's get you to the hotel we use for new arrivals. You can rest there and eat dinner, and we will come by tomorrow morning at ten."

Regina started to sob. The young representative wasn't sure what to do.

"Oh, my goodness. Did I say something wrong?"

Regina regained her self-control.

"No, not at all. You just don't know what I've been through. Seeing you here, waiting for us, feels so welcoming."

It's been so long, and I've been waiting for a fresh start like this.

Since she was so used to arguing for everything she needed from Morris, Regina knew that she needed to manage her tendency to challenge everyone, including the JFS counselors who were only trying to help.

The next day, inside their office in West Los Angeles, the counselors suggested the most convenient place to live where the children would have easy access to good schools. Rhoda, a volunteer with JFS, instructed Regina about the steps she needed to do to get settled into her new life.

She sat next to Regina on a trolley that took them to a furnished one-bedroom apartment on St. Charles Place near Rimpau Boulevard in the Fairfax section of Los Angeles, a largely Jewish community not far from West Hollywood. The bedroom had one bed and a crib. The living room had a bed and a daybed sofa that could sleep two children comfortably.

Everything seems bright and new compared to the heaviness in Chicago.

Regina was exhausted but grateful.

"I hope you like your new home," said Rhoda. "Just take it easy and rest. We gave you some money to buy food, and your rent has been taken care of for two months."

It's too early to consider what I must do next, but that time will come soon enough, like tomorrow. For now, let's get some food and some sleep!

The next morning, Regina dragged herself out of bed, poured cereal for breakfast and took the children to their new school on Saturn Street, which was not far from their apartment.

She introduced herself to the school principal, who took her information and files about the children.

I can't rely on charity forever, but I don't know yet what else I can do.

Regina's English was still not good enough to secure a job, and she hadn't had time to practice or take classes to reach the level she would need to qualify as a translator.

The next day, while the children were in school and Dorothy napped on the floor, Regina took their laundry to the utility room in the basement of the apartment building. A woman putting her clothes into a dryer eyed Regina and said hello in Polish.

"It's so nice to find another Polish woman to talk to," she said. "My name is Aliza, and we live on the second floor in 203."

"It's so nice to meet you. I'm Regina, and we also live on the second floor in 206, just down the hall."

"How are you settling in? You must be exhausted from traveling all the way from Chicago all alone with four children."

"Yes. I got sick of the ice and snow. I figured that if I must be on my own, I might as well be warm."

"Well, it should be easier here for all of you. It never gets very cold at all, and we certainly have no snow."

"My family is just me and my children. Their father, if you can call him that, lives in Texas and seems to have forgotten he has a wife and children."

"I'm sorry, Regina, I didn't mean to upset you."

Regina sighed.

"I'm sorry. It's okay. I'm just dealing with so much right now. Morris has disappeared and I don't receive any help to take care of my kids."

Son of a bitch.

"Did JFS have any suggestions? They will not let you starve you know."

"Yes, yes, of course. But how long can they support us? Right now, I don't know what to do."

Regina sat down and started to cry.

Just talking about it is overwhelming. I hate myself for being so bitter. I never liked feeling this way in Poland, and I don't like it now, either. I wish I could just be happy and grateful for all the help we've received. I want to feel light and cheery and live the American dream.

"Oh, my goodness, Regina, I'm so sorry. I didn't mean to pry."

Aliza bent down and put her arms around Regina.

"Does JFS know you have no support?"

"I'm supposed to see them tomorrow at their office."

Aliza stood up and took Regina's hands.

"Tell them exactly what you told me. They need to know you have no support from your good-for-nothing husband. You can't just sit here wringing your hands. How are you supposed to pay rent and buy food? See what they suggest. They do not want you to starve or lose your place to live through no fault of your own. If you like, I will go with you while the kids are in school."

Chaja Fajga was right. I married a man I didn't really know.

Aliza's offer made Regina cry again.

"You really want to come with me?"

"Regina, I received a lot of support and friendship when I got here, and it made a big difference. You need the same thing, and it's nothing to feel ashamed about. President Teddy Roosevelt started a program called Children and Families, and they helped us and lots of other immigrants. I'm sure JFS will help you apply."

Regina nodded.

"If we go in the morning, we should be back in time for when your kids get out of school. The office is not far from here. Can you meet me in the lobby at ten tomorrow?"

"Of course. Thank you so much Aliza."

Regina went upstairs, changed Dorothy's diaper, and gave her a bottle.

The next morning, after she walked the children to school, she and Dorothy went to the lobby. Aliza had a little boy, named Natan, who was four years old.

"Let's take the trolley on San Vincente to Fairfax."

"How much is the trolley?"

"I've got it," said Aliza. "You can bake me something sometime."

"Why are you doing this, Aliza? I don't know how I can repay your kindness. You don't even know me."

"I know you are a woman with big troubles through no fault of your own. If I can help you get back on your feet, then it's a mitzvah on my part."

When they arrived at the offices, a woman at the front desk took Regina's name, made some notes on her circumstances, and asked her to take a seat and wait. It wasn't long before she was called to see someone.

"Hi Regina, I'm Leah, your intake counselor. You have some serious problems, don't you?"

Regina nodded.

"You and Morris are legally married, but since he has abandoned you and the children, you need to file for support and should probably get a divorce so the court can sue for support on your behalf. Do you understand?"

Regina shuddered when she heard the word "divorce."

Again! It sounds so final. No one in our family has been shamed like this. I can't believe I'm discussing this, let alone so openly.

"How do I do that? No one knows where Morris is right now."

Regina tried not to cry.

"We will help you. In the meantime, it appears you will need support to pay your rent after the two-month subsidy ends. You will also need money for food and clothes. We work with Catholic Charities, and they are very good. We will help you file for support from a government program called the Children's Bureau. Please fill out this paperwork I will give you. I gather you can read and write, yes? If you need help with the English, we can assist you. You speak Polish, right?"

"Yes, and Yiddish and Russian."

"That's impressive, but you must improve your English right now."

Regina nodded.

After she completed the paperwork, Leah said they would make an appointment with the local court and send Regina a notice about when and where to appear.

"Someone from the federation will meet you there and represent you."

Before Regina left, Leah gave her coupons for food at the Catholic Charity Food Bank.

"There are several trolleys that go that way from your apartment. Just tell the driver where you want to go. They all know it."

For the first time in months, Regina felt some relief from the fear she felt that she could end up on the street with her children. She knew they would have food now, and that the rent would be paid for a while longer.

Why must it be like this? Why have I been reduced to a charity case? What would Mama and Papa think if they knew?

Regina continually thought about Morris and kept replaying their demise in her head.

I need to stop, but I can't. I want to know what made him grow so cold.

Regina got to know the trolley lines that took her to the food bank and the JFS office. They filed on her behalf for a divorce from Morris, and asked for alimony and child support, but so far there was no word from him, and all the official letters were returned, marked as undeliverable.

46

Surgery and Tears

Regina woke up with a sharp pain in her abdomen. When she tried to stand, she doubled over, holding her stomach.

What is wrong with me?

"Louis, please come here and help me stand up."

Louis tried to help her take a few steps.

"Momma, what's wrong? Why are you holding yourself?"

Regina didn't answer. All she knew was that she was in pain and needed help. She would not be able to walk the kids to school or care for Dorothy.

"Louis, I need to see a doctor. You must stay home today and watch the children. There is plenty of food in the house and I'll leave you some money just in case. I'll be back as soon as I can."

She got herself dressed and hobbled down the stairs and walked to the corner where the bus stopped. She boarded the next one that came, not paying attention to where it was supposed to go. As she boarded, she doubled over in pain, and her forehead dotted with sweat.

"I need to go to the hospital. Would you take me there, please?"

"Oh my God! Are you okay?" the driver said.

Regina held the railing with one hand and her stomach with the other.

"Folks, we are making a short detour."

"Don't worry about the fare," he said.

He drove the bus as close to Los Angeles County Hospital as he could and stopped a block away on State Street. The driver pointed out the hospital to Regina.

"I'm sorry I can't get closer. You see it?"

"Yes. Thank you."

A passenger further back stood up.

"I'll help her to the front door. If you have to go, I'll get the next bus."

Regina held onto the stranger as she carefully reached the sidewalk. They walked slowly to the hospital, where a young woman greeted them in a thick Eastern European accent.

"Can I help you?"

"Yes! This woman needs help."

Regina nodded.

"I need to see a doctor. Please."

The stranger wished her luck before he went back to the bus.

The desk clerk watched Regina shaking and saw how she was clutching her belly. She instructed a man behind her to bring a wheelchair.

While Regina's English had improved, it was not good enough yet for a medical discussion. The doctor put out a call for anyone who spoke Polish or Russian to come to the exam area. When a woman arrived and introduced herself to Regina in Russian, she was relieved. She winced as she described her symptoms and then they asked her for her medical history.

A young man in a white coat appeared with her chart.

"Mrs. Butlaw? I'm Doctor Yelowitz. I'm here to see why you are in so much pain. I'm going to touch your belly and I'll try not to hurt you."

After the translator explained what he said to Regina, he gently pressed on Regina's abdomen.

"Mrs. Butlaw, I'm afraid you have an infection in your gall bladder. It isn't terrible, but we must remove it right away. If we don't, you could be in serious trouble. Can we register you for surgery later today?"

Regina waited for the translator and nodded.

What choice do I have? The doctor is so young, but he sounds like he knows what he's doing. I must trust him and hope for the best.

The nurse gave her a shot of codeine for the pain and as it gradually took effect, Regina began to feel fuzzy. Soon, she became too foggy to understand what was being said or what was happening to her. She didn't recognize the woman who seemed to appear out of nowhere.

"Mrs. Butlaw, I'm Hannah from Jewish Family Services, remember me?"

Regina barely nodded.

"I'm here to get some information so we can get you the help you need. You have four children?"

Regina managed to tell Hannah about her kids and where they lived. She also reminded her that her husband was out of the picture.

"Regina, where are your children right now?"

"They are at home with Louis."

"How old is Louis?"

"Eleven. He's a very good boy and a big help."

"Thank you, Regina."

Hannah walked out of the room and returned a few minutes later. Regina and a nurse were waiting for an anesthesiologist to administer ether.

I don't know what's happening right now, but I hope my children are safe.

When Regina woke up from surgery early that evening, she felt pain in her abdomen. She began to retch, even though her stomach was empty. A nurse offered her a basin and water.

"Where am I? Did I have surgery?"

A nurse standing nearby responded.

"Yes, Mrs. Butlaw. It's all done. Everything is fine. You may not feel great for a bit, but the nausea will pass and then we will get you something to eat. In the meantime, if you can drink some water, that will help."

Regina winced, trying to clear her vision. She was still groggy from the anesthesia. Slowly, she became aware of her surroundings.

"Where are my children? I need to check on them. Louis is taking care of them, but I need to go home."

"I will get the social worker to answer your questions. I know someone went to your house earlier today."

Regina vomited again into the basin. She struggled to sit up and fell back against her pillow.

"Please, I need to know they are okay. Please."

The nurse left, leaving the basin with Regina. A few minutes later, a new woman came in and introduced herself.

"Mrs. Butlaw, I'm Mrs. Levinsky from Jewish Family Services. Your children are safe with two Jewish families until you are well enough to leave the hospital. You will be here for a few days before you can go home. We couldn't let them stay in the apartment alone."

"What do you mean? Louis can take care of them. Where are they?"

"They are too young, Mrs. Butlaw."

"Louis is eleven. In my country, he is old enough. He's a good boy and very capable."

"Not in this country. The laws are different here. We have placed them with two families because we didn't have one that could take all four of them. It's only temporary until you get home."

Regina was shocked.

"Mrs. Butlaw, here in the United States it is not considered appropriate to leave a young boy with three little girls, with one as young as two. We placed them where they are safe. It is only until you are home."

Regina broke out in a sweat and retched again.

I don't understand why they took them away and separated them, too. I've failed my own children. They must be terrified. Who are these strangers taking my children?

Regina couldn't think straight and soon fell fast asleep.

47

The Orphanage

Regina tried to put the pieces together from what she had experienced over the past several days, beginning with when she entered the hospital, had surgery, and woke up feeling nauseous, groggy, and out of control.

The world was spinning around her. She closed her eyes.

Did I hear them right? My children were taken away and put in foster care? What does that mean?

Mrs. Levinsky met Regina before she was released from the hospital.

"I want to let you know about your children. Louis and Dorothy have been placed with the Newmarks, a benevolent Jewish family with ties to the movie industry in Los Angeles. They can sleep in the same room, but in separate beds of course. Rose and Josephine are with the Cohns in Beverly Hills, a family that owns several grocery stores in downtown Los Angeles. They have two children of their own in high school, and they have an extra bedroom they make available to us for Jewish foster children. So, all your children are in good hands."

Regina was too stunned to respond.

Two days, later, the pain in her abdomen had eased enough for her to stand and walk slowly around the ward on her own. After four days in the hospital, Regina returned home, healthy, and mostly healed. She was instructed not to lift anything for at least a week and to continue to take it easy until she had her stitches removed in a couple weeks.

Adinah, a short woman with curly brown hair, was another counselor assigned to Regina's case. She picked her up from the hospital to take her home. On the way, they stopped by the JFS office so Adinah could fill out paperwork for the hospital that showed the agency was paying Regina's bill.

This also gave Regina a chance to see the documents the legal team had filed on her behalf, including petitions for divorce and monetary support. Since it would take some time to settle this case, Regina had no way to support herself or her children.

As she sat in a chair across from Adinah, Regina didn't know what to say or what to do.

This doesn't seem real.

She put her head in her hands.

"I don't understand what's happened since I went into the hospital. You filed for divorce from my no-good husband. And now, my children are in foster care in two different houses. What's next?"

"Regina, I know this is not what you expected when you went into the hospital. You didn't know it at the time, but you were very ill, and we had to focus first on your health. It's a good thing you got that operation when you did. Otherwise, I hate to think of what could have happened. You could have died, Regina! And then, your children would not have their mother."

They don't have their mother right now!

"It takes a while for the divorce process to resolve so we can go after your husband for support. Even though he hasn't responded, the law says there must be a certain amount of time to declare his absence official. Meanwhile, we will help you find work while the court resolves your circumstances."

"I am very willing to take a job, but I must take care of my children, too. Who will watch them while I'm at work, and how much will it cost?"

"Regina, I see on your naturalization papers that you did leather work in Warsaw. Is that right?"

"My father was a leather worker, and he taught us some of what he did. I did translation work in Polish, Russian, and Yiddish. I am learning English, but it's not going as fast as I hoped. Is there a job here for someone like me?"

"That's impressive. I don't know of a translation job right now. We know a leather factory in the Los Angeles area, in the city of Hawthorne, that makes furniture and gloves. We can help you with that after the girls get settled."

Regina nodded, more out of habit than approval.

"In the meantime, Regina, whatever you earn will not be enough to take care of your children. Your stipend from us will run out in two months and I'm afraid your salary will only be enough for you. I'm sorry to say that we need to make some hard decisions."

"What do you mean?"

"We think it would be better for your daughters if they live at the Vista Del Mar Jewish children's orphanage in Los Angeles, at least until they finish school. Louis is old enough to stay at home with you. We will continue the legal process to help you pay rent and get food for you and Louis. I'm sorry, Regina. It's not fair to keep him out of school to be a full-time babysitter."

Regina nodded.

"And you don't want the government to step in and put your girls in public foster care because you can't support them. Really, it's better for them and for you if they are in the Jewish orphanage."

As Regina looked at Adinah, she struggled to absorb this unexpected news. Ever since Morris stopped sending money home, Regina had faced a series of problems.

Now, everything points at me as a parent who can't care for her children.

Regina was worn out, and she knew that fighting wouldn't help her case, but she felt overwhelmed and couldn't control herself.

"An orphanage? What are you doing to my children? First, you take them out of my home and put them with strangers, and now you want to put them in an orphanage? What kind of Jews are you?"

Adinah handed Regina a box of tissues and waited.

"Why do you think this is a good idea? My children have a mother! They have parents. One is just a no-goodnik, but I'm right here! I love them, and I want to take care of them. You are making it look like I'm abandoning them. How are they going to feel about that?"

"Regina, I understand everything you are saying. But we have experience with this, and children in these situations usually feel fortunate when they get to Vista Del Mar and see how wonderful it is. It's not like some institutions you hear about that are more like prisons. Vista is a very caring place, and they have enough money to take good care of these children. The entire Los

Angeles Jewish community contributes so that these children can have the best of everything, including medical care."

Regina rocked back and forth.

"What will I do without my girls?"

"We will take you to the facility so you can see what it's like. I think you will feel better once you see how nice it is."

Regina had no more energy to fight what she could see was a losing battle. *They're right. I can't take care of the girls, certainly not by myself.*

"Okay, you win. I can't take care of them, right now, but I will soon. This isn't permanent, right?"

"We don't know until we see what happens with your divorce, Regina, and your support from Morris, and how much you earn from your job."

"Okay, what's next?"

Adinah escorted Regina back to her apartment, which felt eerily quiet without any children. She was exhausted and wasted no time curling up in bed and going to sleep.

48

Another New World

Two days later, Regina had regained enough strength to focus on seeing her children. She was terrified at what they would think, especially if they thought she was abandoning them.

The orphanage was located on 22 acres on Motor Avenue in West Los Angeles. It had been built with what was considered a new childcare design that had proven effective in other cities.

Its strategic location had benefits, as it was bordered by two major movie studios: MGM and 20th Century Fox. The studios donated costumes and let the children visit to watch movies.

Vista Del Mar had a main ranch house and five two-story cottages that housed the children by age and gender. The site included a superintendent's home, an infirmary, a laundry, and staff housing.

Each cottage had a house mother who lived with the children. The first floor had a living room and kitchen, and some had a piano. On the second floor were five bedrooms, enough to house 20 children.

When Adinah and Regina arrived at the administrative building, a man with balding white hair and a kind face approached them. He greeted Adinah before turning his attention to Regina.

"I'm Joseph Friedman. I'm guessing you are Mrs. Butlaw?"

"Yes, thank you. I'm Regina Butlaw."

"Thank you for coming. Can I get you a glass of water before we begin our tour?"

"No, thank you. You must know I'm not happy about my girls coming here. It isn't my idea, but I don't seem to have a choice."

"I understand, Regina. Adinah has filled me in on all the details and please know I'm aware of how this must feel for you."

"I doubt it."

Friedman didn't respond.

"Let me show you the cottage where the two older girls will stay."

Regina and Adinah followed Friedman to the cottage where Rose and Josephine would live. She met a couple housemates and saw the bedroom where the girls would sleep. It was full of books and dolls. Two of the four beds were empty.

As they left the cottage, Regina saw the infirmary and was surprised to see an outdoor pool, gymnasium, tennis courts, baseball diamond, paint shop, and a playground with swings and a barbeque pit. A health cottage was open 24 hours a day with a staff of registered nurses. It also provided tutoring in case a child missed any time in school.

Regina learned that every night after dinner the children pulled out their books to study and Mr. Friedman visited each cottage to see who needed help with their homework.

This is impressive, but it's all so terribly sad.

Regina had questions for Mr. Friedman.

"What ages are the kids here?"

"The youngest are between three and four. They must be potty trained, and the house mothers assist with everything else."

"What about children younger than three?"

"They stay in foster care until they are old enough to come here."

This was another knock to Regina's fragile state of mind. She realized that Dorothy wouldn't be with her sisters or even her brother for a year or more. Instead, she would be living with strangers.

"Thank you for the tour. I'd like to leave now."

Regina turned away and headed for the administrative building.

"Regina, I'm sorry I didn't tell you about the parents of the children who are here."

"Parents? I thought these kids didn't have parents."

"A good many of them do, but like you, for whatever reason something hasn't worked out, so they live here, usually until they graduate high school. We encourage parents to visit on weekends, so their children don't think they have been abandoned. We even like them to take their children out for the weekend, if possible."

I have no more words. This place is at least a bit better than I expected.

As they walked to the car, Regina pointed a finger at Adinah.

"You didn't tell me about Dorothy. Are you trying to trick me? Who is she going to live with for the next year? I don't have any say in it, do I?"

"I'm sorry, Regina. I should have told you before we came here. This has been a lot to deal with, I'm sure."

"Explain to me again when I can see my children."

"Any time on weekends. They are not being kept away from you. They are still your children, but for now they need to be somewhere where they will have enough food and proper medical care."

"Now what?"

"Now, you get to visit and hug your children."

Adinah smiled, but Regina said nothing.

Oh my God, I don't know if I can do this.

"We will pick up Rose and Josephine from the Cohn's house and you can ride with them back to Vista and have some time with them. Louis can go with you to see his sisters, and then we will take you both home. Dorothy will stay with the Newmarks. You have seen that she is well cared for there."

"I can see them now?"

"Yes." Adinah said.

Regina closed her eyes and tried to breathe.

This is all too much. I must keep myself together when I see my girls.

The reunion was brief and full of tears before Adinah and Regina returned with Rose and Josephine to the Vista Del Mar campus. The girls held Regina's hands as they walked to the office, and as they waited there, they sat silently and hugged each other.

When Mr. Friedman appeared, he greeted them with a smile.

"Let's see. You must be Rose? And you are Josephine? Welcome to your new home. We are so pleased you are joining us."

Despite his cheery banter, the girls were unsure of what was happening.

Friedman sat down and leaned forward to address the children.

"I want you both to know that you are here because your mother loves you and she wants to be sure you get everything you need, like food and medicine. She is not giving you up. You are still her daughters. How long will you be here? I can't answer that, but if you are here, we will do everything we possibly can to take good care of you."

Regina tried to keep her composure as a woman entered the room.

I still can't believe this is happening.

"We will take you to the cottage where you will share a bedroom with two other girls about your ages. This is Mrs. Brandt, who oversees the cottage. She will explain how things work. If you have questions, you can ask Mrs. Brandt. You can always come see me, too. You are not alone here. Everyone at Vista Del Mar is here for you."

"Give your mother a big hug," said Mrs. Brandt, "and then let's go find your beds and a snack."

As the girls held onto Regina, they began to cry.

"Nooo, I don't want to go with you," said Rose. "I want my mama. You can't take me away!"

Regina held Rose, tears streaming down her cheeks.

"You see what you are doing to my family. They want to stay with me."

Josephine sat still, crying softly.

Friedman suggested that they give Regina some time to say goodbye to her children. He leaned down so he was face-to-face with them.

"I know this is hard for everyone. We have many children here who would rather live at home. Their parents also feel bad because they would rather have their children with them. But parents also want to be sure that their children have enough food to eat. Your mother will always be your mother and she can come and see you every weekend."

Friedman waited as Regina sat with her girls.

Crying and yelling will not change anything right now. I must finally accept that this is the best thing for Rose and Josephine.

Regina stood up and nodded at Mr. Friedman, Adinah, and Mrs. Brandt.

"My dear girls, don't worry. Everything will be okay. I will see you in a few days. Go now with these nice people. They will get you some good food to eat, and I will bring you some homemade sugar cookies this weekend."

After Rose and Josephine left with Mrs. Brandt, Adinah and Regina were driven to the Newmark's home to pick up Louis. When they arrived, he was sitting on the front steps with his valise and a scowl on his face.

"Mama, they lied to us! They said it would only be a few days!"

Adinah intervened before Regina could reply.

"Louis, you are right. I told you it would only be a few days, but your mother was very sick, and she needed time to get better before she could go home from the hospital. I'm sorry that things have changed and that it will only be you living with your mother, at least for now. We weren't trying to deceive you. I promise you that."

"That wasn't very nice of you, what you told me before."

"I didn't tell you anything wrong on purpose. I didn't know what was going to happen. I believed you all would go home together, but it's better that Dorothy stays here, and Rose and Josephine live at the orphanage, at least for now, until we can help your mother change her situation."

"Why can't we all live together, like before?"

Louis choked back his tears.

"I'll explain why things are this way. You are old enough and smart enough and grown up beyond your years, so I think it is only fair to tell you."

Regina nodded to Louis so he would listen.

"Your stepfather, Morris Butlaw, is living in Texas, and he is not sending home any money for your mother or for you and your sisters. Without that money, your mother can't pay for the apartment or for food or clothes."

Regina listened as Louis stared straight ahead.

She's telling the truth, and he's old enough now to hear it.

"Why doesn't Morris send money? Can't they make him?"

"We are trying."

Regina went inside to hug Dorothy.

"Okay, I'm ready. Let's go home."

She put her arm around Louis as they headed to the car.

49

The Visit

As soon as Adinah's driver stopped the car outside Regina's apartment, Louis jumped out and ran upstairs and went straight to his bedroom.

"I think someone is happy to be home," Adinah said.

Regina stood in the middle of the room, still sniffling from her visit with Dorothy. No one said anything as Louis came out and hugged his mother.

"Just a reminder, you can see the girls at Vista Del Mar any time on the weekend, and Dorothy, too."

She handed Regina a packet of papers.

"This is information about the girls with addresses and phone numbers, so feel free to call and check in."

Regina nodded as she hugged Louis and wiped her eyes.

"I'll leave you two for now. Unless there is anything else you need."

Regina grimaced and looked at Adinah.

I know I shouldn't do this, but I can't help myself.

"Haven't you done enough already? It's easy for you to say I can call and visit my children while they live away from me. Am I supposed to feel lucky that my daughters are in an orphanage and in foster care? I have news for you. I'm going to get them home very soon. You'll see."

Adinah turned to leave.

"Remember that you have my contact information if you need it. Have a good evening."

She turned and closed the door behind her. Louis sat on the floor with one of the books the Newmark's had given to him. Regina wandered around the apartment, mumbling to herself, and checking in on Louis.

"What has happened us, Louis? I need to see the girls soon to be sure they are being taken care of as they should."

Regina sat at the table and shuffled through the documents Adina had left for her, including copies of the divorce agreement and those suing Morris for support. A second pile contained documents for Rose and Josephine, and the third pile concerned Dorothy's foster care. The smallest pile was paperwork from JFS, showing the support they would get for another month while she looked for a job.

Who am I kidding? I don't have leather making skills. Papa took me to work with him a few times, but I only learned a little bit, certainly not enough to get hired as a genuine leather craftsman.

Regina didn't expect that translating documents from Polish to Yiddish or Russian was a skill that anyone in America cared about, especially since her English was still not very good.

Thank God Louis is home with me.

After dinner, she and Louis read one of his books together because Regina wanted to check his English skills and improve her own.

The next day, she went to school with Louis so she could explain his absences to the office. She hoped they would not punish him.

After all, it wasn't his fault.

As they approached the counter, a woman greeted them. Regina answered in her best American accent.

"Good morning. I am Regina Butlaw. This is my son, Louis Butlaw."

To Regina's surprise, the woman responded in Polish.

"Good morning, Mrs. Butlaw. How can I help you?"

"Louis had to miss school last week because I had an operation, and he was taking care of his sisters. It wasn't his fault."

Even though the woman responded in Polish, Regina was surprised that so many people in the area were Jews from Germany, Russia, and Poland.

"I'm sure this will not be a problem as it was a family issue."

Regina waited while the woman went inside the office and returned with a folder.

"What grade are you in, Louis? Fifth?"

271

"Yes, Ma'am."

Since Louis had missed a lot of school during all their moves, he had been held back a year, but he was now doing well.

"I see you were absent last week from Tuesday until Friday. Your mother was sick, and you stayed home with your sisters?"

Louis nodded.

"Well, Louis, since you missed several important assignments, I'd like you to make them up at home if you can. If not, we can have someone work with you after school. I don't want you to fall behind because then you will not understand the new lessons."

Regina didn't appreciate that Louis had to do any extra lessons.

It's not his fault that he missed school, and how much could he have missed in just a few days? They already kept him back a year, and now he's being treated like a dumb kid.

"Excuse me, but why does my son need to do a special class? He's smarter than any of the kids in his class. I'm sure he already knows the assignments."

Louis looked down as the principal's assistant waited a moment before she answered Regina.

"Mrs. Butlaw, I have no doubt that Louis is a very bright boy. However, the school requires that some assignments must be completed. I'm sure Louis will complete these easily and then he will be all caught up."

"Okay, so now what?"

"Let's get Louis back into his class. I will go with him now and explain everything to his teacher. She will take it from there, Okay, Louis?"

Louis nodded.

Why is everything such a fight?

"Louis, I will come for you after school so we can walk home together."

Regina was not pleased about how she felt the school was treating them.

It looks to me like they think my son is an ignorant immigrant.

Los Angeles
1920

50

Blindsided

Fifteen months later, the time had finally come to arrange for Dorothy to transfer to Vista Del Mar. Regina was mildly surprised by Adinah's request to come to her office that week. Dorothy was three-and-a-half, old enough to join her sisters at the orphanage.

I had hoped to have them all with me by now.

She had a job at a nearby bakery, but she still wasn't making enough money to feed and clothe all the children and pay to have someone watch them while she was at work.

More paperwork, I guess. America loves paperwork.

When she arrived at Adinah's office, Regina was surprised to see Jacob and Aviva Newmark. She knew them from her many visits to see Dorothy, but now she was more than ready to thank them and never see them again.

I want my daughter out of the foster care system. Not that the Newmark's hadn't been nice, but I want more control over Dorothy's life.

Adinah greeted Regina with a warm handshake.

"Regina, so good to see you. You look well. Have a seat. Of course, you know the Newmarks."

"Yes, of course."

"I'll cut to the chase, as I'm sure you want to be home when Louis arrives. We have something to talk to you about concerning Dorothy."

Regina's eyes narrowed.

"What are you talking about? Is she okay? Is she ill? What happened to my daughter?"

Regina almost shouted with alarm.

"No, no, she's fine. I'm so sorry, I didn't mean to alarm you."

"Well, what then?"

It feels like my life is just one disaster after another. Why can't things be simple? Just once, please God.

"Why are you wasting my time if nothing is wrong? And who is with Dorothy now?"

Adinah and the Newmark's shot looks at each other.

"Regina, Dorothy has been with the Newmarks for well over a year, and they have grown to love her like a daughter."

"Of course, you would love her. She is an adorable and loving child. How could you not? You were lucky to have her."

"The Newmarks would like to discuss something with you."

"So, discuss. Why are you doing all the talking, Adinah? Can't they talk? Is something wrong with their voice?"

She shot a look at the Newmarks.

"I'm sorry Regina, we don't mean to have Adinah talk for us," said Jacob. "You know we have had Dorothy with us for a while now."

"Fifteen months. I can count."

Yes, and it has been an amazing time watching her grow."

"So, what about you, Mrs. Newmark? You are unable to speak?"

This conversation feels odd, and it's making me uncomfortable.

"I'm fine, Regina. My husband said it best. We have had an amazing year with Dorothy."

"So, let's get to the point," said Jacob.

"Yes, let's do that."

Regina's attitude put the Newmarks on edge, and Jacob waited a moment before he continued.

What do these people want? I have better things to do right now.

"Regina, we would like to adopt Dorothy."

For a moment, Regina said nothing. She wasn't sure she heard what they really said.

Adopt my daughter? Are these people out of their fucking minds?

"Are you serious? Adopt Dorothy? She is *my* daughter! Mine! You can't take that away."

275

Regina stood up to leave. Adinah jumped out of her chair.

"Please, Regina. Please hear them out."

"No. I will not hear anyone out."

She looked coldly at the Newmarks.

"I do not want Dorothy in your house any longer. I can take care of her now, and I want her home immediately."

Adinah started to speak.

"No, no, no. You heard me. Everyone in this office heard me. You cannot adopt my daughter and that's final."

The Newmarks looked at each other, unsure what to do.

What the fuck is the matter with these people that they think I would even consider letting them adopt Dorothy?

"You must be sitting in the sun too long, drinking cocktails or something, if you think I would let anyone adopt my daughter!"

Regina turned to Adinah.

"Are you part of this scheme? Do you also want to take my daughter away from me?"

"Regina, I just learned of their request and it's my job to let them ask you. It doesn't matter what I think."

"I want to see Dorothy right now. Let's go to your home so I can pick her up right now."

Adinah stepped in.

"No one is going to take Dorothy away from you, Regina. You said no, and that's final. You can accompany Dorothy to Vista Del Mar if you wish."

"If I wish? I get to make a wish now?"

"Regina, please."

I can't believe they tried to do this to me.

"What time should I be there?"

"Be at the Newmarks at nine on Sunday morning. Dorothy will be ready, and you can go with us to the orphanage and have your visit with Rose and Josephine. Of course, Louis can come along, too."

"Fine."

Regina calmed down, knowing the Newmarks couldn't adopt Dorothy and were not going to fight with her. She sighed and looked at them.

I've been terrible.

"I'm very sorry, I didn't mean to yell at you. I know you have taken very good care of Dorothy when I couldn't. I can understand why after all this time she would feel like your family."

She stood up.

"I appreciate everything you have done for Dorothy."

She turned and walked out without another word.

On Sunday morning, Regina rushed Louis through his breakfast, and the two of them hurried to the JFS office. She had a bag of cookies from the bakery and felt more excited than usual about seeing her daughter than she'd been in months. While the Newmarks never discouraged Regina from seeing Dorothy, they hadn't exactly encouraged it either.

Well, that's over. The girls can finally be together again. But when will they come home? How much longer must I wait until I make enough money? It's more than just money for food and clothes and medical care. There are so many things that children need.

Just thinking about it all overwhelmed Regina.

"Okay, Louis, it's time for us all to be together, even for a few hours!"

Adinah greeted them with her usual cheery disposition.

"Good morning, Regina. Hi Louis. I'm sure you are both excited to get Dorothy today and see Rose and Josephine!"

Regina nodded, afraid to say anything that would make her burst into tears in front of her son.

Relax now. The Newmarks are not trying to steal Dorothy.

They drove to the fancy neighborhood where the Newmarks lived, on Oakhurst Drive off Gregory Way in Beverly Hills.

Jacob was holding Dorothy in his arms as he opened the front door. She held a small stuffed animal to her chest. Aviva came up behind them with a valise. Regina could see that her eyes were red and knew she had been crying.

This is so awkward. These two good people have taken such wonderful care of Dorothy and it's no surprise that they've come to love her. I must let them know how grateful I am.

"Thank you so much for taking care of Dorothy. I'm sorry I yelled at you. This has been a terrible time being separated from my children. Please take these cookies as a small way from me to say thank you. I'm sure the orphanage will let you visit her if you like, and it will be okay with me."

"We would love that. Thank you, Regina We will check to see how that works. We don't want to confuse her."

Regina took Dorothy's hand as they headed to the car. When they reached the orphanage, Dorothy hugged Regina tightly, barely letting go as they got out of the car.

I wonder if it would've been better to keep her home for a week, but Mr. Friedman suggested that another transition would not be good for Dorothy.

They walked together to meet Mr. Friedman, who greeted them with a big smile and hugs for Adinah and Regina.

"So, this is beautiful little Dorothy! Regina, you have been truly blessed with such a wonderful family."

Regina was heartened by such a warm welcome. She didn't know what to say, but she smiled.

After signing several official documents, Regina, Dorothy, and Louis were surprised when Rose and Josephine walked into the office. They ran to Regina for hugs and knelt to hug Dorothy.

"You got so big! Do you remember us, Dorothy?"

"Dorothy, how old are you now?" Friedman said.

"I'm three and a half."

"We have three other girls here your age here. They will be glad to have you join them as the fourth in their room."

Dorothy clung to Regina.

"No, I want to stay with Mama."

Regina hugged Dorothy tight and nestled into her soft, red hair.

"Schatzeleh, I know this is hard, but I will see you every weekend. And guess what? Rose and Josephine stay here, too. You can see them every day!"

Mr. Friedman bent down to look at Dorothy.

"I have some special cookies here for new children. Would you like one? Would that be okay with you, Mama?"

Regina nodded and smiled as Dorothy took a cookie.

"Dorothy, why don't we show you around and we can bring some extra cookies. This is Mrs. Adelberg, your cottage mother. She will take very good care of you."

She walked them around and explained what she could to Dorothy, especially the cottage where she would live and the one close by where her sisters would be.

"Shall we go to the playground?"

Dorothy nodded, and as Rose and Josephine took her hands, Regina realized this was the perfect time to say goodbye, at least until the weekend. She and Louis watched the three girls skip away and decided to get ice cream on their way home.

This is what an orphanage should be. Except Jewish holidays should be spent with family, like I had back home.

Regina reminded herself that coming to America was her choice.

I can't second-guess myself, even though life here has not turned out the way I hoped. If things get worse in Poland, which I fear will happen soon, perhaps my family will join me, and I will be able to sponsor them.

"So, Louis, what flavor would you like?"

51

The School

Every morning, as Regina watched Louis gobble down his breakfast, she was reminded that this was not the family situation she thought she would have. She never thought she would lose one husband and then another, and then three of her children.

My children will never know their grandparents.

The seders at the orphanage would not have a big table where her son and daughters would be surrounded by cousins, aunts, and uncles, all singing together and hiding the afikomen that the children could run around and try to find after dinner.

All the family rituals from Poland have been lost.

She expected the girls to grow up to become beautiful young women, and that Louis would finish his high school education and maybe go to college.

That was my dream when I left Europe to come to America.

Her marriage to Morris was just one more failure in Regina's life that she had to deal with, and the experience had left her feeling vulnerable and skeptical about trusting people. She didn't trust if people were telling her the truth, and she often felt like everyone wanted to trick her or take advantage of the fact that she was an immigrant woman living alone.

They assume that I don't know if I am being lied to, but I do!

She was exhausted having to be so vigilant all the time, but she had to be on her guard to keep herself and her children safe from those who would take advantage of her situation.

Why do I second guess everything I have chosen in my life? Why don't I have a husband? Why do I suffer so many disappointments? I can't help resenting women who have husbands and their family intact.

In 1927, after Louis finished high school, he found a decent paying job and moved on to build his own independent life.

One down, three to go.

Rose and Josephine were next in line to move back home. Louis sent money to Regina every month to help her pay the bills. For several years, Regina only visited Dorothy at Vista and since she was older, and well-adjusted, she didn't mind that her sisters were no longer there. Seeing them on weekends was good enough.

On a typical Sunday afternoon, Regina brought a bag of groceries for Dorothy, and even though all the girls told her they didn't need any extra food, Regina insisted, so they stopped arguing and just thanked her.

"Hi Mama!"

Dorothy always greeted her mother with a big kiss on her cheek.

"My beauty. My schatzeleh. How is my daughter today? I brought you some goodies from the bakery. They always have leftover cakes and challah that they can't sell, so they let me take it for you."

Dorothy shrugged.

"I know, I know, you can't eat it all. Share it with your friends."

"Thanks Mama. I know they will love it. They always ask when you will come because you always bring wonderful goodies."

On that day, in the spring of 1937, Regina wanted to tell Dorothy what would be expected of her once she moved back home, as her graduation wasn't far away.

"You will leave here soon and can find a good job, Dorothy."

"Yes, Mama, I'm looking forward to being at home."

Toward the end of their visit, Regina started in about the bakery where she had been working for ten years, complaining that the owner didn't pay her enough, and the other workers didn't carry their load, and the customers were rude, and another bakery was undercutting their pricing.

At least the owner isn't antisemitic. He's Jewish!

Dorothy listened and put an arm around her mother.

"Mama, is it possible that you don't need to work there any longer?"

No one had ever suggested that option., but it made sense. Regina worked long hours and was always tired, especially by the end of the week. Now, with Louis, Rose, and Josephine helping with her expenses, she might be able to cut back on her hours or stop working altogether.

Could I do that? I don't know if I could just stop working.

Her life was relatively simple. She had no expensive jewelry, and only a few frocks that she wore repeatedly. She had learned to drive a car, but the used Ford she bought wasn't expensive, and everyone shared the costs.

Maybe Dorothy is right. Who knows what things might be like when Dorothy graduates and moves back home?

On their next visit, Regina and Dorothy caught up on family news.

"What's new with my sisters?" she said.

"Oy, what's new? Josephine has moved back home and got rid of that no-goodnik of a husband of hers."

"Well, I'm glad," said Dorothy, "because she will be happier without him. She can do better. How is Rose, and how is her husband, Franklin? He seemed nice the one time he came here to visit."

"They're fine."

"How is Josephine's job going at the studios? That seems so glamorous. Does she meet a lot of movie stars? If she is going to be on her own, it's so good that she never gave up her job when she got married."

"Everyone wants Josie to do their hair. She is the best, you know. So talented, that one."

Dorothy smiled.

"So, Schatzeleh, you only have a few more months here before you graduate. Mr. Friedman said you need to think about what you will do next, like going to college or getting a job. Do you know what you want to do?"

"I do. Probably secretarial school at Vista. It sounds like a good fit for me, and it will let me work in many different jobs with the same tools. I want to work at a newspaper."

"Good. I'm glad you have thought about it. It's so important that you can make a good living, so you won't end up in the same pickle I did. I want all you kids to be able to take care of yourselves. You never know what life will be like, and you can't count on a man to take care of you. You must be able to take care of yourself."

"You had it rough, Mama. I admire you for fighting through it."

"Oh my God, Dorothy. That's so kind of you. Do you mean it?

"Of course, I do!"

Regina was in tears.

"You don't know what your words mean to me."

Dorothy kissed her mother and suggested they take a walk around the campus. Regina was not enthusiastic about moving around in the heat, but she was so elated by Dorothy's comment that she agreed to go.

Oh my God, what a beautiful thing she just said to me.

Regina was eager for Dorothy to move home, even though she had come to believe that the orphanage had been good for them. All three of her daughters had grown up to be caring, independent-minded young women. She recognized how Vista Del Mar had saved all their lives.

I didn't appreciate it at first, that's for sure, but I must admit now that we were all fortunate that Vista existed.

Regina and Dorothy held hands as they slowly walked the scenic grounds.

Los Angeles
1945

52

Regina's Lament

Dorothy's daughter, Nadine, just turned two, and she and her husband, Joe, had invited the entire family to gather at their house to celebrate. On the way home, Regina sat in the back seat of her car with her granddaughter, Elizabeth, while Louis drove, and his wife Lucy joined him up front.

The birthday party was a family treat. Josephine and her fiancé were there, and Rose and her husband came, too. They were visiting from San Francisco to house hunt, as they were planning to move back to Los Angeles. Louis and his wife Lucy and their daughter were there and, of course, Dorothy, Joe, their son Edward, and the birthday girl, Nadine. Since her birthday came around Hanukah, she received several extra presents.

As Elizabeth napped, Regina enjoyed the ride and allowed herself a moment to reflect for what seemed like the first time in years.

How did I get here? I'm a grandmother! Oh, my God, it feels like it happened so fast.

She compared her situation to what it might have been like if she had never left Poland when she did. From the day she boarded that train to Paris, everything had felt so urgent and stressful, so she enjoyed the fact that she and her family had made it as far as they had in America and that she didn't have to worry any longer about her children's wellbeing.

She knew she was fortunate to have children who were willing to take care of her in every way. She had everything she could need in life, which was so different when she first moved to California.

It feels very sweet now, but it took a lot of heartache to get here.

Regina thought about her sisters and brothers, who would not leave Poland when she did, and how they had to suffer through years of Jewish boycotts and violent antisemitism. She had always followed the news from Europe, especially as the second world war evolved from the ashes of the first.

When German soldiers overran Polish border defenses and advanced towards Warsaw, she was horrified but not surprised when the government surrendered on September 28, 1939.

The Warsaw ghetto was established about a year later and was quickly enclosed by a ten-foot-high wall topped with barbed wire. It was tightly guarded to prevent movement into the rest of the city, and Warsaw's Jews were required to identify themselves by wearing white armbands with a blue Star of David. The Germans closed Jewish schools, confiscated their property, and conscripted Jewish men into forced labor. More than 400,000 Jews were squeezed into the Warsaw ghetto in an area of 1.3 square miles. Three years later, they were slaughtered.

News about her own family had been mixed. Regina learned about her sister Dina and 11 cousins, nieces, and nephews who died in the Bergen-Belsen camps, and others who fought for and lost their freedom and their lives in the 1943 ghetto uprising in Warsaw.

Over the years, letters had been few and far between, and Chaja Fajga was Regina's only real link to the family, but none had arrived since 1941. She admitted that she was glad she had moved out of Poland and settled in France, even though they were in plenty of danger during the war.

Yosef had been forced to quit his job at the leather factory because his boss and friend, Henryk Bolesław, could no longer guarantee his safety.

Regina's parents had managed to survive World War I on Zelman's farm. He had achieved his dream in 1913, building a dairy farm in rural Poland, an hour from Warsaw, that specialized in gourmet cheese, and he invited his parents to work there with him and his wife, a strong farmer's daughter.

Since food was scarce at the time, Zelman's cheese was used by the Polish military to feed the troops. Yosef and Lena stayed there for 22 years until, at the age of 67, Yosef fell under a tractor he was driving. Lena died a year later of tuberculosis. Zelman and his family were still there.

Regina's brother, Aleksander, who served as an aide to General Radko Dimitriev, was fatally wounded when his unit successfully pushed the German Army back in the Battle of the Vistula River in October 1914.

Years later, late in the fall of 1945, just weeks before Nadine's birthday party, Regina received joyful news in a letter from Chaja Fajga. She hadn't heard from them in nearly four years, as they had been living in constant terror, trying to survive the Nazi occupation.

Their letter described what happened in 1941 when a Catholic priest in Paris, who had worked with Aron on an ecumenical project two years earlier, sent Aron, Chaja Fajga and their three children to live with a Catholic walnut farmer in the Dordogne region in southwestern France. The farmer hid them successfully for almost four years in the cellar of his barn, at great peril to his own family. Aron and Chaja Fajga returned to Paris after the war, and Aron became the chief rabbi at the same synagogue where he began his career.

Dina, her husband and two of their children died at Bergen-Belson in 1944. Dina's other two children survived. Her youngest sister, Kejla, died with a rifle in her hand, leading a unit of the Jewish Combat Organization in the Warsaw Ghetto uprising.

That all seems so far away from here, riding along a California highway.

Regina was grateful that her own children never had to experience war, thanks to the choice she made to leave Poland, but she carried a great sadness from what happened to most of her Polish family.

What can I do with these feelings of anger and helplessness? No one would listen to me and look what happened. If it wasn't murder at the hands of the Nazis, it was diseases that couldn't be treated because physicians didn't have the medicines they needed.

It didn't have to be this way.

Regina thought about Morris.

Did he ever wonder about me and his children?

Regina could not comprehend how a man could abandon his children.

What did they ever do to deserve that?

She thought about Leopold. He had remarried and successfully hid some of the staff at the Bund in a cellar he created under his house until soldiers discovered it and sent them to the ghetto where they fought and died.

As she looked out the window, Regina considered the entire arc of her life. She lived thousands of miles and a lifetime away from the Warsaw she once knew and the family she never stopped loving.

Now, here I am, safe and unafraid of my life in America. I was not clairvoyant, not at all, but I couldn't ignore what I saw in front of me. I couldn't pretend it would go away.

Regina was smart about so much, but not when it came to men and love. She had trusted Morris without knowing him much at all. She recognized her failures with Leopold, too. She had trusted him because he was older, and she thought that made him wiser.

It doesn't take a genius to make poor decisions.

She had learned over and over that it was foolish to trust anyone too much because people betray you.

I can only depend on myself, and I must fight for what I want in life.

She remembered the support of the Jewish community in Chicago and Los Angeles when she was sick and destitute with young children.

My children should never have to make the choices I was forced to make.

Ultimately, she knew it was better to struggle than to stay in Poland and die. She built something for her children, and they were now enjoying the fruits of her struggles and their own resilience.

Regina closed her eyes and leaned her head back against the car seat. She felt an ache in her heart, she always did when she thought about her family.

No regrets, Regina, no regrets.

About the Author

Geri Spieler is the past president of the San Francisco Peninsula branch of the California Writers Club and has authored articles in numerous publications, including *The Los Angeles Times*, *San Francisco Chronicle*, *Huffington Post*, and *Forbes*.

She served as a research director for Gartner, a global technology advising company, and she was a regular contributor to Truthdig.com, an award-winning investigative reporting website. She is a member of the Society of Professional Journalists, the Authors Guild, the Women's National Book Association, the Internet Society, and the Book Critics Circle.

In her breakthrough book, *Housewife Assassin-The Woman Who Tried to Kill President Ford*, Spieler reveals the true story of Sara Jane Moore, a mother and doctor's wife who, in 1975, became the first woman who tried to assassinate a president and missed his head by six inches.

Geri lives in the San Francisco Bay Area with her husband, a family of chickens and ten fruit trees.

Upcoming New Release!

GERI SPIELER'S

REVENGE OF THE SISTERS
A TALE OF RETRIBUTION

REGINA OF WARSAW SERIES
BOOK TWO

No one ever said life is fair, but for three sisters raised in a Los Angeles orphanage during the Great Depression, life was doubly unfair. Targeted by students and teachers, each sister suffered a specific event at school that altered her future and kept her from achieving her dreams. Years later, as adults armed with new skills and resources, each woman seeks retribution to right those wrongs and extract justice for past transgressions.

For more information
visit: www.SpeakingVolumes.us

Upcoming New Release!

ANNE SHAW HEINRICH'S

GOD BLESS THE CHILD
The Women of Paradise County Series
Book One

For more information
visit: www.SpeakingVolumes.us

Made in United States
North Haven, CT
01 October 2024

58147832R00189